"All right, then, what are you upset about?"

"You," Jason said.

"Me?" He had completely lost her. "What about me?"

He turned away for a moment, shoving his hands deep into his pockets. Searching for words.

"Look, I don't want to have to do without you."

Was that it? He was afraid of losing his maid? Over the years she'd taken a relatively self-sufficient man and gotten him used to having everything done for him.

"I'll still do everything I've always done," she assured him, trying hard not to let her annoyance show. "Get up, throw up and move on. Your meals will still be made, most likely on time, you—"

"I don't want to have to do without you," Jason repeated, saying the words with more feeling. "If something happened to you, I wouldn't be able to go on."

For one of the very few times in her life, Laurel found herself truly speechless.

Marie Ferrarella

wrote her very first story at age eleven on an old manual
Remington typewriter her mother bought for her for
seventeen dollars at a pawn shop. The keys stuck and she
had to pound on them in order to produce anything. The
instruments of production have changed, but she's been
pounding on keys ever since. To date, she's written over
150 novels, and there appears to be no end in sight. As long
as there are keyboards and readers, she intends to go on
writing until the day she meets the Big Editor in the Sky.

Marie Ferrarella
Second Time Around

THE SECOND TIME AROUND

copyright © 2007 by Marie Rydzynski-Ferrarella

isbn-13:978-0-373-88123-9

isbn-10:   0-373-88123-1

TheNextNovel.com

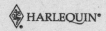 HARLEQUIN®

PRINTED IN U.S.A.

From the Author

Dear Reader,

Considering that I never liked playing with dolls, I was very surprised to discover that I loved being a mother. Loved the whole concept, from diapers to midnight feedings to reading bedtime stories and even to homework-helping at the last possible minute. I was blessed with two children, a girl and then a boy. Sadly, although they'll always be my children, they are not little people anymore. They grew up (it was the daily watering that did it). I miss little fingers wrapped around mine, miss little bottoms nestled on my lap (my dog still sits on my lap, but it's not the same).

And I have to admit, if it wouldn't send my husband into something akin to anaphylactic shock, I would love to have another baby, even though both my kids have graduated college. I know a lot more now (or so I tell myself) and I would be a much more self-assured mother than the one who called the hospital hotline in a panic at two in the morning because her one-year-old was coughing.

But since I can't have another short person of my own, I decided it might be fun to write a story about a couple who thought they had the rest of their lives completely planned and knew what was coming around every corner—only to find themselves pregnant. It's not as upsetting a situation as you might think. After all, they don't call it the miracle of birth for nothing.

As always, I wish you love and I thank you for reading.

Marie Ferrarella

To Dr. Anne Lai, for helping Rocky

If there was anything she looked forward to less than her annual visit to her gynecologist, Laurel Mitchell didn't know what it was.

It wasn't that her doctor was heavy-handed with the examination or made her uncomfortable. On the contrary, Dr. Rachel Kilpatrick, the same doctor who had seen her through all three of pregnancies, had a gentle touch and a fantastic bedside manner. And she was a kind, understanding woman to boot, someone she could talk to about anything that bothered her. Rachel Kilpatrick was not the kind of doctor who just roller-skated by, taking pulses and collecting fees. She genuinely cared for her patients.

No, it wasn't Dr. Kilpatrick that she minded. What she found upsetting was the whole awful experience: sitting there in a cool room, wearing a vest that was made out of thin tissue paper with what could have passed as an extralarge paper towel draped around her lower torso. *That* was what she found so off-putting.

That and the stirrups.

Whose idea were they, anyway? Necessary or not, they

made her think of something two steps removed from a torture rack from the Spanish Inquisition.

But she endured it all like a good little soldier. Because that was what women were supposed to do once a year: troop in, strip down and lie there, thinking of other things while cold steel instruments were inserted in places women of her grandmother's generation never talked about.

Finally the probing and the scratching were over. Dr. Kilpatrick removed the instruments and put the prize she'd secured between two glass lab slides, then placed that on the side counter. Laurel lost no time in dismounting from the stirrups and sitting up. She tried her best to pull her dignity to her and ignore the goose bumps forming on her flesh from the room's cold temperature.

When she raised her eyes to Dr. Kilpatrick's face, she saw that her gynecologist was frowning.

Not a good sign, Laurel thought. The queasiness in her stomach increased, reminding her that the cereal she'd had for breakfast was not resting well. But then lately, very little had. She chalked it up to stress and told herself it would pass.

Dr. Kilpatrick pushed the stool she'd been sitting on back into the corner. She held Laurel's file against her chest and moved closer to the examination table, and to Laurel.

Her eyes were kind as she asked, "How have you been feeling lately, Laurel?"

Laurel bit back a flippant answer. Whenever she was nervous, she tended to make jokes, a habit that drove her husband, Jason, and her sons, crazy. This time, she shrugged.

"Okay, I guess. A little run-down but that's to be expected. I'm not twenty anymore." Her suspicions began to multiply, conjuring up awful images. Her neighbor, Alexis Curtis, had been feeling run-down and she was diagnosed with cancer. The chemo treatments had made her chestnut hair fall out.

Laurel sat up straighter, drawing her shoulders back. "Why? Is something wrong? Tell me if something's wrong," she requested, hoping that wasn't a tremor she heard in her voice. "I can take it." She scrutinized her doctor's face, trying to uncover what the woman was thinking.

Dr. Kilpatrick took in a slow breath, as if bracing herself to rip a Band-Aid from her patient's arm. "Well, Laurel, as they used to say in the old days, you're with child."

"With child," Laurel repeated, dazed. Numbed. Confused. She cocked her head, as if that would somehow shift everything in her head and make her better understand the words. "Whose child?"

Dr. Kilpatrick smiled, amused. "Your child, I'd imagine."

Laurel heard the words clearly, but somehow, they just didn't seem to register. She shook her head, confused. "I'm not getting this."

An almost wicked smile curved the physician's lips. "Apparently, you are, or at least did." Leaning over, Dr. Kilpatrick placed her hand over Laurel's. "Laurel, you're pregnant."

Laurel thought it was a miracle that she didn't swallow her tongue from the shock. But then, this was a joke, right? Some bizarre April Fool's prank just a couple weeks shy of its mark, since it was the middle of April. The doctor was apparently running behind in her attempt at humor.

Very emphatically, Laurel shook her head, never taking her eyes off Dr. Kilpatrick's face. "No, I'm not."

"You just left a specimen of your urine before the exam." Dr. Kilpatrick flipped over a page to show her the results the nurse had gotten. "The test says you're pregnant. Tests don't lie."

Again, Laurel shook her head, this time even more adamantly, refusing to accept this docilely. There was a mistake. This was all wrong. She was exhausted, she had the flu, maybe even walking pneumonia. There was a whole list of possibilities for her condition that didn't have the word "baby" attached to it.

"Test me again," Laurel pleaded. "I need a do-over. I was always careless on tests, always got the wrong answer the first time around." She placed her hand on the doctor's arm. "Please."

"I don't have to take another sample from you, Laurel," Dr. Kilpatrick told her softly. "Your color's changed."

Laurel pressed her hand against her cheeks. Was she running a fever? Well, small wonder. The doctor had just scared her to death. "My color?"

The doctor's smile turned into a broad grin. "Not there." She indicated Laurel's face. "There." With a nod of her head, Dr. Kilpatrick glanced toward the blue "paper towel" that was inadequately pooled about her patient's thighs, indicating the area she was referring to.

Laurel shifted uncomfortably, as if she could actually feel what the doctor was talking about. "It could still be a mistake."

There was sympathy on the doctor's face. "Could be," she allowed skeptically. "But it's really highly doubtful."

Laurel blew out a breath. "Pregnant," she said, still unable to absorb the implications behind the eight-letter word. Still holding it at bay with the last ounce of her strength.

The expression on Rachel Kilpatrick's face was pure sympathy. And perhaps, just a touch of envy. "Yes."

"Me."

The doctor lifted her shoulders, then let them drop. "You're the one on the examination table."

Laurel laughed shortly. This wasn't happening. It couldn't be. She couldn't possibly be pregnant. She raised her eyes to meet the doctor's. "I'll gladly switch with you."

"Laurel, this is a wonderful thing." The doctor gave her hand another warm squeeze. "A miracle."

Miracles were things that you hoped for, prayed for, Laurel thought haplessly. Miracles were things that happened despite impossible odds because you wanted them to. Never in her wildest dreams had she ever wanted to be pregnant at forty-five.

"You bet it's a miracle," Laurel said sarcastically. "It's damn near close to being an immaculate conception. In the last six months, I can count the number of times Jason and I made love on the fingers of one hand."

"Now there's your problem," the doctor teased with a laugh. "The bed's much more comfortable for that sort of thing." And then, because her patient looked so sober, so upset by the news that usually brought tears of joy to so many of her other patients, Rachel sat down on the examining table beside Laurel and placed an arm around her patient's shoulders. There was compassion in her eyes as she asked, "Is there trouble between you and Jason?"

Jason was one of those easygoing men who was hard to ruffle. But this should definitely do it, Laurel thought. An ironic smile curved her mouth. "There will be once I come home with this."

The doctor shook her head. "Besides 'this.'"

Laurel knew she'd lucked out the day she'd haphazardly picked Rachel Kilpatrick to be her doctor. She could come to her with anything, even after hours. It made her wonder how the woman managed to maintain a private life. But somehow she did. Laurel knew for a fact that the woman had a husband and children.

"No 'trouble.' Jason's just gotten caught up in his old hobby. Trains," she explained.

Her husband had been a collector when they'd first met. At that time, he had only three engines to his name. Over the years, under the guise of building up sets for their sons, he'd bought more and more. But they hardly ever even got out of the box once he brought the trains home. He was storing them. And then suddenly, last Christmas, they'd all come out of their boxes, every last one of them, and began showing up in almost every room in the house. She'd managed to convince Jason that he needed to have them all in one place. He settled on two, the bonus room and the garage, both of which looked like miniature Grand Central Stations these days.

"We've got tracks all over the garage. The cars are parked outside." She'd had to find a cover for hers because she didn't want the elements getting to the paint job. "Now he's talking about setting up something outside in the backyard." Actually, he was doing more than talking about it, but she didn't want to take up the doctor's time.

"So, see, this will work out just fine."

Laurel looked at her, not following the doctor's reasons. "And how do you figure that?"

"Well, if you give him a son, Jason will have an excuse to play with the trains. Give him someone to run the trains for."

They already had a son, Laurel thought. As a matter of fact, they had three of them. Three big, strong, strapping boys. None of whom were in that getting-on-their-knees-and-playing-with-trains stage anymore. Besides, Jason didn't want another son—he wanted a heavy-duty transformer to help run his trains over longer distances without losing power.

Laurel looked at the doctor, feeling overwhelmed and helpless as well as exhausted. "What I'll be giving him an excuse for is leaving home."

Dr. Kilpatrick rose from the table. "I think you're selling your husband short."

It wasn't so much a matter of selling Jason short as it was having been privy to his dreams all these years. He had a plan for their future. And that plan definitely didn't include morning sickness and swollen ankles.

"You don't understand, Doctor," Laurel sighed. "Jason and I are in a different place now than we were twenty-five years ago."

"Yes, for one thing, you're far more experienced now than you were then."

That wasn't what she meant. "Twenty-five years ago, Jason wanted enough kids to populate his own professional baseball team. Now he's satisfied with just enough to play four-handed poker with. Occasionally. What he wants to do is travel, do all the things we couldn't do back then because we had kids."

Oh God, pregnant. I'm pregnant.

"How am I going to tell him that after all these years, we're back to square one again? Less than one. Zero. How am I going to tell him that he's got to wait another eighteen years before we go on that road trip he's been planning? By then, they won't let him drive because they'll have taken away his driver's license."

The exaggeration made Dr. Kilpatrick laugh. "Jason's what, one year old than you?" Laurel nodded, letting another from-the-bottom-of-her-toes sigh escape. "That makes him forty-six. I don't think he'll be ready to be put on an ice flow just yet. Besides, haven't you heard? Forty-six is the new thirty-six." She patted Laurel's shoulder. "Forget about this early-retirement business," she advised, referring to something Laurel had told her earlier about her husband's plans. "It's highly overrated. Being involved keeps you young. Babies keep you young," she emphasized. "This way, he still has retirement to look forward to." Crossing to the door, Dr. Kilpatrick paused for a moment, a fond expression on her face. "Sometimes, the looking-forward-to-something part is even better than actually getting that 'something.'"

"You want to come home with me and explain that to him? Maybe he'll believe it if he hears it coming from you."

Her hand on the doorknob, Dr. Kilpatrick stopped and turned around. "What, that you're pregnant?"

"No, that looking forward to something is better than having it."

Dr. Kilpatrick smiled. "Look at the positive aspects—"

What possible positive aspects could there be about being pregnant at forty-five? "Right, I'll be the oldest mother in kindergarten."

The look the doctor gave her said she knew it was just the shock talking, nothing more. "No, you're better off financially than you were when you had your other children. And you're definitely more experienced. You know what to expect."

"Yes, morning sickness for five months." And one hell of an explosion when she broke the news. She couldn't think of one person who was going to be happy about this unexpected twist.

"Afterward," the doctor gently prodded. "Remember how afraid you were when you brought that first baby home? How you thought you'd drop and break him? How everything was this big mystery? Every rash, every cough had you fearing the worst? Now you'll have the advantage because you'll know what you're doing."

Laurel remembered the early years and, yes, she'd learned from them. Learned that she could survive and, most of all, learned to expect the unexpected.

She laughed drily. "Obviously you've had an easier time

with motherhood than I have. Each one of the boys was different. Each one refused to play by the rules his brothers set down." She had great kids, but it had been an uphill battle with each one of them. There'd never been any coasting, not even with the youngest one, Christopher, who'd been the most like her.

He wasn't going to be the youngest one anymore, she suddenly thought. How was Christopher going to like that? "Every time I thought I knew what I was doing, I didn't." And it had been exhausting, physically and emotionally. Laurel raised her eyes to the doctor's. "How am I going to go through that again?"

The doctor answered her question with a question. "Would you change anything if you could?"

"What do you mean?"

Just for a second, Dr. Kilpatrick moved back into the room. "If you could erase one of your sons, go back and not have him, would you?"

Laurel didn't even stop to think. "No."

It was obviously the answer the doctor had expected. "Then how do you know you won't feel that way about this one?"

Laurel shook her head. Things were getting jumbled, twisted. "Because with this one, I'll be forty-five years old. Because with this one, I won't be able to run and play."

The doctor opened her chart and glanced down at the notation she'd made earlier. "You still get in a game of tennis now and then, don't you?"

It had been an exaggeration. Wishful thinking on her part.

She was too busy with the demands of her career and personal life to spend much time on the courts. "More then than now."

The doctor closed the chart again, accepting the correction and going from there. "Running is not a requirement with children."

The hell it wasn't, Laurel thought. "I guess your kids were less active than mine. Mine were born running." At least it felt that way. "I get tired just thinking about it." And then it suddenly dawned on her. "Is that why I've been feeling so tired lately? Because I'm pregnant?"

Dr. Kilpatrick's smile filtered into her eyes. "That would be my diagnosis."

One mystery cleared up—and she wished with all her heart that it'd had an easier solution. "I beat you to it. That means you can't charge me."

"All right," Dr. Kilpatrick agreed, tongue in cheek. "I'll just bill you for the urinalysis. And the friendly advice."

She could use some advice, Laurel thought. Real advice. "Which is?"

"Enjoy."

Laurel rolled her eyes as she crossed her arms before her. "Easy for you to say. You don't have to face a man who's stockpiling tons of brochures on summer cabins from three different states."

"He'll be thrilled," the doctor promised.

"He'll be in shock," Laurel countered. Real concern began to set in. What if the news was too much for Jason? "Got a smelling salts I can take with me?"

Dr. Kilpatrick opened the door. "You have my number. Call if you need me."

Laurel laughed. "That's all Jason needs. An ob-gyn attending to him."

Laurel's smile faded the moment the door was closed again. She slid off the table, trying to stay one step ahead of the numbing shock that threatened to completely swallow her up.

This was absurd.

Unreal.

How in heaven's name could she be pregnant? Weren't eggs supposed to dry up at her age? She slipped on her underwear, then hooked her bra. Wasn't that what the whole ticking-biological-clock thing was all about? Having babies before it was too late? Before she couldn't have any? It looked as if she could go on having babies until she was an octogenarian.

Laurel pulled her turtleneck sweater over her head, then punched through her arms.

"This breaking news," she mumbled to herself in disbelief. "Eighty-seven-year-old Laurel Mitchell has just given birth to her twentieth baby. Someone stop this woman for the good of humanity."

With her panty hose still in her hand, Laurel leaned her hip against the table and sighed. How had this happened? She knew how it happened, she upbraided herself, putting on first one leg, then the other. She'd gotten lax. At the end of last year, she'd given in to Jason's pressure and finally stopped taking her birth control pills. He thought it wasn't too much of a risk.

Well, guess what, big guy, we're pregnant. How's that for a risk?

She was on the cusp of menopause, experiencing her own personal heat waves while others were bundling up in sweaters and jackets. She'd assumed that her birthing years were over. That any occasional romp she enjoyed with her husband was deemed safe for all concerned.

Well, you deemed wrong, Laurie old girl.

Old girl.

God, she was too old for this. Too old for morning sickness. Too old for prenatal vitamins and too old to be chasing around after a toddler.

Yet, here it was, happening.

She spread her hand out over her as-yet-flat stomach. There was a teeny-tiny occupant inside now, no bigger than a speck. But he was growing. Growing by the moment. Frowning even as she stood here in this nice, pastel-colored room, agonizing over it.

Him, she corrected herself. Agonizing over him. All she'd ever managed to produce was boys. There was no reason to believe this newest passenger would be any different.

Oh God, this was different.

She was forty-five, for crying out loud. What was God thinking, letting her get pregnant?

"This isn't funny," she murmured, looking up toward the ceiling. "Not funny at all."

And the one who would be laughing the least would be her husband.

Slipping on her shoes, she closed her eyes. How was she ever going to explain this to Jason?

CHAPTER 2

Pregnant.

She could remember the first time she'd ever heard that word applied to her. She and Jason had been married just a little over a year. Jason had graduated from UCLA just that past June and she was set to get her liberal arts diploma that coming June. They felt empowered, as if nothing could stop them. The whole world was wide open for them and they were going to take advantage of it. Right after they took a little time off to do some traveling. That had always been the plan: graduate, then travel a little bit before settling down to a job and starting a family.

The best-laid plans of mice and men…

When Dr. Kilpatrick had told her she was pregnant, her reaction had been bittersweet. Being pregnant meant closing the door on being young and carefree. It meant opening the door to parenthood, which was something both of them wanted and anticipated with relish—sometime in the near future, but not right at that moment.

"So we're a little ahead of schedule," Jason had laughed when she'd told him the news.

She'd come home with a loaf of French bread and candlesticks, intent on creating as much of a romantic setting as she could before telling him. Jason had gotten the news out of her within ten seconds of her closing the door to their tiny furnished apartment.

He'd hugged her, lifting her off the ground. He'd stopped short of spinning her around when she'd protested, saying her stomach contents were threatening to revisit the outside world.

"What about the road trip?" she'd reminded him when her feet were firmly planted back on the floor again. She knew he'd had his heart set on it and had spent weeks planning it, in between going to work. There were maps littering every available flat space in the apartment, many of them with red lines marking possible routes to take.

With a wide grin, he'd shrugged it off. "Plenty of time for a road trip once this little fella makes his debut." He'd patted her stomach, then suddenly dropped to his knees, resting his cheek against her abdomen and talking to her belly button as if it was a direct connection to the baby within. "Don't give your mom any trouble, now. She really doesn't look very good in green."

She'd loved Jason so much at that very moment, she'd thought her heart was going to burst. "We'll go on that road trip as soon as the baby's old enough to travel, honey," she'd promised him with feeling.

Jason rose to his feet, a dazed, happy look of disbelief on his face. "It's a date."

And then he'd gone on to seal the bargain with a deep,

amorous kiss that had made her recall just how it was that she'd gotten into this state to begin with. Because Jason had undone her so quickly, she had completely forgotten all about taking any precautions against this very thing.

But as soon as Luke—named after Jason's late father—was old enough to take on the overdue road trip, Morgan was more than just a gleam in Jason's eye. He was a bump in her stomach. A rather large bump.

Christopher came two years later.

Within a few months after her twenty-fifth birthday, Laurel found herself the harried mother of three children, all under the age of five. Her own mother presented her with a large eleven-by-fourteen book meant for the elementary-school set entitled, *Where Babies Come From*.

Her mother's idea of a joke, Laurel had thought at the time. "I know where babies come from, Mother," she told the woman who had only given birth to two children herself. "They come from heaven, holding a small piece of it in their chubby little hands when they arrive."

And she'd meant that with all her heart. Because holding her babies in her arms was like holding heaven.

But that didn't mean life was peaceful by any stretch of the imagination. Her three, overactive boys had each been a trial in their own unique way, sending both her and Jason to the edge of their tempers and to the center of their ability to love.

It was, all in all, a trial by fire. Three trials by fire. But there wasn't a minute of that hectic, insane life that she would have eliminated—with the possible exception of when Morgan had brought home that jar of black widow spider eggs and they had hatched overnight. The babies had gotten loose, crawling out of the holes he'd punched in the top of the metal lid.

Frantic, envisioning them all dying of spider bites in their beds, she'd almost insisted that they move out of the house. Jason had her agree to a compromise by getting an exterminator at a moment's notice.

But even the black widow spider incident had had its upside. Because of that, when she'd gone to the local real estate agent, she wound up getting friendly with the man who ran the agency. So much so that she began to seriously think about getting a part-time job selling houses as a way to bring in extra money. True to his word, Ed Callaghan signed her up with his agency the very day she passed her course and received her real estate license.

She found that she was good at finding just the right house for people. And just like that, Laurel had a career. A career she still had and a livelihood she could easily count on. When the last of her boys had gone into the first grade, she began to put in more hours. Now she had three plaques on the wall of her cubicle proclaiming her to be the saleswoman of the year. Jason called her his go-getter.

Go-getters didn't go get pregnant. Not if they didn't want to be, she thought glumly as she drove onto the main drag within the city she'd called home for the past twenty years. Once upon a time Molten Parkway had been nothing more than a two-lane road that went from one end of the town to the other, the only path to either of the two freeways that went through Bedford. But now they were a city, not a town, and Molten was a major thoroughfare with three lanes whizzing by in either direction.

Whizzing, that was, in the off hours. During peak hours, the road was clogged with cars either intent on taking one of the two freeways back to wherever it was they came from each morning or returning home from some other region. Molten Parkway found itself the scene of the eternal Southern California shuffle of vehicles. And it was getting worse with each passing month.

Laurel had seen Bedford, like her family, grow over the years. Often she found herself wishing that Bedford would finally stop growing and stay the way it was.

She never thought that she'd find herself wishing the same thing about her family. Certainly not at this stage of her life.

She remembered right after she'd brought Christopher home from the hospital and she and Jason had captured a quiet moment to themselves after Luke and Morgan had collapsed into a fitful sleep.

The two of them had stood over the baby's crib, absorbing the fleeting, rare silence, watching the brand-new third addition to their family sleeping.

And then, suddenly, Jason had broken the silence. "Three," he'd said.

The single word had come out of the blue, surprising her as much as it confused her. She'd looked at him, puzzled, waiting for an explanation. When none came, she'd asked, "What?"

Jason had turned to her and then lightly kissed her forehead, his lips barely touching her skin. Tingling her soul.

"Three," he repeated. "I like the number three." And then, in case she didn't get the reference, he added, "Three sons."

She'd cocked her head, trying to discern something she thought she'd detected.

"Is that finality in your voice?" she'd asked, recalling how he'd talked about having a houseful of kids while they'd been in school.

"It is," he replied, nodding his head as if reviewing his own thoughts and finding them good. "Any more and we might not be able to provide them with everything they'll need." He leaned over the crib, tucking the blue blanket around his small, new son. "Might not be able to give them enough of ourselves, either. Not if equal shares are being handed out."

She'd laughed then and kissed his cheek. As always, he was the soul of reason. And she agreed with him. Three was a good number, even though it was one more than she had hands.

"I do love you, Jason Mitchell."

He'd put his arm around her shoulders then, pulling her closer to him as he murmured, "Yes, I know," into her hair.

"We'll have that road trip someday soon," she'd promised.

She sighed now.

Someday just got a little further away.

CHAPTER 3

Laurel's already overworked heart rose up to her throat as she pulled up before the two-story Colonial house that highlighted their steady rise in the world. It was their third house in twenty years. They'd lived here for a little over seven years now.

It felt like home. More so than the other two, smaller houses.

But it wasn't sentiment that had her heart lodging itself in her windpipe. It was the sight of Jason's navy-blue sedan. The sedan he'd been talking about trading in for a sportier two-seater. He'd been talking about doing this since Christopher had gone off to UCLA almost two years ago. She thought it was her husband's way of coping with empty-nest syndrome. Hers was to look forward to the next visit from one or more of her sons.

It was two o'clock in the afternoon. What was her husband doing home?

Damn.

That wasn't the word that usually came to mind when she thought of her husband. But she'd counted on having more time to pull herself together, to figure out what words to use in order to break the news to Jason—that there would be a baby in their future and it wasn't because one of their sons had accidentally dropped his guard and gotten a girl pregnant.

How could this be happening to her?

Laurel pulled up into the driveway and left the car parked next to his—she had no choice since he'd taken up every square inch of the garage with his train layout. After a deep, fortifying breath, she got out of the vehicle. She took her time locking the door and activating the antitheft alarm.

Of course, she was stalling. Eventually, she was going to have to go in and face the music.

For the time being, Laurel decided to table the "big revelation" in favor of finding out just what Jason was doing home in what amounted to the middle of the day. He rarely came home before six o'clock, usually closer to seven. It seemed to her that the higher up he went in the advertising agency where he worked, the less time he actually had for himself. For them.

Which was why he'd sounded so wistful lately when he talked about chucking everything and taking an early retirement.

Still moving in slow motion, Laurel unlocked the front door. Her hand on the doorknob, she paused to take another deep breath before turning it. She might have leaned on it a little too hard. The next thing she knew, she found herself pitching forward into the house, thrown off balance because the door was being opened from the inside.

"About time you got here," Jason declared, catching her.

He was grinning the grin that transformed him from the

forty-six-year-old ad executive to the young man she'd fallen so hard for the first time she laid eyes on him. He'd been grinning then, too. But at Bernadette O'Hara, who wore her sweaters so tight everyone in high school used to wonder how the five-foot-five dark-haired girl managed to keep her circulation from being literally cut off. At least, all the girls wondered. The boys were all too dazed to be able to put together more than three words into a semicoherent thought without drooling.

All except Jason, she'd discovered, much to her delight.

Jason was deeper than that, deep enough not to be taken in by such superficial things as overdeveloped mammary glands and the underdeveloped material that strained to cover them.

With his hair a deep chestnut-brown as yet unassaulted by any stray gray hairs, Jason was still as boyish looking as he'd been back then. Still as trim and muscular, too, even though a few more pounds had found their way onto his torso. They'd settled in across his chest and biceps, not his waist. She still bought all his pants from that same small section marked "size 30 waist."

Won't be able to say that about you pretty soon. You're going to be size elephant.

"I didn't realize you'd be here," she told him now, slipping off her coat. She tucked it into the hall closet, leaving it on a hook. Right now she didn't think she could handle something as complicated as a hanger. "What are you doing home?"

"Waiting for you." Jason brushed his lips against hers. It

was then that she realized he was holding a bottle of champagne in his hand. Backing up, he held it aloft like the first rider across the finish line at the Kentucky Derby. "I almost started celebrating without you."

"Celebrating?" she echoed.

He knew?

Laurel tried not to sound as nervous, as unsettled, as she felt. It took effort to keep her voice calm. "What are you celebrating?"

There was a smattering of disappointment in his eyes, as if he was surprised she could have forgotten, what with all the hours he'd put in and all the Saturdays he'd spent in his office at home, trying to make things come together for him.

"The Aimes Baby account. It's ours," he declared, referring to the project for the agency he'd been working for these past fifteen years. Then he gleefully corrected, "Mine." Jason let the words sink in before embellishing. "The baby food, the diapers, the toys, all mine."

"We'll have to add on to the house," Laurel quipped, trying very hard to focus on his joy and not her own dread.

"Very funny. I'm talking about the account." As if she didn't know, he thought with affection. Laurel had always taken an active interest in his work. More than he did in hers, he was sorry to admit. But then, he was the one who needed bolstering at times. She had always been tireless, always confident. He didn't know how she did it. "They loved my ad campaign," he told her needlessly since he was the main one pitching to the company. His dark green eyes were shining as he went on. "This means a bonus, a raise and a lot of other perks. Jon Aimes approved the campaign personally. You know what this means, right?"

Her brain felt like Swiss cheese. She didn't even know her own middle name right now.

"Tell me what it means," she coaxed in a voice that wives had been using for centuries to humor husbands who were dying to disclose details.

"It means that we have an in with his other companies, as well. *I* have an in with his other companies as well," he emphasized. "This makes me a very important asset to Chandler, Wallace and Mitchell." His grin was so wide now, it threatened to split his face. "Sky's the limit, Laurie," he declared.

His enthusiasm about to overflow, Jason propped the bottle against his thigh and began working the cork loose. "I told them I needed some time off before I could throw myself headlong into the work. They were a little skeptical at first, but I convinced them. I told them I'd take a laptop with me and e-mail them anything I came up with."

"Laptop?" Laurel repeated. Every second, her brain was shrinking, reducing in size to whatever might reside in a single-cell amoeba.

"Yeah. I figured we'd take it on our road trip. You didn't think I'd forget about the road trip, did you? I know it's not going to be for as long as we anticipated, and I will have to do some work, but it'll be great, I promise, honey." He saw the look on her face and put his own interpretation to her expression. "I know, I know, I was going to taper off, working toward an early retirement, but this just fell into my lap." He conveniently forgot about the long hours he'd put in to get this to fall into his lap. "This was just too good to pass up, you know? And we'll take that longer road trip once all this is squared away. Scout's honor."

The cork finally came loose and went shooting into the living room like a large, beige-colored bullet. Jason laughed as foam came pouring out.

"Wow. I had no idea those things could go that far. C'mon, honey, follow me," he urged, hurrying into the living room, a trail of foam marking his path.

There were crystal glasses on the coffee table and he quickly filled first one, then the other. Once he put down the champagne bottle, he picked up both glasses and offered one to her.

"Here."

But Laurel kept her hand at her sides and she shook her head. "No, I can't."

Jason was nothing if not tolerant. "I know, I know, it's not five o'clock yet, but this is a special occasion, honey. I promise I won't tell the alcohol police. They won't bust you." Picking up her hand, he tried to press the glass into it.

But she kept her hand clenched, refusing to take the glass even though there was nothing she would have rather done right now than down its contents—maybe even the whole bottle. But the reason she wanted the drink was the very reason she couldn't have it.

"No, Jason, really, I can't. I can't have a drink of champagne. Or anything alcoholic."

The perfectly shaped eyebrows she had always envied drew together in a concerned line as Jason looked at her. "Why? Aren't you feeling well?"

She felt inches away from recycling her lunch. "So-so."

And then he remembered. The excitement left his voice. "That's right, you went to see Dr. Kilpatrick today. What did she say? Something's wrong, isn't it?" he guessed, afraid to let his imagination go any further. "Can you take something for it? Can it be cured?"

Terminated, maybe, but not cured. And she wasn't about to consider the former. So she shook her head. "Not really."

Jason's festive mood was gone. "Honey, is it something serious?"

She pressed her lips together. The moment of truth was here. "That all depends. Do you think a baby is serious?"

It was his turn to repeat words in confusion. "A baby?"

Laurel nodded. It was time to drop the bomb. She couldn't stall any longer. "Jason, I'm pregnant."

The glass he'd been holding slipped from his suddenly numbed fingers. Champagne pooled on the light gray carpet, then slowly sank in.

Like a drowning man going down for the fourth time.

CHAPTER 4

Laurel swallowed the few choice words that sprang to her lips regarding the pool of champagne swiftly vanishing into her recently steam cleaned rug. Hurrying into the kitchen, she made a beeline for the sink and opened the cabinet doors beneath it. Housed there were all the cleaning products she needed for any emergency.

She snatched up her ever-faithful can of extrastrength rug cleaner and a clean cloth. The red can and its brethren had served her in good stead, eradicating pizza, spilled cans of soda and beer and the very pungent evidence of not one but three very intense cases of stomach flu.

Stunned and overwhelmed, Jason came to and followed her into the kitchen. He moved like a lost traveler in a foreign land.

"You're kidding, right?"

Turning on her heel, Laurel narrowly avoided colliding with him as she went back into the living room. Time was of the essence when it came to fighting any and all stains. The carpet was no longer new and not nearly as resilient as it'd once been.

Moving around Jason, she dropped to her knees by the coffee table and sprayed the stain. She knew he was waiting for an answer and wished she could give him the one he wanted. But that wasn't possible.

"Do I look like I'm kidding?"

Jason found himself addressing the top of her head. "You look frazzled," he told her quite honestly. "But it's not a look I haven't seen before."

Dabbing at the stain, she glanced up at him. "I'm frazzled because I'm pregnant."

Jason seemed about to slip into shock. "Stop saying that."

She began to rise to her feet again. He took her elbow and helped her up.

She didn't feel pregnant, Jason thought, remembering how heavy Laurel had been during the last pregnancy. She'd gotten so large, he was afraid she'd never get her figure back. But she had. And he liked it. Liked having her as shapely as she'd been the day they got married. Ralph Peters, one of his associates, lamented that his wife looked twice as large as she had when they were first married. Ralph always spoke about Laurel wistfully, telling Jason what a lucky dog he was. He was lucky, no matter what her size.

Laurel drew her elbow away from him. As she'd left the doctor's office, she'd been ambivalent. More in shock than anything else. She certainly hadn't wanted to get pregnant again. Didn't want to *be* pregnant. But listening to Jason, she suddenly felt very protective of this tiny seed within her. Protective and defensive. And suddenly, despite her condition, very alone. She and Jason had always been on the same page no matter what the issue. Sometimes he was at the top and she at the bottom, or vice versa, but always the same page. The look in his eyes told her they were volumes apart.

She didn't like the feeling.

"The baby's not going away if I stop saying I'm pregnant, Jason." She went back to the kitchen to return the can and the cloth to their rightful place. Housework could be handled better if it was divided into a thousand small components rather than tackled on a grand scale.

"Pregnant," Jason echoed again, shaking his head. "How could this have happened?"

"The usual way, Jason." Laurel shut the cabinet again and returned to face him. "There's a mama bee and a papa bee and the papa bee pollinated the mama bee."

He still couldn't believe it. "You're sure? You're absolutely sure you're pregnant? There's no mistake?"

There was no mistaking the hopeful note in his voice. She closed her eyes, feeling increasingly alone by the second. Maybe she should have told her best friend or her sister first. Or her mother. But Jason had given her no choice. He'd been here when she hadn't expected him to be.

"The doctor's sure." She opened her eyes again. "The stick turned blue, the rabbit died, how many different ways do you want me to say it? I'm pregnant."

He stared at her, confused. "The rabbit died? They still use rabbits?"

He would latch onto that, she thought. He did things like that when he didn't like what he was hearing. Focus on a minute, extraneous tidbit and blow it out of proportion.

"It's just a figure of speech, Jason. But I am pregnant." She took a breath to try to calm down. Her stomach remained queasy. "Now that I think of it, this is just the way I felt with Luke."

Jason tried to put the cork back into the bottle and failed. A perfect afternoon had suddenly fallen apart. He gave up with the cork, tossing it aside. "You had Luke over twenty-three years ago."

She waited for him to continue. When he didn't, she pressed, "Your point being?"

Jason shrugged uncomfortably. He felt like a man walking through a minefield. But he had to make her understand. "My point is that women with twenty-three-year-old sons don't get pregnant."

And what the hell was that supposed to mean? she thought, struggling to keep from losing her temper. She began to pace back and forth around the sofa. She'd been through this often enough to know that it was the hormones talking. They were playing Ping-Pong with her emotions. Having her husband say asinine things didn't help, of course.

"Is that some kind of a law?" she asked. "Because if it is, I was out of town the day Congress passed it."

"Laurel, stop pacing." Then, when she didn't, he caught hold of her shoulders and held her in place. Or tried to.

She pushed away his hands. "Why? So you can get a clear shot at me?" Okay, that was over the top, she told herself. "Sorry, I can't help it. I'm exhausted and yet, there's all this pent-up energy inside of me. Just like with Luke," she repeated, her tone daring him to deny her statement.

"Pregnant," he repeated again. The word kept attacking him from all angles, seeking entrance into his brain. He just couldn't handle it and he sank onto the sofa.

Because she had nowhere else to go, Laurel lowered herself down beside him. Deep within her soul, she wanted her husband, her partner, her best friend of so many years, to tell her everything was going to be all right. That he wasn't upset or angry about this bizarre twist their lives had taken. And that he was going to stand by her, no matter what. Stand by her and rub cocoa butter onto her swiftly expanding abdomen to prevent stretch marks, the way he had all the other times.

All the other times, she reminded herself silently, they had been much younger. Jason had been much younger.

Oh God, this was going to be a nightmare. And when she woke up, she was going to be alone. In her mind's eye, she could see Jason running for the hills. Who wants to be married to a forty-five-year-old pregnant woman?

She blew out a breath. "So."

The word hung in the air between them, waiting for more. Begging for more.

"So," he finally echoed, then turned to look at her. As she watched, his expression changed from that of a man who had just dived into a foxhole, shell-shocked, to that of a man who had suddenly seen the course of action opening up before him. "You can't have it," he told her, his voice firm.

She blinked, stunned.

Jason was the type who refused to kill crickets in the house. He captured them and set them free on the patio. He couldn't be saying what she thought he was saying. "Excuse me?"

"You can't have it," he repeated, his voice carrying just a shade less conviction than it had a moment ago.

"What do you mean, I 'can't have it'?" she demanded. "This isn't some rich piece of cake that's going to send my diet into a tailspin—this is a baby. I *already* have it. I'm pregnant. With child," she added, using the terminology Dr. Kilpatrick had used when breaking the news to her. She fought back the wave of horror that was mounting within her. "Jason, you're talking about a human being here."

There were a score of theories as to when a fetus became a living being. He couldn't summon one to back him up. "There's a debate over that at this stage."

She stood up indignantly. "Not to me. You can't just sweep it away like that."

Didn't she understand what was at stake? He rose, trying to put his hands on her shoulders. Trying to form a unit. "Yes, I can."

There was anger in her eyes, anger mixed with disappointment and deep, deep hurt. "Look, I'm sorry this messes up the plans you've been dreaming about these last few years. They were my plans, too, but—"

"Is that what you think? That I'm upset because we can't take a—a stupid road trip?"

"Well, aren't you?"

"Hell, no." And then because his denial wasn't strictly

true, Jason backtracked a little, correcting himself. "I'm disappointed, sure, but the whole road trip idea is becoming sort of an unattainable goal, like Shangri-la."

"Is it the summer home?" she asked. "Because we could still build one, just not as big and maybe not quite in the location you wanted—"

He cut her short. "It's not the summer home."

She'd run out of things to guess. "All right then, what are you upset about?"

"You."

"Me?" He had completely lost her. "What about me?"

His gift of gab, the very thing that helped him pitch the ads he so cleverly constructed, left him when it came to speaking from his heart. He wasn't a man who bared his emotions. He turned away for a moment, shoving his hands deep into his pocket, searching for a way to anchor himself. Searching for words.

When he spoke, he addressed the words to the wall. "Look, I don't want to have to do without you."

Was that it? He was afraid of losing his maid? Over the years, she'd spoiled him and she knew it. She'd taken a relatively self-sufficient man and gotten him used to having everything done for him.

Her own fault, she thought.

"I'll still do everything I've always done," she assured him, trying hard not to let her annoyance show. "Your shirts will still be ironed, your meals will still be made, most likely on time, your—"

"The hell with my shirts. The hell with the meals," he retorted.

For a second, because he had her really confused, Laurel stopped talking. Confusion had her resorting to quips.

"Okay, you'll be wrinkled and hungry. I wish you'd told me that years ago. You would have saved me so much time every week—"

"I don't want to have to do without you," Jason repeated, saying the words with more feeling. And then, because his wife eyed him as if he had suddenly started speaking in several foreign languages, all at once, he was forced to elaborate. He hated being made to say every word. She was supposed to be able to read between the lines. "If something happened to you, I wouldn't be able to go on."

For one of the very few times in her life, Laurel found herself truly speechless.

CHAPTER 5

The silence in the living room continued, stretching out like a long, silken thread until Jason couldn't take it anymore.

"Say something," he urged.

Laurel felt tears stinging her eyes, threatening to spill out. She knew they were there partially because of the king-size hormonal blender into which her emotions had been tossed. But the tears had also sprung up because words of affection from Jason, any sort of affection, were as rare as a blizzard in July in Southern California. It had been years since he'd said anything romantic. He rarely expressed his feelings for her, he just expected her to know.

The breath she let out was ragged. "I think that's one of the nicest things you've ever said to me."

Jason looked at her as if she'd lost her mind. "I'm talking about you dying."

"No," she contradicted, "you're talking about love." She wasn't going to let him bluster his way out of this. He'd said something nice and she was holding him to it. Laurel touched his face, every single available space within her welling up with affection. "I'm not going to die in childbirth, Jase."

He took her hand, but rather than pushing it aside, he pressed it to his cheek. Just for a moment. And then he moved it aside. "How do you know?"

"All right." She inclined her head as if to give him his due. "I can't give you a written guarantee. But I also can't give you one that says I won't die in a traffic accident because I got hit by a car while driving down to Newport Beach. Or that I won't die choking on your mother's extra dry turkey next Thanksgiving. But," she went on, a smile curving her mouth, "I'm reasonably sure I won't die in childbirth. More sure of that than I am about not getting hit by a car or choking on your mother's turkey," she added for good measure.

Jason sighed, taking her hands in his. He forced himself to look her straight in the eye as he tried to make her understand the full extent of his concern. "Laurel, don't take this the wrong way." She looked at him warily, waiting. "But you're old."

She pulled her hands away and turned from him all in one motion. It turned out to be a little too fast, because the sudden movement made her feel dizzy. Shutting her eyes made it worse, and she swayed. The next thing she knew, Jason had his arms around her, holding her steady. Getting her bearing, she pushed him away from her.

"I'm all right," she ground out between clenched teeth. "And I am *not* old."

Jason held his hands up before him, as if to push away what he'd said, or at least the way he'd said it. "Okay, bad choice of words."

"Horrific choice of words," Laurel corrected vehemently. "Forty-five is the new thirty-five," she told him, echoing Dr. Kilpatrick again. "And thirty-five is not old."

"What I'm trying to say is that you're too old to have a baby."

Even though she'd said the same thing to her doctor not more than an hour ago, hearing her husband say it to her had Laurel up in arms. Suddenly, she didn't feel too old to be a mother. She didn't feel any older than she had when she'd had Luke, Morgan or Christopher. Why was he behaving this way now of all times, when she needed him to be supportive?

News stories she'd read came to her out of nowhere, backup statistics she now lobbed at Jason. "There was a Russian woman who gave birth to a baby at sixty-seven last year. Five years ago, there was an actress in Hollywood who used to be on a sitcom in the seventies. She gave birth to twins. Guess how old she was?"

"Haven't a clue."

No, she thought, he didn't. In so many ways.

"She was fifty-one years old. And the babies are fine," she told him triumphantly, as if their condition was her own personal victory. "Women are giving birth to their first babies later these days. And that's where the real risk lies, with first-time births. I've already had three babies. My body's broken in." She saw the look in his eyes. "Not broken down," she informed him tersely, second-guessing what he was thinking. "Broken in. This'll be a piece of cake for me."

He wasn't convinced. She could see that by the way he set his jaw. She loved the man dearly, but when Jason came to a conclusion, he stuck by it as if he'd been put there with crazy glue. "Would you like to talk to Dr. Kilpatrick?"

This was a losing battle. He'd been with her long enough to know that. It wasn't that he relished the idea of what he was proposing; it was just that if he had to make a choice between Laurel and a baby, it would be Laurel each time. He didn't want to look back and find himself wishing that he had made a choice when he had the power.

"What I'd like to do," he told her, "is talk some sense into you."

He made it sound as if this was all on her. As if she'd somehow done this all by herself. Maybe he needed to be reminded of how this kind of thing worked. "Hey, this isn't my doing alone, buster. As I remember, I had help."

These days, by the time he got home from work, he was far too tired to think of making love with his wife. The job drained him. And when he did have spare time, he wanted to use it putting together the train layouts that had been sitting in boxes for, what was it, almost two decades now?

But every so often, Laurel would come to him with that look on her face, wearing something sexy and sheer. And there was this particular perfume she wore on those occasions. A man couldn't think when the space in his head was all taken up with that scent.

"You seduced me," he accused.

She threw her hands up. "You found me out. I put engine oil behind my ears and made noise like an AmTrak passenger train leaving the station."

The deadpanned statement brought a laugh out of him.

Laurel breathed a sigh of relief. At least he was laughing again. The sound instantly made her feel more mellow.

"It's going to be all right, Jason," she promised, putting her arms around him and leaning her head against his chest. "Really."

Funny how things turned out, she thought. She'd been hoping Jason would comfort her about what was ahead and here she was, reassuring him instead.

Jason kissed her forehead. His breath lightly fluttered against her skin as he asked, "So, how far along are you?"

She did a quick mental calculation, remembering the last time they'd made love. The time before that was too far in the past to count. "Three weeks."

He glanced at her, surprised at her precision. "There's room for error."

She moved her head slowly from side to side. When it came to their life together, the man remembered nothing. While she, on the other hand, remembered everything. "There's no error."

Jason pressed his lips together in a reproving frown. "I want you to get a complete checkup."

"That was what today was supposed to be about," she reminded him, not that she expected him to remember that, either. Jason had a habit of not retaining information unless it had to do with either his work or his hobbies. She counted herself lucky that he remembered the boys' birthdays, although he tended to forget the years. As far as listening went, her husband had gotten "uh-huh" down to an art form. "Dr. Kilpatrick gave me a complete physical."

"More complete," he insisted. "Blood work, an amniocentesis." He saw her frowning. "You know, like you did with Christopher."

With Christopher, there had been some complications at the outset and she'd wanted to make sure the baby she was carrying was all right. Personally, she'd thought it was like being harpooned. She didn't see a need to go through the ordeal the test represented this time around, since all she felt was queasy.

But she kept that to herself because she didn't want to create too many waves right now. Now that she'd calmed down, she could see that Jason was obviously trying to come to terms with the bombshell she'd just dropped on him.

That made two of them, she thought. "Yes, sir, Dr. Mitchell, sir." She saluted.

His eyes narrowed even further. "I'm serious, Laurel."

"I never thought you weren't."

He couldn't tell if she was deadpanning again, being sarcastic or for once, being serious. He changed the subject. To a degree. "Did you tell your mother?"

"Not yet." She'd been too dazed to call anyone. And then she smiled as she thought of her mother. "This is going to knock her for a loop. She thought we were going overboard when we had Christopher." Her mother's philosophy had always been simple: two hands, two kids. According to her, there was a divine message there.

He looked down at her flat stomach. "This time, she's

right." When he raised his eyes again, the sad expression on Laurel's face tugged at his heart.

"Aren't you the least little bit happy about this?" she asked.

"So little I might be overlooking it." And then, because he could see that his flippant answer really bothered her, he made an effort for Laurel's sake. "I love kids, Laurie, I always have. You know that. It's just that I thought, at this stage of our lives, we were done with diapers, baby food and toys all over the living room, and were moving on to the next chapter of our lives."

"Just think of this as a slight detour. A chance to relive a piece of our lives."

"Why? We did it right the first three times," he told her.

"We'll do it right again," she said with more conviction than she actually felt. "Besides, now that you've landed the Aimes Baby account, we can get a few free toys and perks," she teased. Forcing a smile to her lips, she threaded her arms around his neck. "It's going to be all right, Jason," she assured him again. "It really is."

"Right," he echoed.

Jason did his best to infuse his voice with feeling, but he just couldn't seem to manage it. The word came out so flat that had it been a reading on a hospital monitor, the patient attached to it would have been pronounced dead.

But that, he supposed, was to be expected. Men who were in shock often registered no emotions.

CHAPTER 6

The office of Bedford Realty Company looked like a miniaturized Swiss chalet, inside and out. The scent of wood, finely crafted and highly polished, greeted the client the moment he or she entered the small, two-story building. Those who worked there were completely oblivious to the scent, having long since lost the ability to detect either the wood or the lemon polish applied nightly.

When Laurel walked in that morning, only Jeannie Wallace, her best friend of ten years, was in the office, seated at her desk. Because of the Mercedes parked in the reserved spot, she knew that the manager, Ed Callaghan, was in the back, most likely looking over the number of sales that had been brought in this month. Beyond that, the office was empty.

She'd debated keeping her news to herself for a while, thinking it might be better that way. But Jeannie only needed to take one look at her face to know something was up.

"C'mon," she urged in her no-nonsense voice, "spill it."

So she did.

For a total of ten seconds, Jeannie said nothing. And then she found her voice. "You're kidding."

Laurel laughed softly to herself. "Funny, that's the same thing Jason said when I told him."

Jeannie's wide mouth curved ever so slightly. She and her husband, Jonas, socialized with Laurel and Jason on a fairly regular basis. She knew all about Jason's plans for the future. "Before or after he got up off the floor?"

Laurel turned on her computer out of habit rather than any specific need to view anything. She kept her schedule in her head as well as on the hard drive. Other than putting in a call to the First Escrow Company of Bedford to find out what was holding up the process for the Newtons, one of her recent sales, she didn't have anything on her agenda.

"After."

Jeannie pursed her lips and shook her head. There was humor in her eyes. "Pregnant, huh?"

Laurel was really having a hard time getting accustomed to the idea. She'd had the same problem the first time around, but then it had been because she was walking on air. That wasn't exactly the case this time. "You don't have to grin like that."

Jeannie leaned back in her chair, which creaked its protest. "I'm just thinking better you than me." Her eyes swept over her friend's petite frame. "I always thought you could stand to gain a few pounds. If I was the pregnant one, they'd have to start reinforcing the chairs around here." The idea made her laugh. At close to six feet, Jeannie was what was politely referred to as heavyset. It never seemed to bother her. Jeannie had always seemed comfortable in her own skin. "I'm lucky Jonas likes his women big." And then her grin widened. "Or maybe he's the lucky one." Pushing away from her own desk, Jeannie, still seated, brought her chair around closer to Laurel. Her eyes were a tad more serious as she asked, "So, how do you feel about it?"

She kept asking herself that same question, Laurel thought. She shrugged in response. "Numb. Nauseated."

Jeannie waved her hand at the words. "Besides that. Those are givens."

Laurel paused for a moment, thinking. Examining. She raised her eyes to Jeannie's. "Happy, I guess. Scared." Despite the fact that they were alone in the front office, she lowered her voice in case Callaghan entered in. "I mean, when I had the others, my body was pretty resilient. Back then, my skin bounced back." She looked down sadly at her flat stomach, knowing that was just a temporary state. "This time around I might end up looking like a stretched-out alligator bag by the time all this is over."

"Not you, Laurel. If I know you, you'll be exercising right through the whole ordeal." Realizing that the word had the wrong connotation, she corrected herself. "I mean, experience."

They'd been friends too long to start pretending now. "No, you got it right the first time. Ordeal's the right word for all this." Laurel sighed, shaking her head. Thinking of the months ahead. The distended stomach, the swelling of every part of her that made rings and shoes too tight. As for the clothes… "I'm going to have to get all new clothes," she realized suddenly. "I gave away the last of my maternity clothes after Christopher was born and we decided that three kids were just about as far as we wanted to go."

Jeannie chuckled. She reached over and patted Laurel's hand. "Well, looks like you're going to have to go shopping, girl." As always, she focused on the bright side. "Shopping's fun. They've got a lot cuter clothes now for pregnant women than when we were at that stage. Originally," she tactfully added. "Wendy and I went shopping just the other Saturday," she went on, mentioning her five-months-pregnant daughter. "I can take you to this new boutique—"

Laurel held up a hand. She wasn't ready to start thinking about buying maternity clothes yet. According to the doctor's scale, she was three pounds lighter than she was when she'd come in for her last checkup. "This isn't another excuse for shopping."

"Sure it is. Everything's an excuse for shopping." Jeannie adored shopping. It had long since been decided that Jonas, an actuary with a major insurance company, was the bread-winner of the family. Her salary went for the frivolous, non-essentials. Once in a while, there was something in it for Jonas. "Shopping is therapeutic, and it helps the economy." She drew herself up as if delivering a proclamation. "Shopping is almost a patriotic duty."

Laurel grinned as she shook her head. "You should have been a lawyer."

Jeannie tossed her head. Newly colored strawberry-blond tresses bounced over her ample shoulders. "I thought about it, but there was too much studying involved. Selling houses is a lot more fun." She leaned in, her voice lowering. "Have you told anyone else yet?"

Laurel shook her head again. She'd thought about it, several times. Had even reached for the phone more than once last night. But ultimately, her courage had flagged. "Not yet."

Jeannie looked at her, puzzled. "Mother, sister, sons?"

The answer didn't change. "No."

"Why?" Confusion gave way to suspicion. "Are you thinking of—?"

"No," Laurel cut her off, not wanting to even hear the option mentioned. By the end of yesterday afternoon, she'd firmly made up her mind to have this baby. Full speed ahead and damn the torpedoes. "I'm not. I just don't have the oomph to go through this five separate times and face those surprised, skeptical and maybe disapproving looks five times over."

Jeannie's solution was simple. "So, don't."

That didn't solve anything. "Right. And what, just tell them I'm gaining all this weight around my middle because my metabolism suddenly decided to die?"

"No, tell them all at once. The whole family. Five with one blow. Like ripping off a Band-Aid. It'll be quick. Just call a family meeting, or whatever it is those gatherings are called. That way, if someone in the group starts asking you what the hell you were thinking, hopefully someone else will jump in to your defense and tell them where to put their opinions."

The thought made Laurel laugh. Jeannie always had

that effect on her. Nothing every fazed her. "Safety in numbers, huh?"

"That's about the size of it."

Laurel thought about it for a moment. She knew that Christopher had classes, but he was free in the evening, as were her other two sons. Her mother was busy with her clubs, but she could set aside a few minutes for her oldest born. And as for Lynda, well, she didn't do much of anything except go to work and come home these days. She was still reeling from her divorce, something that had come upon her totally out of left field.

All five at once. She liked the idea, Laurel thought. It would be a lot easier this way. "Maybe you have something there."

"Of course I do," Jeannie answered cheerfully. "Haven't you noticed? I'm brilliant." The sound of a small bell was heard ringing. They both looked over toward the front door. A lone man entered. "Speaking of being brilliant, looks like we've got ourselves a live one. Why don't you take him?"

They each took turns with clients. She'd been up yesterday afternoon before she'd gone in for the exam that changed everything. "Isn't it your turn for the walk-in?"

"Yeah, but I'm feeling generous. Consider it your first baby present." She looked back at the handsome stranger. He was standing near the door, his hands clasped behind his back as he glanced from photograph to photograph. "Besides, I've got a feeling he's just interested in getting the lay of the land, so to speak." Her lips twitched. "If he were serious, he would have sent his wife ahead first."

"Maybe he doesn't have a wife."

Jeannie pretended to reconsider. "Maybe I shouldn't have given him away so fast."

"Too late," Laurel said, rising to her feet. Sparing her friend one last grin, Laurel walked toward the potential client.

Tall, tanned, with a beautiful thick head of almost black hair with a few distinguished strands of gray, the man was wearing a pair of crisply ironed navy slacks and a striking blue shirt beneath his sports jacket. The shirt was just vivid enough to bring out his eyes. He was examining the array of properties currently up for sale as displayed on the long bulletin board.

"Is there something I can help you with?" Laurel asked as she approached him.

He turned toward her after a beat, pausing just long enough to finish reading the description beneath one of the houses. The smile that came to his lips as he saw her spoke of many things. Houses was not among them.

Laurel felt something electric shoot through her.

"I can think of a few."

His voice, low and rhythmic, was vaguely familiar. But it was like a fleeting thought that wouldn't allow itself to be pinned down. The man's voice probably reminded her of someone else, she decided.

She put on her most cheerful customer-friendly face. "Are you looking for a house?"

"That would be why I'm here," he replied, amusement highlighting his features.

"To buy or rent?"

"To buy. I always buy."

It was probably her imagination, but she could have sworn he was looking at her as if she were a property he was considering owning.

CHAPTER 7

There was nothing going on, Laurel silently insisted the next moment. Just more of her hormones going berserk. The man was merely looking at her, nothing more.

"Sounds promising," she heard herself saying. "Just what did you have in mind?"

The prospective buyer's eyes swept over her, seemingly taking measure of her from head to foot. "Something nice."

Okay, maybe she wasn't imagining it. The man was obviously kibitzing. Out to kill a few hours for whatever reason. And she wasn't all that sure she liked what he was thinking—even though a small part of her was flattered and the truth of it was, she was desperate for a compliment.

Just a sign of things to come, the little voice in her head taunted.

Laurel could remember the tail end of each of her three pregnancies, when she felt as if she was doomed to be eternally round and distended. Eternally fat. She could remember being desperate for someone to look at her eyes when they spoke to her instead of her stomach. Even more desperate for a kind word about her appearance that didn't include the phrase "You're positively glowing" in it. Every pregnant woman knew that wasn't glow—that was sweat from being forced to carry around so much extra weight.

"I'm afraid that you're going to have to be a little more specific, Mr.—" Laurel stopped abruptly, realizing she'd neglected something. Three weeks pregnant and she was getting forgetful already. "I'm sorry, you never told me your name."

"Manning," he told her. "Robert Manning." He said it using the same cadence that James Bond employed whenever he introduced himself to someone.

Her eyes narrowed as the name nudged something in the back of her brain. Just as his voice had. What *was* it she was trying to remember?

Rather than drive herself crazy, she tucked the thought away and put her hand out. "I'm Laurel Mitchell."

Strong tanned fingers enveloped hers. And held her hand a beat longer than was comfortable. He was staring into her eyes as if he was searching for something. Or someone.

Laurel felt her breath shortening even as it lodged itself in her throat.

"Laurel," he repeated slowly. There was warmth in his voice. Warmth that seemed to be spreading out all around her. "I used to know a Laurel. Laurel Taylor."

Who *was* he? "I used to be Laurel Taylor," she heard herself saying, the words dripping from her lips in slow motion as she frantically searched through her sluggish memory banks.

He nodded, pleased. "I thought so." And then his smile

grew as if he'd just told himself an amusing private joke. "You don't remember me." It wasn't a question.

She should have. God knows, she should have, since there was no earthly way she could have possibly forgotten someone who looked like this man. But there was no clear recollection of him in her memory.

Someone else in her position might have attempted to bluff her way through this, but that would only be buying embarrassment further down the line.

Laurel shook her head. "No, I'm sorry, but I'm afraid I don't."

He looked pleased that she hadn't pretended otherwise. "I was Bobby back then. Bobby Manning," he said in case she'd forgotten his last name. "And about a foot shorter than I am now." He laughed, recalling. "With the body of a beanpole. Glasses, a haircut that would have made Prince Valiant proud, courtesy of my mother. I was the class geek," he added, making it sound like an afterthought rather than the painful experience it had once been.

It came back to her.

Laurel's mouth dropped open. The man before her was much too good-looking to have ever been Bobby-not-the-man Manning as the boys in her high school class had always taunted whenever he was around.

Robert laughed then, the sound of which brought to mind a cup of rich, dark hot coffee on a cold winter morning. "I see you remember."

She felt a slight blush creeping up her neck and cheeks, although for the life of her, she couldn't have said why. She'd never been among the ones who'd taunted him. She'd even taken a few to task for being cruel, not that it had gotten her anywhere or made them stop. There was no reason for her to be embarrassed. And yet, the feeling that she was a glowing shade of bright pink wouldn't abate.

Laurel forced a smile to her lips. "I would have never recognized you."

"That was the whole idea." He looked like a picture of confidence. What an incredible difference, she thought. "Money lets you do those kinds of things."

Was he talking about plastic surgery? Not that she'd ever thought there was anything wrong with that. If you could fix something, fix it. Now that she thought about it, his nose seemed smaller than she remembered. But the rest of him looked to have benefited from nature and hard work.

She replayed his words in her head and realized she'd glossed right over the most startling part. "Money?" The Bobby Manning she'd known had worn hand-me-downs. That was part of the reason he'd been the butt of so many cruel jokes.

He nodded. When he spoke, it was matter-of-factly rather than bragging. It reminded her that he'd always been modest. Brilliant, but modest. She was glad he'd done well for himself, especially after what he'd gone through as a kid.

"I created a few dot-com companies that *didn't* go under once the craze was over. I sold a couple, kept one. Things have been good for me." Crossing his arms before him, he leaned a hip against the counter. His focus was completely on her. "And for you, too, I see. You're just as beautiful now as you were in high school."

She could feel the pink hue getting darker. With effort, she shrugged off his compliment, wishing with all her heart Jason could say something like that to her.

"I have a few miles under the hood."

He laughed softly, shaking his head as if to deny what she'd just said. "Must be way under the hood, because it doesn't show."

Laurel continued to feel warmer, so much so that she was surprised she wasn't perspiring. Was she feeling like this because of her new condition, or because the faulty thermostat Callaghan kept promising to have fixed "any day now" was still acting up?

She refused to believe it was because the frog-turned-prince was gazing at her with bedroom eyes.

Laurel cleared her throat and took a step back, creating a little more space between them.

Out of the corner of her eye, she could see Jeannie watching her, watching *them*, as intently as she watched her bevy of soap operas on her days off.

Business, Laurel thought. She needed to get back to business.

She turned her back on Robert and referred to the wide bulletin board. It represented their best listings, but it was only a fraction of what they had to offer. "You said something about wanting to buy a house. How many bedrooms were you thinking of?"

When he didn't answer immediately, she turned back to

him. The smile on his lips seemed to say that he was only thinking of one bedroom. The master bedroom.

What's the matter with you? Are you pregnant with a demon child? You never used to think like this.

Maybe she was having her own midlife crisis, she thought. God, what a time to have one, while she was pregnant.

"There's just me now," Robert finally replied. "So two, three. Nothing very overwhelming."

He'd said "now," which meant the condition had been different before. He'd been married. Recently? "Divorced?" she guessed.

Robert pressed his lips together just for a moment before answering, as if the word was still difficult for him to say. "Widowed."

She felt terrible about stirring up the pain she saw in his eyes. "Oh, I'm sorry."

Robert nodded, accepting her condolences. He took in a breath, using it as a buffer between himself and the past. "It's been a little over a year now. I'm trying to move on."

She nodded, thinking she must seem like a dummy to him. "Best thing to do." It was a lame thing to say, but nothing else came to mind.

"New house, new location." He looked at her for a moment before adding, "New challenges."

She was imagining that, right? That bit of eye contact, the zip that shot through her? The man was a grieving widower. He wasn't hitting on her. "Starting up a new dot-com company?"

"It's on the books," he admitted. "Something I've been

noodling around with. In the meantime, like I said, I still have one left and it has been giving me and mine—my parents—" he clarified, "a good yield."

He mentioned his parents, but no one else. "No children?"

"No, why?"

She moved toward the nearest computer and pulled up a file that had a number of nearby listings. "Well, if there were children, I'd show you some good locations near the schools. But if that's not a factor, I can show you properties that are situated away from the schools. It would be quieter for you."

"I like quiet," he told her. "Although not too much quiet," he qualified. "Too much usually lulls me to sleep."

Laurel crossed to her desk and picked up the leather-bound notebook Jason had given her when she'd sold her first house. She tried not to notice the smirk on Jeannie's face.

Opening the notebook, she began to make notes as she crossed back to Robert. "Price range?"

He shrugged. "Whatever."

Well, that was certainly cavalier, she thought. "Excuse me?"

"Money is not a consideration here," he told her. "Like I said, I've been very lucky. I can afford to buy whatever pleases me."

It sounded like a proposition.

Or maybe she just wanted it to. Laurel banked down her runaway thoughts and told herself to act like a Realtor.

"We have houses that start anywhere from six-hundred thousand dollars to ten times that," she informed him. "Care to narrow down the neighborhood just a little?"

"Why don't we start somewhere in the middle and work our way up?" he suggested.

"Sounds like a plan," she answered glibly, wishing her imagination would stop getting carried away with every word Robert Manning uttered. He was looking for a house and she, apparently, was looking for affirmation. Affirmation that should be coming from Jason, Laurel reminded herself, not from a man who had triumphed over his shortcomings and made good.

CHAPTER 8

Laurel managed to take exactly two steps past the office threshold before Jeannie came rushing up to meet her.

It was nearly three-and-a-half hours later. There were five other real estate agents in the office now, four women and a man. They were either on the phone or talking with clients. Three "civilians" were in the office, seated on chairs directly beside the various desks. The sound of voices, point and counterpoint, buzzed in the air.

Only Jeannie was a free agent at the moment. Her desk, Laurel noted when she glanced over in that direction, was littered with files. Having fallen behind in her paperwork, the way she periodically did, she'd obviously spent the afternoon trying to catch up.

And just as obviously, Jeannie had been watching the door for her return, Laurel thought.

Paperwork, she knew, bored Jeannie to tears. The woman craved drama, mystery and live interaction. Apparently, in lieu of her beloved soap operas, which provided all three, Jeannie had decided to declare her all three, at least for the afternoon.

"You were gone a long time with Mr. Hunk." There was no missing the implication pulsating behind each word. Laurel paused at the main bulletin board to move the pin beside her name from the box labeled "out" to the one labeled "in." "Anything worthwhile come of it?" Jeannie pressed.

"His name is Robert Manning," Laurel told her, hoping Jeannie would stop referring to the man as "Hunk." She made her way to her desk. "We went to high school together. And I was showing him houses. A whole bunch of houses." Draping her trench coat over the back of her chair, she glanced past her shoulder at the other woman. "Fifteen in all before he finally decided he'd had enough."

Hearing something that piqued her interest, Jeannie had stopped listening to the rest of what Laurel had said. "You went to high school together?" She shifted around to the front of the desk as Laurel sat down. "You never mentioned that there was anyone that gorgeous in your background."

"That's because he wasn't." She could see the simple disclaimer just raised more questions. Laurel took a fortifying breath and added, "In my background or gorgeous."

Jeannie clucked and shook her head. "Time for glasses, Laurel." Instead of returning to her own desk and sitting down, Jeannie planted herself in the chair meant for incoming clients. "I told you it would catch up to you, all that fine print you always insisted on reading."

Laurel supposed it wouldn't hurt to give her friend a few more details. Jeannie would just continue to chip away at her until she got what she wanted.

"Bobby—Robert," she corrected, "didn't look like that when I knew him."

Interest continued to grow in Jeannie's soft brown eyes at a very prodigious rate. "A late bloomer?" she guessed.

"Very late," Laurel confirmed. She lowered her voice, leaning in toward the other woman. "And before you let that overactive imagination of yours take you running down soap-opera lane, all I did was show him houses," she enunciated clearly. "Is that understood?"

Jeannie's expression all but shouted, "Yeah, right." Out loud, she asked skeptically, "For over three hours?"

Jeannie, Laurel thought, needed some romance in her life. *Don't we all?*

"They're not exactly located on the same block," she pointed out. "It takes time to go from one property to another. Time to look around. Time to call the owners and let them know someone was coming." She wasn't saying anything that Jeannie didn't know, she thought. The other woman had been at the game the same amount of time she had.

Jeannie looked disappointed. After a beat, she shrugged away the potential vicarious experience, making the best of it. "So, did you make any headway?"

She and Robert had driven from one house to another, each a little more elegant, a little more expensive than the last. He'd found something wrong with each one of them, apologizing even as he turned them down as potential candidates to be considered.

It got to the point that she doubted his sincerity.

Her back ached, her feet ached and her mouth ached—from smiling. And talking. Robert had asked a great many questions about each house they viewed. "He said he hasn't found the one he's looking for."

A glimmer of a knowing look reentered Jeannie's eyes as she looked at her. "Maybe he wasn't talking about the houses."

Okay, enough was enough. Admittedly flattering though the attention might have been, there was reality to consider. Laurel lowered her voice even more, until her words came out in a low growl. "Jeannie, I'm pregnant, remember?"

"They say that pregnant women are desirable."

"No, pregnant women *want* to be desirable," Laurel contradicted. God knows she had in her last three pregnancies. This time, the need was almost immediate. But that was because Jason had kept returning to the fact that she was "old." "And who exactly are 'they'?"

Jeannie spread her hands. "They. Them. The ones in the know."

Laurel shook her head. "The ones who pretend to know."

A touch of pity entered Jeannie's expressive eyes. "Boy, pending motherhood has made you cynical."

Laurel glanced around to see if anyone else in the office was listening to this exchange. But everyone seemed to be caught up in their own worlds. She was safe to try to make her point.

"I'm not pending, Jeannie, I *am* a mother, remember?" she said with as much feeling as a whisper could sustain. "And please, don't say anything to anyone." She glanced at the woman whose desk was closer than the others. "I'd really rather Sally Houseman didn't find out before my sons did."

Jeannie nodded, as if that was already understood. "I take it you didn't tell Mr. Hunk about the little bun in the oven, either."

"Manning, his name is Manning, not Hunk and my condition has nothing to do with the sale of a house," Laurel fairly hissed. Just then, the phone on her desk began to ring. "Now, if you'll excuse me, I've got to take that."

Jeannie reluctantly rose to her feet as Laurel reached for the receiver.

"Laurel Mitchell," Laurel said as she placed the receiver to her ear.

"I think I'd rather think of you as Laurel Taylor," the whimsical voice on the other end of the line told her.

Stunned, it took Laurel a second to find her voice. Out of the corner of her eye, she saw Jeannie watching her with interest as she retreated to her own desk.

What was he doing, calling her? She'd left Robert in the parking lot not more than two minutes ago. At the time, she'd assumed he was going to go home. Or rather, to his parents' house, where he was staying until he found something of his own.

"Did you forget something?" she asked him.

"Yes. I forgot to ask you if you'd like to go out for a drink later after you finish. Maybe do a little catching up."

They'd covered some ground while she drove him from property to property. Obviously not enough ground in his opinion. Or was there something else on his mind?

Warmth began to creep up her neck again.

Pregnant and hot flashes. Terrific.

"Laurel, are you there?" she heard Robert ask when she didn't answer.

She cleared her throat. "Yes. I'm sorry, I was just checking my calendar." It was a lie, but it was all she could think of at the spur of the moment. "I'm afraid I can't tonight. I have a previous commitment."

The previous commitment was one she'd yet to make. She'd already decided to gather the family together tonight to tell them about the baby. The longer she put it off, the greater the chance that one of them was going to find out by accident. Either she or Jason would let something slip. This wasn't the kind of thing that she wanted to just haphazardly come out. If nothing else, this deserved some kind of announcement.

"With my husband," she added, realizing that Robert might misconstrue her words to sound as if she was taking a rain check.

"Bring him along," Robert invited. "I'd like to meet the man who snagged the queen of the prom."

The queen of the prom.

That had been her, all right. About a million light-years ago. She was surprised that Robert knew about that. They hadn't traveled in the same circles. He hadn't had a circle at all when he was in high school.

She was being silent again, she realized. "I didn't know you went to the prom."

The quiet laugh caused more warmth to travel along her body. She valiantly ignored the sensation. "I went stag. To see how the other half lived." She could almost hear him smiling. "I wanted to ask you to dance, but I figured I didn't have a shot. There were just too many guys around you."

All that was a blur in her past. "That was a very long time ago."

"Not that long," he contradicted gently. "You still look like a prom queen."

Oh God, why couldn't Jason say something like that?

Feeling a bit self-conscious, she laughed. "One who has been left back a dozen years or so. Look, I really can't make it tonight, but maybe another time. I'd like you to meet Jason." *Maybe some of you can rub off on him.*

"Just name the time and the place," Robert told her. "I'll look forward to it. And call me if you have any other listings to show me."

"Count on it."

Laurel replaced the receiver in its cradle, a very odd feeling rifling through her.

"Can't get enough of you, huh?"

She almost jumped. When had Jeannie crossed back to her desk? "He just wanted to get together to go over a few details."

"The corner of your mouth twitches when you lie," Jeannie informed her cheerfully. "Just thought you'd want to know." She winked. "Just in case."

"Jeannie, I need to see you for a minute." Callaghan called out from the threshold of his glass-enclosed office.

Saved by the office manager, Laurel thought, as Jeannie reluctantly left her.

She watched as Jeannie walked into the manager's office, then she reached for the phone again. She had phone calls to make if this family meeting was going to be a reality.

CHAPTER 9

"Is this going to take long, Mom?" Christopher Mitchell called out as he let himself into the house. At five feet ten inches her youngest son was blond like his brothers with an athletic build that was the result of years of swimming. Seeing the rest of his family already in the living room, he went to join them. "I'm taking out a new girl tonight and I don't want to be late."

Luke, the oldest, was perched on the arm of the sofa farthest from the doorway. "You're always taking out a new girl." His tone was lofty and a tad patronizing as he regarded his brother.

Dutifully, Christopher paused to kiss his grandmother, seated on the sofa. He nodded at his aunt and his mother. In his bid for independence, he was in the midst of distancing himself from all his so-called childhood practices, such as hugging and kissing his mother and aunt. In his mind, his grandmother was ancient and scheduled to die at any moment, so she came under a different criteria.

As he stepped away from his grandmother, he shot Luke a contemptuous glance. "Better than being stuck with just one."

Luke pulled back his shoulders defensively. He took his brother's retort as a direct slam against the woman he intended to marry in four months.

"I am *not* stuck," Luke retorted. "I happen to love Denise."

"Or so she tells you," Morgan quipped. Easily the tallest of the three, he was reclining languidly on the other end of the sofa, his long legs stretched out before him like two limbo poles at rest.

"Are you saying you think I'm—" Luke's lips began to form the letter *p* but since he was in a room with not only his mother, but his grandmother and his aunt Lynda as well, he switched directions swiftly and said "henpecked," instead.

"Wouldn't dream of it," Morgan answered, quite deliberately sticking his tongue into his cheek as he grinned.

"Guys, put a lid on it," Lynda ordered. "This is your mom's show. The sooner you stop trading barbs, the sooner she'll tell us what this is all about." Sitting on the edge of one side of the love seat that she shared with her mother, Lynda looked up at her older sister impatiently. "What is this all about, Laur?" she asked.

"Yeah, what's the big mystery, Mom?" Luke chimed in. He glanced toward his father, but the latter's face was impassive. No clues there. "Why couldn't you just tell us over the phone?"

It might have been easier in the long run, Laurel thought. At least she wouldn't have worried about seeing the looks on their faces. Too wired to sit, she was the only one standing in the room. Jason had taken a seat off to one side, like an observer.

As if this could have all happened without him.

"Because I wanted you all to find out at the same time so there'd be no hurt feelings about who was first. Also I don't have conference calling for six."

"Six," Morgan repeated, nodding his head thoughtfully. His eyes slanted over toward his father. "So Dad knows."

She glanced at her husband. Jason had taken the seat facing the love seat. It placed him on the same side of the room as everyone else. And not her. Laurel couldn't help wondering if he knew it made her feel isolated.

Me versus them. We're supposed to be a team, Jason. I'm not supposed to be out here on my own.

Hormones again.

In the past few days, she'd felt them bouncing around like Ping-Pong balls on steroids. She'd hit highs and lows she'd never experienced before, not even when she was pregnant with Luke. And entertaining thoughts she could never even utter in confession. Being pregnant at forty-five was certainly different.

"Yes," she acknowledged, "Dad knows."

Christopher made no effort to hide the fact that he was looking at his watch. "Are you going to tell us anytime soon?"

"How about a clue?" Morgan interjected drolly. "First word? Sounds like?" he coaxed, as if playing a game of charades.

She smiled to herself. Morgan was her clown. Her peacemaker. The perfect middle child. Except that he wouldn't be the middle child anymore. At least, not alone. He would have to share that position with Christopher now. She wondered if that would bother him. Probably not as much as having his mother pregnant, she decided. Although, of the three, she imagined Morgan would probably take the news the best.

"Maybe," she finally said.

"Maybe?" her mother, Debra Taylor, repeated. She looked at her in confusion. Her mother did not like being confused. It made her feel as if she wasn't in control. They shared that, she and her mother. Always wanting to be in control.

Sometimes the Fates conspired against you, Laurel thought philosophically.

"It sounds like 'maybe,'" Laurel elaborated, then corrected herself. "Or rhymes with 'maybe,' actually."

Christopher and Luke looked at each other. None of this was making any sense to them. Or to her sister by the expression on Lynda's face.

"What rhymes with 'maybe'?" Christopher asked.

"Glad to see our money wasn't misspent on your college education," Jason interjected drily.

Laurel struggled not to glare at him. *Great, first thing he says and it's a joke*.

"Baby," Lynda said suddenly. "Baby rhymes with maybe." Having said that, she was no more enlightened than she'd been a moment ago. "What are you trying to say, Laurel?"

Feeling stranded, Laurel leaned over toward her husband. "Jason, back me up here."

"You want me to tell them?" He asked the question as if something dire was about to be revealed, something he wasn't really responsible for. What was the *matter* with him?

"Tell us what?" Debra demanded. "One of you say it already."

"Why does Dad have to back you up?" Luke asked.

Debra's sharp blue eyes narrowed. "Laurel, are you thinking of adopting a baby?"

"Is that it, Mom? You're adopting a kid?" Every syllable Christopher uttered had *protest* written all over it.

"Mom, do you—?"

Luke got no further as Laurel cut in. "No."

Luke breathed a sigh of relief. "That's good to hear."

Only Morgan continued watching her, keeping his silence. The expression on his face told her that he had already put one and one together and gotten three.

"No, I'm not adopting," Laurel corrected. "Having."

Luke nearly fell off the sofa's arm. "You're thinking of having a baby?"

"Are you out of your mind?" Lynda was on her feet, as if the mere action would bring her sister, her normally very logical sister, back to her senses.

"Mom, you can't have a baby at your age," Luke declared, horrified. "You're…not young." He'd nearly blurted out the word "old" and had stopped himself just in time, knowing that would most likely only set his mother off.

"Mom, you can't have a baby." Christopher echoed his older brother's words, adding, "It's too gross."

Morgan drew in his legs and rose from the sofa. He crossed to his mother, dwarfing her by close to a foot. He put his arm around her shoulders and looked down into her face. "Mom?"

He knew, she thought. She took a breath. "It's too late for the can't part," Laurel answered.

The smile on Morgan's lips was pure understanding. She could have thrown her arms around him. But this wasn't about being grateful for the one who was supportive; it was about getting everyone else on board. Including Jason.

"You're having a baby," Morgan said softly.

Laurel pressed her lips together, suddenly wanting to cry. That's all she needed, to have them think she was coming apart at the seams.

She nodded. "I'm having a baby."

It felt like a confession instead of the happy announcement she'd hoped it would be.

Morgan gave her a quick, warm hug. "Looks like Christopher isn't going to be the baby of the family anymore."

He sounded rather amused by that, Laurel thought.

CHAPTER 10

The next moment, as if someone had just shot off a gun, signaling the beginning of a major event, everyone swarmed around her. Morgan took a step back as his two brothers converged on her from the right, while Lynda and her mother filled up the remaining spaces on the left.

Only Jason hung back from the crowd, observing the rest of the family without comment, like a physics professor monitoring a science experiment in a state-of-the-art laboratory. His detachment bothered her more than words could express. For the very first time in her marriage, she felt at odds with him.

Christopher seemed particularly distressed as he approached her. "Mom, how'd this happen?" He obviously was having a great deal of trouble coping with the news now that it was out in the open.

Luke hit his younger brother's chest with the back of his hand, the way he used to when they were little boys. "How do you think it happened? Didn't they teach you anything in school?"

Laurel wasn't sure if he was putting his brother on, or if

this was Luke's way of coping with the shock of finding that his parents still had an active, or at least semiactive, sex life.

Christopher looked a little green around the edges as his eyes shifted back toward his mother, shock and accusation mirrored with the dark green orbs. "I don't *want* to think about how it happened," he cried, suppressing a shudder.

"No one's asking you to go there, Chris," Jason said sternly.

Glancing in her husband's direction, Laurel flashed him a grateful smile. *Finally*, he'd said something that sounded as if he was on her side here. It was a start.

And then, holding her breath, she slanted a glance toward her mother, the woman who, nineteen years ago, had trouble understanding what would have possessed her to want to add a third child to the group. She'd fully expected her mother, never a shrinking violet, to voice some sort of criticism about this turn of events.

But Debra Taylor moved her younger daughter aside and threw her arms around her firstborn. Laurel was as stunned by her mother's unexpected demonstration of affection as she had been the other day by Dr. Kilpatrick's diagnosis.

"Mother?" she asked uncertainly from the middle of a very warm embrace.

She felt her mother's smile blossoming, spreading out to encompass both of them. "Well, if anyone cares, I think it's wonderful."

Laurel drew back from the smaller woman, staring at her as if she had sprouted another head. Or possibly a pair of wings. "You do?"

"Sure." Debra's smile widened, the area around her eyes disappearing into a wealth of wrinkles. "As long as it's happening to you, not me," she added with a broad wink.

Joke or not, she realized her mother meant it. She was really happy for her. The way she had been when Luke and Morgan had been on their way. The way she later was once Christopher had made his appearance. Laurel breathed a sigh of relief. She'd been resigned to fighting everyone on this, one by one or en masse. This was turning out not to be so bad.

"God, Mom, you have no idea how much that means to me," Laurel said as her mother impulsively hugged her a second time. She allowed herself a moment to linger there, remembering when she'd been a little girl and there'd been no safer place than her mother's arms.

Her eyes strayed toward her sister. Lynda hadn't said anything yet and there was a confused look on her face. Easing herself out of her mother's hug, she went to her sister.

"What?"

Lynda looked self-conscious at being caught in the middle of a thought. She shrugged, glancing away. "Nothing. It's just that I thought you …you know—" Lynda looked back at her "—couldn't."

Obviously, there were a great many holes in her education as far as menopause went. "Well, looks like I could and I did."

Debra waved her hand at Lynda, dismissing her younger daughter's question and turned back to Laurel. "How are you feeling?"

The question, Laurel thought, was very typical of her

mother. Health had always been her primary concern, especially since her husband died. Debra Taylor was the classic kind of mother, one who had you wearing a sweater when she felt cold.

"I feel relieved," Laurel admitted. She blew out a breath to underscore the feeling.

Debra shook her head, her recently refreshed and dyed blond hair moving back and forth about her face. "No, I mean healthwise."

She shrugged in response to her mother's question. "A little nauseous."

"That's because you're afraid the baby's going to come out looking like another Christopher," Morgan quipped, his mouth curving in his father's smile.

Christopher glared at him. The butt of both brothers' jokes while he was growing up, he was still overly sensitive to their teasing comments. "I wouldn't talk if I were you," he ground out, then went on to ask, "Cracked any good mirrors lately?"

It was only a matter of time before Luke was drawn in. She wasn't about to allow this to disintegrate into a knockdown, drag-out squabble between the brothers.

"All my sons were and are beautiful," Laurel declared, raising her voice in order to be heard above the din.

Although, she added silently, she had been worried about Christopher for the first three months. He'd come out with his head misshapen and he'd resembled an old man who had a perpetually sour stomach. But within six months, he was on his way to being as good-looking as his brothers and now he was probably the best looking of all three, although she would have never said as much out loud, not even to Jason.

"Boys aren't beautiful, Mom," Morgan interjected, a tolerant look on his face. He was obviously attributing her slip to her present condition, as if pregnancy somehow stopped the flow of blood to all vital organs, most assuredly the brain.

But she shook her head and declared with a laugh, "They are to me." She put her arms around the shoulders of the two closest to her, having to stand up on her tiptoes despite her high heels. "At least the three of you are."

Debra interpreted her daughter's response in her own way. "So, this is going to be another boy?"

"I don't know yet." She removed her arms from around her sons, coming down on her heels again. "I haven't had any other tests done, other than the one that indicated I was pregnant."

Debra frowned. She had never been known for her patience, or for waiting things out until the person felt like telling her something. She always jumped into the heart of the matter. "What are you waiting for?"

"Courage."

The word had come out before Laurel thought to stop it. She quickly glossed over the slip, even though it was truer than she'd like to admit. She'd always been the one to forge ahead, to let nothing stop her. For the most part, she liked to think of herself as being fearless, not someone who worried about consequences. Yet here she was, taking baby steps. Hoping for approval. She wondered if that was due to a hormone imbalance, because this was certainly nothing like her normal self.

"And I wanted to let you all know about the baby before any more time had gone by."

"So when are you having the test to determine gender?" Morgan asked.

"It's called an amniocentesis," she told him, and then shrugged in response to the question.

She really hadn't thought that far in advance, certainly not when it came to wondering about the baby's sex. A part of her felt she knew what it would be. She'd always had boys. There was no reason to think that she might have something else.

Even though a part of her secretly hoped…

No, healthy was all she was hoping for. Boy, girl, pony, as long as it was healthy, that was all that counted in her book. Well, okay, maybe not a pony, she amended silently. But healthy. Healthy was all that counted. Which meant that she was going to have to see about having the test done, not to determine gender, but to make sure everything was all right. Great strides had been made with in vitro surgery to correct certain conditions even before the baby was born.

It was a marvelous age they were living in, she thought. And her children would see an even more marvelous one.

"Soon," she assured Morgan. "I think there's a proper time frame for it. I have to talk with my doctor about it."

"Do you want a girl?" Christopher asked.

She glanced toward Jason to see if he had an opinion to offer. Once, she knew, he'd had his heart set on a girl, but that had faded after Morgan. With Christopher, they'd both just assumed the baby would be a boy. And here she was, with another chance at the baby lottery.

The idea of having a girl thrilled her to death. Not that she didn't love each of her sons dearly, but a daughter, well, there were things you could do with a daughter that you couldn't with a son. There were rituals to pass down through generations and, while she would have never traded even one of her sons for a daughter, she had to admit, however secretly, that it was nice to entertain that possibility at the outset.

Christopher glanced at his watch again, shifting impatiently. "Okay, any other bombshells you want to drop on us? Like one of us was really adopted, or something like that?"

"Nope, no other bombshells," she assured him cheerfully. "You're free to see your girl of the week." Catching her youngest off guard, she brushed a quick kiss against his cheek.

"I've been seeing her for three weeks," he protested.

"My mistake."

Laurel did her best to look properly contrite as Christopher quickly hurried out the front door.

"Sorry, Mom, but I've got to fly, too," Luke told her less than a minute after his youngest brother left. "I promised Denise I was going to pick her up at her place for dinner and a movie." He looked at his mother for a moment, then shook his head. "Oh God, wait until I tell her the news."

Bidding everyone else goodbye, Luke was almost out the door when he came to a sudden, almost skidding halt. He swung around to look at his mother. "Mom, the wedding's in four months. Are you still going to be able to attend?"

Tucking her arm through his, she turned him back around toward the door. "I'm pregnant, Luke, not in a coma," she told him with a laugh. "Even if I was, wild horses couldn't keep me away from your wedding."

Luke's eyes swept over her form as he pressed his lips together. "I wasn't exactly thinking about you missing the wedding—"

And then the light dawned on her and she understood. "You were thinking about how Denise might feel if I took some of the attention from her because by the time the wedding comes, I'll look as if I'm smuggling beer kegs to a frat party?" He wasn't saying yes, but she recognized guilt when she saw it. "Don't worry, Luke, I'll pick something out that won't let everyone know your mother's been fooling around with your father." She saw color rising to her oldest son's face.

"Barring that," Jason told him as he moved next to Laurel, "I can always throw a sheet over your mother and we'll pretend she's a mystery gift."

"Yeah, okay," Luke mumbled, more to himself than to anyone there. It was painfully clear to him that his parents thought of this as some big joke. But then, they didn't have to face a woman whose mother had been planning her wedding ever since she'd begun eating solid food. "I'll give you a call," he said into his chin as he hurried out the door.

"You shouldn't torture him like that," Morgan commented, referring to his mother's response. "Luke embarrasses easily. Must have something to do with his repressed childhood," he deadpanned.

His mother was the most open parent he'd ever known. Unlike his brothers, he'd always felt comfortable around her. Comfortable enough to ask any question and hear any answer. Growing up, he'd always thought of himself as being fortunate because he'd had her for a mother instead of some of the mothers his friends had.

"So," Debra said as if some huge hurdle had been met and conquered. "Are we going to celebrate the good news?" She looked at Jason expectantly.

Laurel grinned. "Is that a hint that you want to go out for dinner, Mother?"

Debra shrugged, spreading her hands out wide. "Out, in, it doesn't matter. As long as the meal is taken together with the family. What about you two? Are you free?" she asked, glancing from Lynda to Morgan.

Morgan had temporarily moved back home after graduation, intent on saving his paychecks until such time as he had enough for a down payment on a condo. On occasion, his evenings meshed with those of his parents. Tonight seemed like one of those nights.

"I've got nothing planned, Grandma," Morgan told her. "Celebrating sounds like a good idea to me."

"Well, then that's settled," Debra began. "So—"

"I have to go," Lynda interrupted.

Debra made no effort to hide the annoyance her younger daughter's declaration generated. "Where do you have to go?"

"Someplace," she said forcefully, refusing to elaborate any

more than that. Crossing back to the love seat, she picked up her purse. Lynda slipped on her coat even as she made her way back.

"Wait, I'll walk you out," Laurel volunteered, hurrying after her.

Lynda stopped to fix her collar. "No, you stay," she ordered, then attempted to smooth over the way she'd snapped by adding, "Don't want to risk catching a cold now, do you?"

Without breaking stride, Laurel grabbed her own coat from the rack. "That's why God invented coats," she told her sister, quickly slipping hers on.

The second they were outside the door, and out of earshot of the others, she took hold of Lynda's arm, stopping her from going to her car. "Okay, Lyn, what's up?"

Lynda turned but avoided looking at her as she asked innocently, "What do you mean?"

"Well, I didn't expect you to exactly do handstands over this news, but I thought you'd at least be happy for me."

"I'm happy," she retorted.

"I've seen happier faces on the news when the camera pans a crowd of people who've just found out they were being laid off." Laurel made it clear she was not about to let her sister go without some kind of explanation. "What's wrong?"

"I don't think getting pregnant at forty-six—"

"Forty-five," Laurel corrected her patiently.

"Forty-five," Lynda repeated, then waved her hand at the number. "Whatever—is such a good idea."

Neither had she, on the outset, Laurel thought. But she'd gotten very used to it very quickly, and now, if she didn't think of the obstacles and didn't allow any wet blankets to dampen her enthusiasm, she was rather happy about the idea.

"Well, it's not like we planned it," she allowed. "But now that the baby's on its way—" Laurel stopped abruptly, something sad in her sister's face catching her attention. She was familiar with the look from years back. Lynda was brooding.

Because she was pregnant?

That didn't make sense. "That's not it," she decided out loud. "All the other times, you were always the first one to be excited for me." She remembered when she'd told her about being pregnant with Luke. Lynda wouldn't stop begging until she'd promised to make her his godmother. She'd bought gifts for him for weeks before she was finally stopped.

Lynda shoved her hands into her pockets, staring off down the street at the two little boys attempting to play soccer. Four and five, they kept missing the ball each time they tried to kick it.

"I'm just being more logical these days. That happens when you grow up."

Laurel read between the lines. "This is about Dean, isn't it?"

Lynda glanced at her sharply, a denial hot on her tongue. Then she sighed, as if defeated. "I was supposed to be a mother by now. It was my turn this time, not yours. And yet, look at you. Three with one on the way. Even at this age, you're doing it better than I could."

The divorce had hit Lynda hard, blindsiding her. Dean

hadn't been caught fooling around, hadn't taken a walk to the candy store one evening, never to return, hadn't even announced that after thirty-four years, he'd suddenly realized he was the wrong sexual orientation. He'd just looked at her over toast one morning and said that he didn't love her anymore. That whatever he'd felt for her, for no apparent reason, was gone. He wanted to get out of the marriage so that he could find the one he was meant to be with. Leaving her reeling and emotionally stranded. The family had rallied around her, but it still didn't help the wounds heal. And Laurel knew it.

She put her arm around Lynda's shoulders, but her sister pulled away, keeping her hurt to herself. "I was just lucky to find Jason, that's all. But your turn will come."

"When? When will my turn come?" Lynda demanded angrily. "Just before they close the casket? Is that when I'm going to get my shot at being happy?"

Although her emotions were pretty much strung out because of her condition, Laurel did her best to sound understanding. "Lynda, you're thirty-five, not ninety-five. Nobody's closing a casket on you just yet." She smiled at her encouragingly. "It'll happen."

Lynda made no effort to keep the bitterness from her voice. "Yeah, I hear romances run rampant in old folks homes."

"You're not set to enter one of those for at least another year or two," Laurel said. And then she put her hands on her sister's shoulders, refusing to let Lynda shrug them off. "C'mon back inside, Lyn. We'll go out. All of us. Like the old days."

A half smile played on Lynda's lips. "In the old days we

used to go to those family-style restaurants where we'd spend half the meals if not more chasing after Luke, Morgan and Christopher, trying to get them to sit down and eat."

Laurel grinned. "I'll see if I can get Morgan to run around the table once or twice for old time's sake," she said, squeezing her sister's shoulder. "What do you say? Sound good?"

Slowly, a smile began to emerge. "Yeah, why not?"

Laurel nodded, then stopped just before she opened the front door again. She turned to look at Lynda.

"Dean was a mess, Lyn."

"Yeah, I suppose." Her voice was full of pain and just a little wistfulness. "But he was a gorgeous mess."

"Maybe so," Laurel allowed, "but there's something better out there for you."

Lynda whispered, "Promise?"

Laurel drew an x over her heart, then held up her hand in a solemn oath. "Cross my heart and hope to die."

"I'll hold you to that, you know."

Laurel paused. "The dying part?"

Lynda shook her head. "No, the promise part."

Laurel grinned again. "I'm not worried."

"Sure, why should you be?" Lynda laughed drily. "You're pregnant."

"Trust me, your turn'll come. And I for one am going to enjoy every lovely minute of it." Laurel opened the door and called, "Hey, everybody, we're going out." She didn't bother taking off her coat. Instead, she looked at Jason. "I don't feel like cooking."

He raised an eyebrow. "Is this a preview of the next nine months?"

"Eight," she corrected. She was over three weeks along. "And maybe."

Jason nodded, agreeably, going to get his jacket. "Just so I know."

CHAPTER 11

"I guess they'll survive," Laurel said as she placed her hairbrush back on the bureau. It was later that evening and she and Jason were getting ready for bed. Morgan had gone out again shortly after they'd returned, saying he'd be home before midnight. They were alone in the house.

She glanced into the mirror to see Jason's reaction to her words.

"Why shouldn't they survive?" Jason kicked off his shoes. The left landed near the closet, the right found a home near his side of the bed. He tried to keep the resentment out of his voice. "They're not that directly affected."

Habit had her picking up his shoes and arranging them side by side within his portion of the closet. "Excuse me?"

Jason shrugged, as if debating whether or not he'd chosen the right words. "All right, they're your sons, your mother, your sister, but they're not the ones who are going to be lying on that table in eight months, biting off their lower lip as they're struggling to push out a brand-new life."

Was he aware that he'd just awarded her the family, giving

up any claim to them? It might have been *her* sister and *her* mother, but they were *their* sons.

With an inward sigh, Laurel decided it wasn't worth bringing up. However, she couldn't allow the second half of his statement pass. Pride wouldn't let her. "I never bit off my lower lip."

His laugh told her that he begged to differ with her memory. "Came damn close with Christopher."

There were times when all that seemed as if it had happened yesterday instead of over two decades ago. Vivid memories returned to her as she changed out of her clothes and into the nightgown she favored.

"If I did, it was just that I didn't want to scream in your ear."

He sat down on the edge of the bed, pitching his socks one at a time in the general direction of the hamper in the bathroom. He missed by several feet. "I would have moved away if you hadn't had a death grip on my arm. Took me five days to get the feeling back."

After hanging up her clothes, Laurel turned to gather his socks and deposit them into the hamper. She glanced toward her husband, a fond smile playing on her lips. He was coming around, and she simply had to be patient. "I never knew you were prone to exaggerating."

His mouth curved faintly. "Must be the company I keep."

Once he took off his shirt, then his slacks, Jason let them drop where he stood and pulled on the pair of very worn cutoffs he wore to bed. He yanked on a faded Angels T-shirt. Holes had begun to form beneath each arm, but he remained blissfully oblivious to them. He was nothing if not loyal, even when it came to clothing.

Jason moved back the covers and slid into bed. For a moment, he watched his wife in silence. Watched her pick up the clothing he'd just absently discarded. Watched and thought about how he'd seen her do this exact same thing night after night for what seemed like eternity. There was something strangely comforting about the familiar sight. Something comforting about having her here with him.

His conscience nudged at him. He had taken all this for granted, had assumed it would always be this way. Nothing just continued. Everything was finite. Some things sooner than later.

Uneasiness reared its hoary head again. "Are you sure about this, Laurie?"

After depositing Jason's clothing on a chair, wondering what it took to educate such an intelligent man to do a few simple things like hang up his clothes, Laurel turned to look at him. He'd asked the question so softly, for a second she thought she'd imagined it. But he was watching her like someone who expected an answer, so he must have said it. So much for thinking he was coming around.

Maybe it was going to take him a little longer.

Her hand slipped protectively over her stomach. There was a part of her that was proud of her flat belly, proud that, at age forty-five, she looked more than ten years younger. She was sacrificing a great deal for this tiny invader she had not knowingly invited into her life.

But in her heart, there was no other path she wanted to take.

"I'm not having this conversation again, Jase," she informed him with finality. "This baby isn't some afterthought I can delete with the press of a button on the keyboard." She paused. She didn't presume to know what was best for any other woman in her position, but she knew what was right for her. "I can't just sweep it from my life."

"I know," he said quickly. "You're right and I wouldn't ask you to, it's just that…" An expert at capturing what it was a client wanted to convey in an ad, Jason had never been any good at putting his own feelings into words. "If I had to do without you…"

"You'd drown in a sea of your own dirty clothes within a month." Laurel grinned, slipping into bed beside him. She kissed his cheek fondly. "I know perfectly well that if I died, you'd wind up standing in the middle of the living room, naked, looking for your car keys."

"Not funny, Laurie," he said so fiercely he almost took her breath away.

He was really worried, she realized. Suddenly, she was filled with love. "Don't worry, I've got no intention of dying."

His expression was stony. "It's not always up to you."

"Yes it is. I've got a deal going with God. He gave me this list of things to accomplish before my time down here is over." A whimsical smile played on her lips. "I'm so far behind now, I can never die, so you have nothing to worry about."

He laughed as he kissed her forehead. And then, as he put his arms around her, Jason kissed her again.

On the lips.

With feeling.

Laurel could feel the heat rising within her body even as she banked down her surprise. It had been a while since Jason had wanted to make love to her without her initiating. She'd begun to think that was the way he wanted it.

Apparently not.

She felt his fingers coaxing her nightgown from her shoulders. The next moment, his lips had moved there, creating a web of kisses that fed into one another. A warm smile filtered all through her as her body temperature rose several more degrees. She could feel his body hardening with desire.

She couldn't help thinking how lucky she was, still in love with the same man after all these years. And having that man still in love with her.

Restraining herself because all she wanted to do was rip off his beloved T-shirt and frayed cutoffs, she drew back for a moment. This *was* her husband, right? Not some sexy clone programmed to pleasure her.

He looked at her quizzically. "Something wrong?"

No, nothing was wrong. Everything was perfect. Absolutely perfect, she thought. But she couldn't help asking, "Isn't this what got us in trouble in the first place?"

"So?" He tucked her body beneath his and the familiar fit hardened him even more. Making him want her with a fierceness that never ceased to amaze him. "What's going to happen? You're going to become more pregnant?"

She pretended to consider his question seriously. "I

remember once reading about a woman who was pregnant with twins, but when they were born, the doctor discovered that they were each conceived at different times. One baby was actually chronologically two months younger than his brother."

He gave her a look that said he didn't know whether or not to believe her. He shrugged his shoulders and they moved against her. "I'll chance it."

"Sure," she laughed. "It's not your body you're playing Russian roulette with."

"Nope." His arms beneath her, Jason gathered her even closer. "It's your body I'm interested in playing with."

She melted against him. Melted into him. All these years later and it was almost like the first time.

Damn lucky, she thought again.

"Talk is cheap," she told him. "Show me."

The smile that unfurled along his lips was positively wicked. She could feel her pulse racing. "Your wish is my command."

Her breath was already growing short. Laurel's eyes fluttered shut a moment before she let herself sink into the kiss that was very much, as the old Doors song went, lighting her fire.

"Pregnancy agrees with you," Jeannie decided the following morning after watching her walk in.

Laurel could feel a spring in her step and a glow from last night that had yet to be extinguished. With any luck, she could bask in the feeling for the remainder of the day.

Jeannie was eyeing her as she sat down, eager for details. "I take it everything went all right last night?"

Laurel's eyes widened. "Last night?" she echoed, surprised. "How did you—" And then she realized what Jeannie was referring to. "Oh, you mean with my telling the rest of my family about the baby."

"Yes," Jeannie replied, "but whatever you were thinking looks a lot more interesting." She propped her head on her upturned hand, looking as if she was settling in for the duration. "Want to talk about it?"

Laurel allowed a mysterious smile to play on her lips. "A lady never tells."

Jeannie pushed her chair away from her own desk with her foot, propelling herself toward Laurel's in one smooth motion. "No, but a best friend does." She gave Laurel her best pleading look. "Throw me a bone, Laurel."

The woman made it sound as if she lived a cloistered existence. "You're married, Jeannie."

Her words were met with a huge sigh. "That's exactly why I need a bone. *Because* I'm married."

Maybe their signals had gotten crossed, Laurel thought. Her friend looked too eager for someone asking details about an encounter between a husband and wife. "This is about Jason."

Jeannie's face fell. "Not Mr. Hunk?"

"No, not Mr. Hunk." Laurel did her best not to laugh.

"Always said you had more than your share of luck, Laurel." And then she smiled wistfully. "Lord knows I wouldn't kick Jason out of bed, either."

"Well, you'd better if he's in yours."

Jeannie raised her hands in surrender. "Sorry, no infringement intended." She ducked her head in closer, even though it was still only the two of them in the office. "So, your husband is responsible for that rosy glow on your face." That established, she returned to her original question. "Everyone okay with this new addition, or did you chicken out at the last minute and tell them you were thinking of putting a 'new addition' on the house instead?"

"No chickening out," Laurel informed her. "And the family is fine with it."

As fine as could be expected, she added silently. And Jason would come around, she promised herself. It was simply going to take more time than she'd anticipated.

But Jeannie was no longer listening. Her attention had zeroed in on the front door. The bell above it had just gone off.

"Oh-oh, heads up. Mr. Hunk is back. Whatever perfume you're using, lady, I want some. Make it a bathtub full," she amended.

Laurel barely heard her. Her eyes were on the front of the office. Robert Manning had entered and was heading straight for her.

CHAPTER 12

Reaching her desk, Robert smiled warmly at her. He wore a navy-blue suit with a pearl blue shirt that once again brought out his eyes. It occurred to Laurel that someone had to have taught him how to dress.

She wondered if that same advisor was available for Jason, who wore suits only because he had to. At home, he was the last word in comfort, with jeans that had been pressed into service years ago and shirts that only disappeared from regular use if she kidnapped them and sent them away to Goodwill.

"I was in the neighborhood," Robert told her, "and decided to stop by to see if you have any more listings to show me."

"Is that anything like etchings?" she heard Jeannie ask under her breath, her words addressed to no one in particular.

Rising from her desk, Laurel waved a hand at Jeannie behind her back so that Robert couldn't see, hoping to silence her friend before she said anything audibly enough to embarrass her. She remained on her feet because, for some reason, standing made her feel as if she had more control over the situation.

"As a matter of fact, a few more went on the market as of this morning." Something, maybe intuition, had made her check the

Web site on her laptop before she'd driven in this morning. "I think you might be interested in seeing a couple of them."

Seeming pleased, Robert spread out his arms. "I'm all yours."

Behind her, she heard Jeannie make a little noise and sigh. By the expression on his face, so did Robert. Smiling, he moved around her and put out his hand to Jeannie.

"Robert Manning," he introduced himself.

Like someone in a trance, Jeannie slipped her hand into his. Her eyes never left his face. "Jean Wallace. Jeannie to my friends," she added quickly.

"Jeannie," Robert repeated with a nod of his head, as if to approve of the name. "I hope you'll allow me to call you that."

Allow? Laurel thought. Jeannie was practically begging him to use her nickname.

"Absolutely," Jeannie breathed.

Amused, Laurel watched her best friend, a woman who was known for her sharp wit and equally sharp tongue, dissolve to the consistency of tapioca pudding left out on the counter overnight during a record heat wave.

Robert smoothly turned back toward her. "So, shall we go?" he asked, then looked over at her desk. "Or are you busy?"

On her desk she had a stack of folders, all neatly arranged and in alphabetical order. But that didn't make the work within them any less pressing. Still, the paperwork she'd intended catching up on this morning was going to have to wait. Although she was a tad skeptical about the validity of his search for a new house, she had to treat Robert as if he were actually planning to buy property.

"I'm here to sell houses," she replied.

Picking up the purse, she began to lead the way out the front door. They passed Ed Callaghan on his way in. The office manager looked pleased to see one of his agents going out on a showing this early in the day.

"My car's right out front," she told Robert as they went through the front door.

He closed the door behind them. "Why don't we take mine this time?"

There was no outright company policy as to whose vehicle would be used when viewing a property. Some of the time, a prospective buyer and agent would meet at the site in question. However, most of the time, when leaving from the agency, it was customary to use the agent's car since the latter was strictly for business usage.

Using the buyer's car, at least this time, made the whole venture seem too personal somehow.

A little too much like a date, she couldn't help thinking.

Especially when she saw what kind of a car Robert Manning had chosen to drive. It was parked several spaces over from the front door. Red and shiny, it was low to the ground and sporty beyond belief. She wasn't much on cars. To her, they were just a way to get her to and from places, a great deal more convenient than having to take the bus. But this one was in a class all its own and it took her breath away.

"A Ferrari?" She ogled the vehicle, then glanced over at Robert.

He ran his hand fondly over the roof, obviously not so

obsessed with his possession that he worried about leaving fingerprints. She liked that.

"Yes, I always wanted one, ever since I was a kid." Robert opened the passenger side door for her. "Do you like it?"

She had no idea why, but she felt her heart rate speed up a shade.

Step into my parlor, said the spider to the fly. Laurel couldn't shake the feeling that the words seemed very appropriate in this situation.

You're letting your imagination run away with you, she upbraided herself.

It was her hormones acting up again, nothing more. All this was perfectly innocent and she was reading too much into it. Somehow, knowing the cause of her disquiet still didn't change anything. For reasons she couldn't—or wouldn't—quite put into words, Laurel felt as if she was poised on the very point of a pin, ready to fall either forward or backward, but either way, destined to fall.

"What's not to like?" she responded. "It's beautiful."

Taking her elbow, Robert helped her ease into the low-slung seat. She caught him watching her legs as she swung them inside the vehicle. She took a deep breath to steady her nerves as he rounded the hood and got in on the other side of the transmission shift.

He shook his head as he buckled up. "'Things' aren't beautiful," he told her, putting the key into the ignition. "Now you—" he spared her a look "—you're beautiful."

Oh no, she wasn't going to fall into that trap. Was not

about to deny his statement and find herself getting sucked into a discussion that revolved around her looks or anything remotely about her. That was definitely much too personal.

So instead, she shook her head. "Oh, I don't know. I've seen some sunsets that were positively breathtaking."

She half expected him to disagree and she was ready for that. He surprised her by seeming to change the subject.

"You were captain of the debating team." It wasn't a haphazard guess on his part. He said it as if he remembered.

Captain of the debating team. The position had been something she'd been proud of. Something, she recalled, that had left Jason pretty much unimpressed when she'd told him about the string of successes she'd amassed during her term in her senior year at Bedford High. It was also a fact that she didn't expect anyone to remember.

"Where to?" he asked.

She gave him the address, still staring at him. "You remember that?" she asked. "That I was captain of the debating team?"

The smile was gentle, reminiscent, as if the past was never very far away for him. "I remember a great deal about high school," Robert told her, then glanced at her as he pulled out of the parking lot. "A great deal."

She studied his profile for a moment when he looked back at the road. He had a very determined chin. Still waters did run deep, at least in his case.

"And you used it, didn't you?"

Robert eased his foot onto the brake as the light turned

yellow. He was too far from the intersection to risk getting across before the light turned red. "Excuse me?"

She thought again that high school had had to be hell for him. In his place, she wasn't sure how she would have fared. "All those negative experiences, those horrible people who got their kicks by picking on you—you used all that to spur you on," she told him. "To make you the man you are now."

Rather than seem annoyed at the reference to his past, Robert allowed a hint of a smile to slip across his lips. The light turned green and he shifted from the brake to the gas.

"Go on."

It was a philosophy she espoused. "Well, kids who have to put up with cruel teasing either go on to become huge successes—or serial killers. I'm guessing it's safe to say that you're not a serial killer."

He laughed at her comment. "Not that I didn't think about it for a while," he admitted, then elaborated. "Getting the likes of Will Turner and Jack Sullivan in some dark, dead-end alley and running them over with my car sounded pretty good at the time. But then I decided that becoming successful and well-off was the best way to go. What's that old saying?"

"Living well is the best revenge?" she offered.

He nodded, a pleased grin on his lips. "That's the one. Funny thing, though. Along the way to my ultimate success, people like Will Turner and Jack Sullivan stopped mattering."

"Well, that's a healthy sign," she commented.

"But other people," he went on, turning to look at her meaningfully, "never stopped mattering."

CHAPTER 13

"Do you know that I used to dream about sweeping you off your feet?"

Robert's tone was so offhand that it took her a moment to get the full import of what he was saying. He'd had a crush on her. And she had been so wrapped up in her own world, in her activities, in being the best at everything that she had hardly noticed him. Certainly not *that* way.

Laurel felt guilty at the oversight—and a little worried to boot. Was this a ruse? Was he just pretending to want to buy a house in order to—what? Grab a little alone time in the car with her? That seemed more than far-fetched. This was real life, not some grade B horror movie about obsession.

Laurel turned toward him as they came to a stop at a major intersection. "Robert—Bobby," she corrected, reverting back for a moment to a past they only remotely shared, "I'm married."

Traffic was moving again. He shifted from the brake to the accelerator. "Yes, so you mentioned yesterday." But then he asked, "Happily?"

"Very." And even if she weren't, she wouldn't admit it to him. There was no way she would give him any false hope.

Yes, he was gorgeous and his attention was flattering, but her heart belonged to Jason. It always had. She was not in the market for a fling, casual or otherwise. It wasn't her style. "And, I'm expecting a baby."

That seemed to catch him off guard. The way it had everyone, she thought. He probably thought she was either putting him on—or out of her mind. "Really?"

She nodded. "Really."

"On purpose?"

Laurel saw him sneaking a look at her stomach. It didn't bear out her words and she was rather happy about that. She didn't mind being pregnant. What she minded was *looking* pregnant. She supposed that made her vain.

"Well, I am now." She lifted her shoulders in a half shrug. "I can't say it was something that either one of us exactly planned." A smile played on her lips. "But I'm getting used to the idea."

"What about your husband?" He searched for a name. "Joshua? Is he getting used to it?"

"Jason," she corrected. And no, she thought, Jason wasn't getting used to it. But he would, in time. He *had* to. They were a team and she needed him now more than ever. She couldn't stand the idea of going through all this isolated from him.

She tried not to dwell on that. "He's worried that something might happen to me. He thinks I'm too old to have a baby."

Robert slanted a look at her, amusement in his eyes. "Did you hit him?"

She laughed. "I was tempted." Jason kept insisting on making them old before their time, like their grandparents had been. She always maintained that a young frame of mind was what kept you going and helped you beat old age. "But Jason tends to be a worrier, so I just let it ride."

"If you were my wife, I'd be worried, too," Robert told her, then quickly glossed over his statement by adding, "But in this day and age, there's a lot doctors can do in case there's some kind of a medical emergency." The four-way stop sign gave him the opportunity to look at Laurel again. "And you look like you've been taking good care of yourself."

"I exercise," she volunteered. Then, because her schedule was so overwhelming, she added, "About twenty minutes every week and a half. Not much more time for anything else." Laurel sighed, suddenly feeling drained and grateful that Robert was doing the driving. During her last three pregnancies, exhaustion would periodically hit her, coming out of the blue and striking without any rhyme or reason. Looked like this time around would be no different. "Things were supposed to get less hectic as time moved on, not more."

He glanced at her. "Do I take a right here?" She nodded in response. He turned the wheel. "Kids keep you young."

She laughed, thinking of what her mother said. "Or age you rapidly, depending on your point of view. Do you have any kids?"

Robert shook his head. He had the window cracked open. The breeze that squeezed in ruffled his hair a little. "My wife and I tried, but we were never lucky enough to have any." And then his eyes crinkled a little. "Why, are you giving this one away?"

"Not a chance." She smiled at his gentle sense of humor.

Leaning forward, she indicated the second house on the right. "Right there, that's the house. Just pull up in the driveway." He did as she instructed. She saw him looking around, probably for a car. "The owners had to move," she explained. "The house is empty," she went on, "so it's going to require exercising some imagination on your part."

"Not a problem," Robert assured her. "I started out designing software for a living. My imagination is alive and well."

"Okay, then let's put it to good use." Laurel opened the door and was about to get out. Robert rounded the hood and presented himself on her side. He cupped her elbow with his hand, helping her from the vehicle. "Someone obviously taught you some excellent manners."

"My wife gets all the credit for that," he told her modestly. "She gets credit for a lot of things, including teaching me how to dress and how to appreciate a good woman."

She heard the wistful note in his voice. He still missed her, she thought. Now that was devotion. "Then you are going to make some lucky lady a wonderful prize package someday," she prophesized.

Taking out her passkey, Laurel inserted it into the lock box and turned it. She felt the lock give. "I'm not sure exactly what you're going to see. This is my first time here."

He nodded. "Consider me forewarned."

She considered him a great deal more than that. He was a catch waiting to be grabbed up. As she talked to him this morning, the wheels had begun turning in her head. Since she'd been a little girl, arranging dates between her fashion dolls and stuffed animals she'd had the heart of a matchmaker. She saw no reason to turn her back on her natural tendency now. All she needed was the proper lead-in. Men like Robert Manning didn't come along every day. Or even once every leap year.

Stepping back, she allowed him to walk into the house first so that she could observe him.

The toast popped and Laurel frowned over the result. The color was too dark, even though she had it set on "light." It was just a shade away from burnt. She put it on a plate and turned her attention to the waffles she was making. Too much of an undertaking on a day she was running behind, she chided herself. But Jason liked waffles.

"You know that guy I told you about?" She tossed the question over her shoulder, then turned to him when she received no response. "The one I used to go to school with? He came in last week to look at some property."

She paused after each sentence, waiting for the light of recognition to enter Jason's eyes. Like all husbands, hers suffered from the malady commonly known as short-term amnesia. He had the ability to sit and appear to listen to every word, only to have absolutely no recall when asked. The habit drove her crazy.

"The one who got rich selling the dot-com companies," she added in desperation.

"Oh, right, him." Finally, the light had dawned. "What about him?" Jason peered at her over the top of the newspaper section he was reading. "Are you thinking of throwing me over for him?"

It was a joke. In reality, he was as secure as a husband could be, especially since she'd given him three and one-quarter children and he was fairly certain she was devoted to him.

She thought about choosing her words carefully, then decided to go in, feet first. There was something to be said for honesty. For the most part, finesse was lost on Jason.

"I was thinking of him for Lynda."

"Are you going to gift wrap him?" he asked drolly. "Or just tuck him under your arm and wait to present him to Lynda at the first opportune moment?"

Ordinarily, she didn't mind being teased. But the pregnancy didn't find her doing anything "ordinarily."

"I'm serious." She had to curb herself from snapping at him. "She needs someone in her life. Dean leaving her like that made her feel like a rank, number-one loser. If I had him here now," she added, her eyes suddenly blazing, "I'd wring his neck."

He looked up from his newspaper again, but just barely. "My money's on you, big Mama."

Laurel froze in the middle of removing the waffles from the griddle. "What did you just call me?"

"Big Mama," he repeated, a touch uncertainly now. "It's a term of affection."

"So is 'dog-faced woman' in some cultures, but not here." She moved over toward the refrigerator. With its shining black exterior, it offered up a bastardized version of her reflection. She looked at it, turning sideways and studying herself intently. "I look big to you?"

Blessed with a keen survival instinct, he backpedaled as quickly as he could. "No, not at all. Tiny. So tiny that when I talk to you, I just throw my voice around, hoping it reaches you."

She frowned, completely unamused. Laurel glanced at her blackened reflection again. "So I'm big."

"Honey, I was just teasing," he pleaded, then closed his eyes as he shook his head. "Oh God, I forgot how sensitive you get when there's more than just one of you in the same space." He made a last-ditch attempt at amends. "You're not big, Laurie. But you have to face facts." He was nothing if not truthful. It was something she both cherished and, right now, hated. "You're going to get that way. You always did before."

History, she thought fiercely, did not necessarily have to repeat itself. Not if she didn't let it.

CHAPTER 14

"You're eating like a bird," Jeannie commented, looking at the meal that Laurel had hardly touched.

They'd gone out to lunch together, the way they did every Friday, stopping at the Village Steakhouse, one of their favorite restaurants. Today there had been something extra to celebrate as well, but Laurel had greeted her serving with less than her customary gusto.

Jeannie regarded her with concern. "It's been almost three months now. You still feeling nauseous?"

Oddly enough, she wasn't. The awful feeling that had haunted her throughout her first pregnancy and had hung on, to varying degrees, for the better part of the other two had completely vanished within a week of Dr. Kilpatrick's world-jarring diagnosis.

Laurel shook her head, still picking at the melting butter on her potato. "No."

"If you're not nauseous, why aren't you eating? Why are you just pushing around your food from one side of your plate to the other?" she asked. "Take advantage of the situation," Jeannie coaxed. "You're eating for two now."

"Yes, but one of those 'two' is the size of a peanut," Laurel pointed out. "Peanuts don't consume very much."

"Well, if you don't want that baked potato, can I have it?"

"Be my guest." Laurel obligingly shifted the steaming vegetable over to Jeannie's plate. It wasn't that she wasn't hungry. She actually was. But the thought of the food applying itself directly to her hips did a great deal to make things look unappetizing. "Anything else?"

Jeannie eyed the steak on Laurel's plate, even as she sank her fork into the potato. "I'll let you know." She took a taste of the baked potato. Her expression indicated that she had crossed over to the other side of the pearly gates. "Mmm, this is good."

"Enjoy," Laurel told her. She didn't bother picking up her knife and fork. Instead, she just looked off, out the window at the traffic that was moving by.

Jeannie sighed as she reluctantly retired her utensils. She leaned in close to Laurel. "Okay, what's wrong?"

Laurel glanced at her, then looked away and shrugged. "Nothing."

"No," Jeannie contradicted. "'Nothing' should be wrong. You just sold Mr. Hunk that semi-castle that Callaghan never thought we'd unload—and made Mr. Hunk think he was happy about it—"

"He was happy," Laurel insisted softly.

She *wouldn't* have sold the house to Robert if he hadn't been. She didn't believe in talking a client into anything. It was only on a whim that she'd even showed Robert the old Myford place. No one was more surprised than she was when

Robert said he actually wanted to put a bid on it. The building was only three quarters finished. Construction had halted when the owner had run out of money. It was considered an eyesore in the neighborhood. But Robert, bless him, had seen possibilities in the place.

He really did have a good imagination, she thought. She'd felt so responsible for his having bought the place that she'd offered Robert the services of her brother-in-law, Jared, who was a licensed state contractor.

He and Morgan went out the next day to meet with Robert and discuss the house's possibilities. Robert seemed very satisfied with the whole arrangement.

Ed Callaghan had been overjoyed when she'd told him. The office manager had called her that night to tell her that the owner had snapped up the bid faster than a catfish swallowed bait. And just like that, Robert Manning had a house. Or three-quarters of one, she amended.

Callaghan had brought out a bottle of champagne to celebrate the sale—at which point she was forced to tell him that she was pregnant.

Champagne and a confession. It was becoming a pattern. Callaghan had seemed leery of the news, until she'd told him she intended to keep on working. He'd congratulated her— and everyone else had had the champagne.

"So?" Jeannie pressed now. "If he's happy, the owner's happy and Callaghan's thrilled to death, what's the problem? Why the long face?"

Laurel debated not saying anything. Or, just chalking it up

to her hormones being out of sync again. But lying had never been her way and holding things in was lying. She turned away from the window and looked at Jeannie.

"It's starting," she said glumly.

Jeannie's penciled-in eyebrows drew together over a very pert nose that had been a gift from a plastic surgeon. "What's starting?"

Laurel pressed her lips together, looking for the right words, the right way to put this without sounding as if she was whining.

This morning, when she'd tried to get dressed, she'd found that the button on her skirt no longer wanted any part of the hole it normally fit into. There was at least an inch between them now. A whole, irreconcilable inch. And when she finally managed to pull the two sides together, pushing the button through the hole, she found that breathing had become optional. And very difficult. It felt as if she had just applied a tourniquet to her waist.

And this was only the beginning. There were at least five more months ahead of her.

"I'm putting on weight," she murmured.

Jeannie laughed, shaking her head. "For my money, you'd look better with a little meat on your bones."

"A little, maybe," she allowed diplomatically, since Jeannie was rather heavyset. She didn't want to insult the woman, but that didn't change how she felt about what lay ahead of her. "But I never started gaining weight so early in my pregnancy."

"They say the body remembers. I read that in a health magazine once. And each time you get pregnant, I guess it remembers a little faster." She grinned, amused. "You get pregnant again and you'll probably start gaining weight the next morning."

"Pregnant again," Laurel echoed. "God forbid." After this pregnancy was behind her, she was going to give Jason the option of either getting a vasectomy, or wearing two condoms whenever he made love to her again.

"So you gained a little weight faster than you expected. What's the big deal?"

The big deal was that by the end of the month, if not sooner, nothing in her closet was going to fit her anymore. She sighed. "I don't have any of my old maternity clothes."

Jeannie broke off another hunk of bread and slathered it with margarine. "Well, that's a good thing," her friend observed, taking a healthy bite of bread. She paused until she'd swallowed. "Styles have changed in the last twenty years."

"Twenty-one," Laurel corrected absently. The last time she'd been in maternity clothes was twenty-one years ago. That was a whole generation ago. What in God's name was she thinking, getting pregnant again?

"Twenty-one," Jeannie echoed. "Even more changes." She grinned broadly at the opportunity this presented for Laurel. "Hey, like I said before, this a built-in excuse to go shopping, honey." Her mailbox was always filled with catalogues. "From what I've seen, they've done some really cute things with maternity clothes these days." She finished off the piece of bread, chewing thoughtfully. "Although I have to say, I'm not too crazy about the bathing suits. Makes you look like you're trying to smuggle a beach ball and not being very clever about it." She turned her attention back to the last of the baked potato she'd scored. "The new slogan seems to be 'pregnant and proud of it.'"

Laurel wasn't sure she'd go quite that far. "I'm not ashamed of being pregnant," she told Jeannie. "I just don't particularly want to stick it in anyone else's face, that's all." And, she added silently, she didn't want to be mistaken for the Goodyear blimp, either.

She caught her lip between her teeth. She could feel herself expanding even as she sat here, with her hips spreading east and west and her breasts determined to sink south. It felt as if she was a lost section in a map handbook.

"Then get big maternity clothes, that's all," Jeannie suggested.

Picturing herself walking into a maternity shop was enough to make her shiver. Unlike Jeannie, who felt that all shopping was good, she didn't want to do this. But she obviously had no choice. Her only other alternative was to walk around wearing a barrel.

"I dread the whole process," she admitted to Jeannie.

Jeannie's fork stopped in mid journey to her mouth as confusion clouded her features. "In heaven's name, girl, why?"

She pushed the remainder of her steak into the wilting cluster of asparagus spears. "Because I'm not looking forward to shopping for maternity clothes standing elbow to elbow with girls who have peaches-and-cream complexions and think that crow's feet means something a crow uses for walking."

"I can go with you," Jeannie offered. She glanced down at her mature figure. "We can tell them we got knocked up together. One look at me and nobody's going to doubt that I'm not pregnant."

Jeannie's unself-conscious remark made her smile. "No, I can do this by myself. But thanks for the offer."

Jeannie turned her attention back to eating. "Hey, what are friends for? Are you going to finish your steak?"

With a laugh, Laurel slid the piece onto Jeannie's plate.

CHAPTER 15

It took Laurel another two-and-a-half weeks to work up the courage to face walking into a maternity shop. Two-and-a-half weeks and five outfits that no longer buttoned or zipped the way they were supposed to.

Examining herself in her bedroom mirror when she'd reached outfit number five, she felt tears filling her eyes. She looked as if she'd been stuffed into the suit and was about to explode at any second.

It was her favorite, the one she considered her "lucky" suit. Though not superstitious, she still felt that if she had the suit on things were more inclined to go her way.

But not anymore.

She needed a new "lucky" suit. She needed a new everything.

There was, of course, an alternative to walking into a maternity shop. She could just buy clothes the next size or two up. But the problem with that was she was only gaining weight in an isolated area. Her waist was expanding. Everything else, including her shoulders, remained just as they had been. Which meant that she was still a size four—everywhere but in her midsection. That appeared to be thickening every hour on the hour. So while clothes two sizes up might accommodate her waistline, they would hang off the rest of her.

Logically, she had no choice but to go to a maternity store. The thought left her far from happy. Every day, she found a reason not to go. But this morning, as outfit number five died, a casualty of the ever-expanding waistline war, she made up her mind. There was no other choice. She had to go shopping.

Still uneasy about the pending venture, she'd briefly entertained the idea of taking Jeannie up on her offer to come along with her. She'd even thought of—God help her—asking her mother to accompany her to the maternity store. She did neither, knowing that both women, especially her mother, would feel compelled to offer a running commentary as they went from outfit to outfit within the store or stores.

Right now, her emotions were in a state of flux, bouncing back and forth between joyous and overwhelmed in less than the blink of an eye. She kept going from "Oh, boy" to "Oh, God," in zero to sixty seconds.

Laurel could just hear her mother commenting about the emotional whiplash she was getting. And asking Lynda was out of the question. Her sister would probably spend the entire time looking wistfully at every single article of clothing within the shop, trying not to cry over the fact that she would never see her belly distended.

"I'm going to die miserable and alone," Lynda had lamented the last time she'd spoken to her sister on the phone. Laurel had curbed the desire to say, *You will if you keep this up*, knowing that pointing out her sister's flaws would do no good. Lynda was going to have to work some of her issues out by herself before she was up to keeping any sort of company with people of the opposite sex.

Laurel had even thought—so briefly that for all intents and purposes, it hadn't happened—of asking Denise to come with her. From the moment Luke got serious with this girl, Laurel had been determined to create a bond between herself and her future daughter-in-law. But currently, Denise was in the final stages of the mother of all meltdowns because of the swiftly approaching wedding. A simple greeting was liable to cause the girl to burst into tears.

She'd smiled to herself, thinking that she and Denise were not all that far removed from each other in their present frame of mind. The wrong look was liable to send her off into a crying jag, too. Except that she was discreet enough to hide it. Denise believed in being open about everything. It was the new truth as far as she was concerned.

So, in the end, Laurel decided to go on her odyssey to the maternity shop alone. Taking advantage of a lull in the office, she'd left Jeannie and a woman named Sonya to deal with anyone who walked in while she was gone. With dread and not a little trepidation, she got into her car—a car that was beginning to feel slightly crammed around the hip area—and drove in to the Bedford Mall where the oh-so-cutely named store, Bun In The Oven, was domiciled.

The walk through the mall was over with before she knew

it, even though she tried to linger over a display of camping gear, something she had yet to work up an interest for.

No more stalling, Laurel silently ordered, forcing herself to cross the last bit of distance to the shop's front entrance. And then, determined, she forced herself to walk in. A soft, tinkling bell announced her. She felt like turning on her heel and going right back out again.

The appearance of another human being, emerging from the back of the store, prevented her from making good her escape. A very perky salesperson, more girl than woman, came even before the sound of the bell had faded away. She looked as if she'd just recently graduated from nursery school and was currently working her way through the elementary grades.

The salesgirl fairly bounced across the room, as light on her feet as Laurel felt heavy. "May I help you?"

Laurel wanted to browse in peace, to look through the various styles and try to find something that wasn't designed for the pregnant twenty-two-year-old. Obviously with the baby salesgirl at her elbow, that wasn't about to happen.

She vaguely remembered that when her mother was pregnant with Lynda, she'd complained about the various skirts with their cut-out panels and how unflattering everything labeled "maternity" was. On top of that, there had been very little to choose from. From the quick scan she'd just taken as she entered the store, it appeared that a lot of designers had been working overtime to take the "frump" out of maternity clothes. They'd succeeded almost too well. The store appeared to be bursting with all kinds of merchandise.

Some things were so pretty, Laurel noted, that they fairly took the sting out of being pregnant.

Here goes nothing.

She tried to return the blinding smile as she said, "I'm looking for some maternity clothes."

"Of course you are," the just barely postpubescent salesgirl chirped. "Or else why would you even come in here?" She paused to giggle at her own words. High-pitched, Laurel rated it as easily one of the most annoying sounds she'd ever heard. "So, what size were you looking for?"

Something in a pup tent, please. Laurel pressed her lips together. "I guess we could try a size six first."

"Oh, then she's tiny, like me," the salesgirl concluded.

Laurel looked at her blankly. There wasn't anyone else in the store with her. "'She?'"

The salesgirl nodded her head, her straight auburn hair moving from side to side. "The person you're buying the clothes for. Your daughter?" she guessed brightly.

This was a mistake, Laurel thought, glancing toward the entrance. Buying larger clothing was beginning to sound better and better.

"No."

The salesgirl, whose name tag declared her name to be "Ginger," cocked her head and squinted her eyes. "Well," she finally said, her words dripping out slowly one after the other, "you look too young to have a pregnant granddaughter."

"That's good to hear." Laurel struggled to bank down her embarrassment. "Because the maternity clothes are for me."

The information clearly took the salesgirl by surprise. Her lips formed an almost perfect circle, but no sound initially came out. Finally, she managed to squeeze out a sentence. "They're for you?"

Laurel thought of simply hurrying out of the store, but she was getting angry. This little snip of a thing with the amoeba-size brain was judging her. "That's what I said."

Ginger's eyes grew rounder. She couldn't seem to process what she was hearing.

"Really," Ginger breathed. It wasn't so much a question as a stunned observation. Her eyes washed over her customer.

Laurel drew herself up. "Really," she echoed with all the dignity at her disposal.

The young girl shook her head in uncensored wonder. And then she said something that turned everything around. "Well, I certainly admire you."

It wasn't what she'd expected the girl to say. "And why would that be?" At this point, Laurel felt herself spoiling for a fight, something to release the aggressive feeling she was harboring.

"Because it's really brave to go after what you want and the hell with what everyone else thinks."

Laurel opened her mouth, ready to retort, to put down, to go straight for the jugular and then vivisect the salesgirl slowly with sharp words and cynicism. But in an odd sort of way, the girl had a point, Laurel realized. She *was* going through with this and saying the hell with what everyone else thought.

Maybe she was being too thin-skinned and sensitive,

Laurel decided. The salesgirl was smiling at her eagerly. Probably had the IQ of a shoelace, Laurel thought.

"Okay, Ginger, I need a whole new wardrobe, so let's get this show on the road."

Ginger looked so excited she seemed to be in danger of heart failure. Laurel could almost hear the sound of an old-fashioned cash register melodically going off as the salesgirl drew her over to the newest rack of clothing that had been brought in "just this morning."

CHAPTER 16

Jason came home after six. Of late, he'd been keeping longer hours, divorcing himself from what was going on at home, from the fear that seemed to be waiting for him every time he did think about his wife's pregnancy. Out of sight, out of mind. But at times, like tonight, guilt would corner him and he'd force himself to come home at a decent hour. He did love her, and that was just the problem. He didn't want the change, the risk this baby represented.

But he did miss Laurel.

Calling out a greeting to her, he'd gone straight upstairs to shed the trappings of his career and put on more comfortable clothing. When he came back down a few minutes later, he went straight to the kitchen, led there by his nose and the tempting aroma of spaghetti sauce in the making.

He found his wife there, putting the finishing touches on what he deemed to be one of his favorite meals. He found his spirit lifting with every step he took toward her.

"I see you've gotten used to the idea of being pregnant." The path into the master bedroom had been impeded by a bevy of shopping bags, all embossed with the logo of a baby popping out of a flowery oven.

Laurel gave the parmesan-cheese container another hearty shake, sending a cream-colored snow storm into the gently simmering red sea. She stirred it until the creamy flurry had disappeared into the sauce.

Glancing over her shoulder at him, she said, "No. Why?"

He paused to open the refrigerator and take out a can of beer. After popping the top, he took a long drag of the amber liquid. He avoided looking at her so as to avoid any reminders of her condition.

"Because I just saw a squadron of shopping bags filled with maternity clothes upstairs and I assume they didn't come here by themselves. Did you buy out the store?" He took another long pull before returning the can back to its shelf and closing the refrigerator again.

"I left the hangers," she quipped, then spared him another glance. "It's either that, or have you come bail me out of jail."

His dark eyebrows drew together in confusion. "Come again?"

"For indecent exposure," she elaborated as she reached for the cilantro. "That's the term they use, isn't it, when someone's naked in public?" Giving the jar two good shakes, she put it back in its place.

A flash of that old feeling came over him. *I miss you, Laurie.*

Jason came up behind her. Wrapping his arms around her shoulders, he drew her to him. She could feel his chest against her back. There was something comforting about feeling him breathe. Jason kissed the top of her head affectionately.

"Nothing indecent about your body."

"Obviously the man has not looked at me for quite a while," she murmured to the pot she was still busy stirring. She had missed his admiring glances, she thought sadly, missed seeing that glint in his eyes.

Releasing her, Jason stepped back and leaned a hip against the counter, watching her. "Yes I have. I distinctly remember sneaking a peek last Christmas Eve when you walked out of the shower."

Right, when she wasn't pregnant, she thought sadly. "Very funny." She took out a package of shredded mozzarella cheese from the refrigerator. Moving the zipper at the top of the package, she removed a handful of the cheese and drizzled it across the sauce. The shreds slowly sank into the surface, then became submerged. "Well, I've grown since then." She dusted off her hands against each other. "A lot."

He looked unfazed by the information. "How many pounds in 'a lot'?"

If he thought she was going to volunteer the number, he didn't know her at all. "That information I'm taking to my grave."

Jason laughed. He thought about taking another drag of his beer, then decided not to. Instead, he focused on his wife's figure. "Know what I like about you being pregnant?"

Still holding the plastic spoon she was stirring with, she

turned around to look at him. "You like my being pregnant?" This was certainly news to her.

He moved his shoulders in a half shrug. "It has its perks," he admitted. Commandeering the spoon from her, he stole a lick. "Perfect," he pronounced.

Laurel took the spoon back and laid it on the spoon rest. "Never mind that." She dismissed his culinary appraisal. "What perks?"

The smile that came to his lips was positively wicked. She hadn't recalled him looking like that in a long time. "Your breasts."

Laurel stared at him. "Excuse me?"

"Your breasts," he repeated. "They get very large when you're pregnant." He wiggled his fingers in the air, mimicking someone massaging something very large and round.

She looked down at herself, as if she expected something to be different. But it wasn't. She hated the way her breasts looked when she was pregnant. Like something that belonged to a matronly old woman. "They get like two large loaves of bread," she complained.

He grinned and moved his eyebrows up and down comically. "Who says that man cannot live on bread alone?"

She sighed and shook her head. Turning her back on him, she picked up her ladle again. "You're a typical male."

"And aren't you glad about that?" he teased, nuzzling her neck.

She felt a burst of desire zip along her skin. It wasn't easy ignoring it. "All I know is that there would be a hell of a lot less pregnancies in the world if men were the ones who had to carry the babies the full nine months."

"You'll get no argument from me," he told her. Unzipping the bag of mozzarella she'd just used, he stole several strands of cheese and popped them into his mouth. "You got the hard part."

The spaghetti was boiling rapidly. She lowered the heat and stirred the noodles a couple of times. "It was awful," she murmured.

"I'm sure it was."

She turned around to face him. "You don't know what I'm talking about."

"No, but I figure if I waited long enough—" he popped some more cheese into his mouth "—I'd catch on."

She blew out a breath, then took the cheese away from him and put it into the refrigerator before he completely spoiled his appetite. "I'm talking about the shopping trip."

He thought, by now, he knew her inside and out. Obviously he needed more lessons. "Since when don't you like buying clothing?"

"Since the 'barely out of grade school' salesgirl thought I was buying clothes for my daughter." She drained the spaghetti in the colander and set it back into the pot to keep it warm.

"Did you tell her we didn't have a daughter?"

"That's not the point."

"No, but it might have stopped her in her tracks," he offered.

Laurel tried again. "She thought I was buying clothes for my *daughter*," she emphasized, saying the words through her teeth.

"We already covered that. See?" he said brightly. "I'm listening."

Laurel rolled her eyes. "But obviously not hearing," she countered.

His expression was affable. "Give me another shot at it."

She reminded herself that men and women didn't think the same way, didn't take offense at the same things, and she should simply be happy he was home for dinner, that he was actually talking to her instead of responding in grunts. "She was telling me I was too old to have a baby."

"The hussy," he declared, obviously seeing some humor in the situation that she had missed. "Did you show her your belly to prove her wrong?"

Turning off the heat beneath the sauce, she frowned at him. "This isn't funny, Jason."

"Humor is where you find it." He took down two glasses from the cupboard and placed them on the counter. "If she upset you so much, why'd you buy so many clothes from her? You could have gone somewhere else."

She paused for a moment, reluctant to admit what had motivated her. The telling trivialized the interaction somehow, when it hadn't felt trivial at the time. "Because then she said she thought I was very brave, to go ahead and do what I wanted and the hell with everyone else."

Jason nodded, amused. "Nice save," he commented.

But Laurel shook her head. "She wasn't bright enough for a save. Her mouth was connected directly to her brain. Whatever she thought came right out, no detours, no pauses."

"You *are* brave," Jason told her, taking her into his arms again, taking her completely by surprise. "The bravest lady I know."

She grinned. "You're only saying that because you're hungry."

"That, and because I want to cop a feel later." He pretended to leer at her. "Remember, big breasts turn me on."

She laughed and shook her head. You learned something every day. "You know, you never said anything about that before."

"I thought it was a given," he said innocently. "I'm a male."

She leaned back against his arms. "Yes, so I noticed. That's what got us into this problem in the first place."

"Takes two to tango, my dear." He nuzzled her throat for a moment, drawing in her scent. He found it more arousing than spaghetti sauce. He raised his head and looked into her eyes. "Want to tango?"

She looked at him in surprise. "Now?"

"That's the general idea."

She glanced back at the pots on the stove. "I thought you said you were hungry."

"I can eat later," he told her. "If I eat now, I might get drowsy. If I tango now, I'll work up an appetite." He pretended to leer at her. "In more ways than one."

"You're serious."

He nodded, raising one hand while still holding her with the other. "I can take a blood oath."

She smiled, pleased but curious. "What's gotten into you?"

He shrugged, then took a stab at it. "Midlife crisis. Maybe

I'm reliving all the other times you were pregnant." He shrugged again. "Or maybe I'm just plain horny."

Amusement curved her mouth. "Or maybe all of the above?"

"Maybe," Jason answered, just before he kissed her.

CHAPTER 17

Jason made love to her, and with her, lyrically. Just the way he had years ago when the fire they felt was new and burned brightly.

Laurel felt an excitement zipping through her veins, fairly screaming with anticipation, as her husband teasingly peeled away her clothing bit by bit. Tantalizing them both.

He hadn't been like this in a really long time, Laurel thought as she returned the favor and slowly separated Jason from his jeans and his pullover. It had been decades, maybe, she decided, drawing his belt out of its loops. Before the word "retirement" had become a regular part of his daily conversation.

Ever since his first day on the job, Jason had made no secret of the fact that it had been his goal to retire. Early if possible.

"Do things while I'm still young enough to enjoy doing them," he'd told her over and over again.

Back then, when they'd married, Jason had thought thirty was old. Well, he was thirty plus more than half that again and as far as she was concerned, he wasn't old. She still saw him as the stud she'd fallen in love with in college.

A very hot stud, she thought as they both tumbled naked onto the bed.

Now, with another baby on its way, Jason's dreams of retirement were going to have to be put on the back burner. Way on the back burner. Certainly his dreams of an early retirement would have to be shelved.

In her heart of hearts, Laurel had to admit she was secretly relieved about that. To her, "retirement" meant the act of retiring from life. In a nutshell, it meant surrendering to the approach of old age and just sitting around, waiting for the inevitable end to finally come. On her own, she would never even think about retiring. There was so much left to do, so much more of life to grab hold of. Retirement was inconceivable to her.

However, she had fully expected Jason to hold the indefinite suspension of his almost lifelong dream against her. Certainly against the baby that was making all this a reality. It would go a long way to explaining why he'd all but abandoned her, coming home late, leaving early, ignoring her whenever she mentioned going to look for baby furniture.

Yet suddenly, here he was, just the way he used to be. The Jason she knew and loved. Maybe he'd finally accepted the baby. Oh God, she hoped so. She'd been miserable without him. He was her best friend and she'd grown so accustomed to sharing everything with him. When he wasn't here for her, the sting of betrayal was almost unbearable.

Thank you, God. Please make this last.

But even in the heat of lovemaking, or maybe because of

it, Laurel couldn't help wondering what had suddenly changed her husband's mind. Or had it changed? Was it something else? Was he so deeply entrenched in denial that he had somehow managed to block out any and all thoughts about the baby's eventual arrival?

"What's gotten into you tonight?" she heard herself asking, the question emerging in small, breathless gasps because Jason had succeeded in raising the temperature in their bedroom. "You're not acting like yourself."

"Is that a good thing, or a bad thing?" he asked, while tracing a path between her breasts with his lips.

Her skin was tingling. She pressed him to her as tiny volcanoes began to erupt in sequence up and down her body. Talking was an effort. *Thinking* was an effort.

"Good…very…good," she finally breathed out the answer to his question. "But I don't understand. Why the change?"

She felt him smile against her belly. Her flesh quivered beneath his lips. "Must be the glucosamine I've been taking," Jason said. "I've upped the daily dose."

She wiggled beneath him, drawing in his heat, his strength. Feeding on the passion Jason was exhibiting. The same passion that could always ignite within her own breast.

"God bless the pharmaceutical companies," she murmured as she raised her hips in a silent offering.

As desire urgently slammed into her, Laurel bit down on her lower lip to keep from crying out. Morgan hadn't been home when they had gone up to their bedroom, but he might have come in after they'd closed the door.

"Here," Jason murmured, "let me."

And then, before she could ask what he was referring to, she felt him gently bite down on her lower lip. Suckling, he ran the tip of his tongue along her tender skin.

She climaxed.

And then again as he thrust himself into her, immediately increasing the tempo of the dance that seemed so new in its familiarity.

She dug her fingertips into his shoulders, trying hard not to scratch him the way she wanted to. Even in the full blast of heat, with her mind winking in and out, she couldn't help thinking that she was one of the lucky ones.

"Maybe he realizes that he's been acting unfairly. Or maybe he's been kidnapped by aliens who left a clone in his place," Laurel concluded flippantly the next morning.

Both in the office early, she and Jeannie had retreated to the alcove that housed a combination sink/refrigerator/microwave oven. The coffee machine stood on the minuscule counter, yielding both fairly decent coffee and hot water, depending on which spigot was pressed. Jeannie had tossed a dollar into the empty coffee can and filled her extralarge mug with black liquid, while Laurel had put in the same amount for hot water that would activate the chocolate crystals she'd deposited into her cup.

She stirred it now, waiting for the crystals to dissolve and the mixture to thicken.

"God knows, I don't have any answers," she confessed

after having given Jeannie a cursory response as to why she seemed to walk on air this morning. Jeannie had looked at her with unabashed envy, asking what her secret was for activating a husband who'd spent the past few years essentially in "sleep" mode. "Jason's acting like he's twenty-five again."

To her surprise, Jeannie accepted the theory and even backed it up. "They say that having a baby later on in life makes you feel young again. Makes you relive your earlier years." She grinned wickedly and added, "Either that, or he's having an affair and he feels guilty so he's sharing the wealth."

Laurel took a sip of her hot chocolate. She hadn't shared with anyone just how withdrawn Jason had been lately and she didn't allude to it now. Holding the cup between her hands, she gave Jeannie a less-than-pleased glance.

"Not exactly something I want to hear at a time when I feel like the incredible expanding woman." And then she smiled. "Besides, I know that Jason is as faithful as the day is long."

To Jeannie, men were only as faithful as the length of the leash around their necks. "Are we talking about a regular day or an Alaskan midwinter day?"

"An Alaskan midsummer day," Laurel countered with utter conviction. There were a few things she knew with a fair amount of certainty and this was one of them. "They're what, twenty hours long?"

Jeannie shrugged, her wide shoulders moving up and then down carelessly.

"Something like that. I was only kidding," Jeannie added before taking a long sip of the inky brew in her mug. "The man knows when he has a good thing going. If I was to pick which of you stood a better chance of being unfaithful, I'd pick you."

Laurel came dangerously close to choking on her hot chocolate. It took her a second to clear her throat and find her voice. "Me?" she cried incredulously. "Why?"

"Not because you're out there looking for it," Jeannie told her. "At least, I don't think you are." She laughed as Laurel raised her mug, pretending to hurl it at her. "But look at it logically. You're the one who has more opportunity to get down and dirty with someone who isn't your husband." She waved her hand about the office. "Let's face it, there are a lot of guys who come through here."

Laurel raised her finger, making a point before Jeannie could continue. "Almost all of whom have wedding rings on their fingers, or at least in their lives."

"Like Mr. Hunk?" Jeannie interjected mischievously. "I saw the way he looked at you."

There'd been nothing suggestive in the way Robert had looked at her, Laurel thought staunchly. And she'd never said anything to Jeannie about his asking whether her marriage was a happy one. She knew what her friend would make of that.

"He hadn't seen me in twenty-five years, Jeannie," she reminded the woman. "If anything, he was probably looking for all the telltale signs of aging."

"The man was drooling," Jeannie contradicted with a finality that said she wasn't about to be argued out of the point. "So, how's he doing these days, anyway?" she asked.

Laurel had told her that her brother-in-law was working on Robert's newly acquired property. "Waiting to have the renovations finished on that castle of his. It's pretty close to completed. Jared's giving it his top priority," she added, referring to her brother-in-law.

"That man has a castle." Jeannie looked at her significantly. "Now all he needs is a princess."

"Princesses don't come pregnant."

Jeannie laughed. "This is the twenty-first century. Things change." Just then, they both heard the bell ring in the front of the office.

"I believe you're up," Laurel said. "Unless you want me to get that."

But Jeannie was already, and mercifully, on her way to the front of the office, to bag a client. "Nope, I'll get it."

Thank you, God, Laurel thought. Taking a seat at the tiny kitchenette table, she went on sipping her hot chocolate.

CHAPTER 18

One of Laurel's main credos was believing that, no matter what, she could find a way to get along with anyone. Jason had once paid her the supreme compliment of saying that if anyone could get along with Satan, she could.

The people who crossed the threshold of Bedford Realty Company bore out her husband's statement. Some clients were exasperating, others the last word in affable. Some knew exactly what they wanted, others vacillated like newly struck tuning forks. She got along with them all and did what she could to accommodate their wishes. Being resourceful and accommodating was part of her job description.

However, Denise's mother, Sarah Wyman—the woman had taken back her maiden name when she divorced Denise's father—was in a category all her own. It was Laurel's unbiased opinion that the tall, statuesque onetime debutante was a great deal less friendly than Satan and a great deal more judgmental. Satan might have had a cloven hoof, but Sarah Wyman had a lethal, razor-edged tongue. One which she sharpened on every available body that had the misfortune of crossing her path.

So it was with no little dread that Laurel agreed to meet with Denise and her mother, as well as the four young women Denise had chosen to act as her bridesmaids and maid of honor, at the exclusive bridal boutique in Beverly Hills. This was supposed to be the final fitting before the wedding. Because being in Sarah's company made her feel like the lone survivor of a shipwreck floating on a leaking rubber raft, "surrounded" by one very quick moving, hungry shark. Laurel brought along a reinforcement for moral support. Lynda.

Laurel saw Sarah the moment she walked into the boutique. Blessed with the kind of skin that would have made a porcelain doll green with envy, Sarah was carefully and artistically made up to an inch of her life. Laurel had it on good authority that Sarah never ventured a foot outside of her bedroom without makeup.

Seeing her enter the shop, Sarah's crystal green eyes—a gift from her ophthalmologist via contact lens—narrowed and her mouth twitched with barely contained amusement.

There was no mistaking where the woman's eyes were focused. On her stomach.

"Eyes front, enemy sighted," Laurel murmured under her breath, taking Lynda's arm and tugging her sister around.

In order to gain entrance, they'd had to ring a bell and be admitted to the store by one of the three saleswomen. The boutique, Giselle's, prided itself on not allowing "just anyone" into their showroom. Clients came through referrals and preferably with a lineage that had originally come over on the *Mayflower*.

"I thought they were going to stick me to see if my DNA was good enough to come into this place," Lynda complained, still looking over her shoulder at the petite older woman who had unsmilingly allowed them admittance to the inner sanctum.

"Lynda," Laurel whispered urgently. "Barracuda, twelve o'clock high."

Her sister turned around just in time to see Sarah descending on them. The expression on the woman's face was slightly pained as she regarded the uninvited invader beside Laurel.

Sarah's eyes were cold. "And this is?"

She was going to make this work, she was, Laurel thought urgently. Family harmony was at stake. Besides, Luke loved this witch's daughter. "My sister, Lynda."

Lynda extended her hand toward Sarah and was left holding it in midair.

"I hope she's not expecting to get her dress here." Sarah was making no effort to hide her distasteful appraisal of her sister. Laurel's intentions of a peaceful détente went up in flames. Thoughts of dark alleys and strangleholds began floating through her head.

"No, not at all," Lynda informed her casually. "I'm having mine flown in from Switzerland. Twelve little myopic nuns are pricking their fingers over it even as we speak."

Sarah raised an eyebrow, clearly not amused. "She has your sense of humor," she said icily to Laurel.

Laurel merely flashed a smile. "It's a family thing."

Sarah made a little disparaging noise that sounded suspiciously like a snort. "I certainly hope not, for Lucas's sake."

"Luke," Laurel corrected for what was probably the dozenth time. The woman kept insisting on calling Luke by the wrong name. "His name is Luke."

The disdain on Sarah's face only intensified. She looked put upon, as if she was attempting to lift trailer trash to a decent level, only to meet with resistance.

"'Luke' is something a farm boy would go by," she told Laurel. "'Lucas' has power, strength."

Laurel struggled to hold on to her temper. She couldn't kill the woman in front of witnesses. "Perhaps, but his name is still Luke. After his grandfather. I can have his birth certificate sent over if you like."

"Whatever." Sarah sniffed defensively. And then her eyes dipped down to Laurel's waist again.

Despite the fact that Laurel could have sworn she felt it thickening on a daily basis, she was still not showing in the traditional sense. There was no telltale, rounded bump on its way to being a mound. At the moment, she only looked as if she'd indulged in one too many chocolate bars on a daily basis for the past couple of months.

"Speaking of whatever," Sarah said, pausing dramatically, "whatever were you thinking, Laurel, dear?"

Laurel heard her sister draw in her breath. Lynda knew, she thought, that the haughty woman had just skated onto extremely thin ice. She stared at Denise's mother intently, her eyes never wavering. "About what?"

"About this." Sarah waved her hand at her middle. "Why on earth would you allow yourself to get pregnant at your age?

To *be* pregnant at your age?" she emphasized in a tone that was both mystified and ridiculing. She didn't bother lowering her voice and it was obvious that the saleswomen couldn't help overhearing. Well-bred to a fault, they gave no indication of listening. But they would have had to have the constitutions of martyred saints not to.

Laurel never faltered. "Maybe because I like children and I don't eat my young."

Sarah's pale complexion instantly acquired color. Laurel watched in fascination, wondering if the woman could get steam to come out of her ears as well.

"Is that a joke at my expense?"

Laurel was the very picture of innocence as she denied any intended offense. "Just a statement, Sarah, nothing more."

She saw the other girls hovering in the background. Even Denise was keeping her distance.

Initially, she hadn't been thrilled with the girl when Luke started bringing her around. She thought of her as a little too cool. But seeing what had raised her, or claimed to have raised her, Laurel was beginning to think that Denise had turned out remarkably well, all things considered. It was evident that Denise had not escaped her mother's sharp tongue unscathed.

"Now," Laurel continued, taking charge and knowing that the very act irritated Sarah beyond words, "since I'm sure we all have to be somewhere else—"

"Anywhere else," Lynda said under her breath, but audibly enough for two of the bridesmaids to hear. The girls both began to giggle, then stopped abruptly the instant Sarah shot a dagger in their direction.

"Why don't we get this final fitting over with?" Laurel concluded.

Sarah wrenched control back. "I imagine they will have to spend the most time on you." She looked over toward the small, slender older woman in black who stood unobtrusively off to the side. "Giselle, is there enough material on Mrs. Mitchell's dress for you to let out so that it can fit her properly?"

The owner of the exclusive shop gave her a tight-lipped smile after glancing at Laurel's figure. "I am sure there will be no problem, madam."

"Obviously Giselle doesn't know the woman very well, does she?" Lynda whispered into Laurel's ear.

"All right, then why don't you see to the bridesmaids and maid of honor first?" Worded like a suggestion, it was more of an order. Sarah waved the four young women toward the dressing room. She didn't expect to be contradicted and she wasn't as the girls meekly shuffled away.

They were yet to be out of earshot when Sarah turned toward her daughter, a triumphant smile on her lips. "I'm so glad you listened to me, dear."

Denise looked at her mother, a little perplexed at the praise. Everyone knew that her mother was not thrilled with the match that had been made. She made it clear that Luke's bloodlines were less than satisfactory.

"Listened to you?" she asked uneasily. "What do you mean, Mother?"

"I'm talking about making sure that the young women in the bridal party weren't pretty." She smoothed down a single stray hair on Denise's head. "After all, a bride should be the most beautiful one at her wedding and, well—" Sarah cocked her head, a look of pity entering her eyes "—you were never really a head turner, darling, so—"

"That all depends if the head is on the neck of a person with a stick up their butt," Laurel said, putting an arm around Denise's shoulders and glaring at her mother. And then she turned to Denise. "We all think you're beautiful, Denise," she told her future daughter-in-law. "Especially Luke." Laurel deliberately emphasized her son's name as she looked at Sarah.

Before Sarah could make any rejoinder, the rear curtain was moved aside and the three bridesmaids came out like a gaggle of geese. The maid of honor was behind them. They had on long, ice-blue gowns with straight skirts and empire waists.

She was getting very fond of empire waists, Laurel thought.

"And aren't they just gorgeous?" she declared, posing the rhetorical question to both her sister and the boutique owner.

Sarah made a cryptic remark, which everyone seemed not to hear. This gave Laurel immense satisfaction.

CHAPTER 19

Lynda waited until after the waiter had placed their orders—Lobster Cantonese for Laurel, Sesame Chicken for her—on their table before answering Laurel's question about what was behind her wide, pleased grin.

"You sure gave it to that stuck-up bitchy woman." Every word sounded like a cheer.

Taking the rice, Laurel scooped out a portion before spooning half the Lobster Cantonese on top. She frowned, not at the praise, but at her own actions. "I should have kept my temper."

Lynda licked the drop of sauce from her forefinger before picking up her fork. "No, you should have decked her."

God knows she'd wanted to, Laurel thought. But that didn't exactly help forge good relations with Luke's future in-laws, or at least, his mother-in-law. She had a sneaking suspicion that Denise's father might have applauded her had he been there. But that didn't change the fact that she should have held her tongue for the sake of peace.

"I don't know what's wrong with me lately," she admitted to her sister. "It's like all my emotions are in this huge microwave oven and they keep popping like corn kernels without any warning." She raised her eyes to her sister. "Most of the time I don't know if I'm going to laugh or cry the next minute."

Lynda watched as Laurel filled her tiny cup with tea before pouring some for herself. She nodded her thanks, then raised the cup in a silent salute. "Welcome to my world."

Laurel set the teapot back down and addressed her meal. Her stomach had been growling for the past half hour but she didn't feel like eating. "No, I'm serious. This isn't me. I've always been even tempered, the diplomat for the family." She'd lost track of all the arguments she'd refereed between her sons when they were growing up.

Lynda allowed herself a taste of her food before answering. "Want my guess?"

"Go ahead."

Lynda took a sip of her tea. "You're pregnant and going through menopause at the same time." Setting the cup down, she picked up her fork again and ate with gusto. "Twice the fun, twice the emotions."

Laurel banked down her disappointment. She'd been hungry all afternoon, but now her appetite seemed to have deserted her even though she was eating one of her favorite meals. Being pregnant was for the birds, she thought moodily.

"There's a scary image," she said as she picked at her meal.

Lynda had been through all this by proxy three other times. It made her an expert of sorts. "It'll level off, it always does," she reminded her confidently. "At least you'll have something to show for it at the end of your crying jags." She sighed. "All

I ever have is a stuffed-up nose." Because the waiter had also brought their fortune cookies at the same time he'd brought their dinner, Lynda selected one and cracked it opened. "How original," she murmured, crumpling the tiny paper.

"What does it say?" Laurel wanted to know.

"You will meet a tall, dark stranger who will sweep you off your feet. Right." Her voice vibrated with cynicism.

Well, this was as good a lead-in as any she could have hoped for, Laurel thought. It was now or never.

"Speaking of which…"

Lynda held her hand up, indicating a time-out until she swallowed what was in her mouth. "Come again?"

"There's someone I want you to meet."

Lynda rolled her eyes. "Oh God, Laurie, please tell me it's not a blind date."

"No, he's got twenty-twenty vision." Her sister gave her a reproving look for the archaic joke. "And practically perfect everything else," she added with conviction.

She could see that, despite trying not to be, her sister was interested. "So what's he doing on the market?" Lynda asked. "Is he some kind of a closet serial killer?"

Why did everyone always assume that if a person wasn't taken by the ripe old age of twenty-five, there had to be something wrong with them, some glaring flaw? Sometimes it was just a matter of the right person not being in the immediate vicinity.

"There's nothing in his closet except clothes and hangers…and shoes," Laurel added with feeling.

"You seem to know a lot about his closet."

"I sold him the house." She knew she'd mentioned it to Lynda because the sale had been such a big deal. But in typical Lynda fashion, her sister hadn't really heard her. There were times what she thought Lynda had to be an honorary male. "And Jared's been retained to fix it up. He and Morgan are almost finished with it."

Putting down her fork, Lynda wiped her mouth. A skeptical look came into her eyes. She was *not* impressed. "You sold him a fixer-upper?"

Laurel knew what her sister was thinking. That the man couldn't afford the prices of the newer homes and had gotten one that was priced to sell quickly because the owner wanted to unload the property. "I sold him the castle."

"The castle?" Lynda echoed. "He bought the castle?" She took a sip of the by-now-cool tea. "He's the one? What is he, some deluded prince?"

Picking up the teapot, Laurel refreshed Lynda's cup and then her own. She felt herself getting defensive for Robert. That would probably tickle him, she couldn't help thinking. After all this time, she was still defending him. Against her sister this time instead of a bloody nose, but the end result was the same.

"He liked the stonework on it. Listen, the castle's unique and so is he." She looked down at her full teacup and decided to pass, even though she'd just poured it. They had a long drive ahead of them before they reached Bedford and she was at that point where for every drop of tea she consumed, three more seemed to materialize within her bladder. She didn't want to be forced to get off the freeway in search of a bathroom halfway through their trip back.

Lynda, meanwhile, seemed to be mulling over a word she'd used. "How unique?" she finally asked.

Ha, gotcha! Laurel could feel herself reeling her sister in. "Well, for starters, he transformed himself from a geek everyone picked on to a man whose name has appeared on the pages of *Fortune 500*." She knew that for a fact because she'd checked.

But Lynda had gotten hung up on an earlier word. "Geek, huh?"

"He doesn't look like what you would expect a geek to look like," Laurel told her firmly. "As a matter of fact, Jeannie refers to him as Mr. Hunk."

Lynda snorted, popping a piece of the fortune cookie into her mouth. "Jeannie has Jonas as her frame of reference."

The fact that the woman was married to someone who reminded most people of a life-size toad didn't alter the fact that Jeannie had an active fantasy life. Most likely it had even contributed to it.

"Trust me, she's called it this time." Laurel paused a beat, wondering if volunteering this would help or hinder things, then decided that if Lynda did go out with Robert, she was going to find out anyway. "I went to school with him."

Fresh interest crossed Lynda's fair-complected face. "Oh?"

"He's a nice guy," she told Lynda. "His wife died a few years ago and I think he's lonely. But selective," she added for her sister's benefit, "which is why he's still single."

"Well, there go my chances."

Laurel sighed and shook her head. She opened the vast cavern that was her purse and took out a small mirror. Holding it up before her sister, she said, "Take a look at yourself, Lynda." When Lynda averted her eyes, she repeated sharply, "Look at yourself." It was now a command, not a suggestion. "You're a beautiful woman."

Lynda pushed the mirror down. "If I'm so beautiful, why did Dean leave?"

Laurel returned the mirror to her purse. "Ever think that might be Dean's problem, not yours? That he doesn't know what he wants and is just one of these people who goes through life, constantly dissatisfied, constantly looking for 'something better' to come up over the hill even when he has something that's out of this world right there in his lap?"

"You're a lot nicer now than you were when we were growing up." Her sister laughed softly, shaking her head in disbelief.

"That's because you were a pain then," Laurel quipped.

Finished with the scraps from her cookie and her meal, Lynda sat back in her chair, her eyes level with Laurel's. "Okay, I'm game. When do I meet Mr. Terrific?"

Yes!

Laurel did her best to keep a poker face. "How about coming to dinner next Friday? I'm having him over for a home-cooked meal, something he said he prefers to restaurant food." She crossed her fingers that Robert would accept the invitation when she actually had a chance to extend it to him.

"Friday," Lynda repeated slowly, thinking. Her work as a

corporate attorney for a leading manufacturing company kept her fairly busy. "I'm not sure…"

"Lynda," she began warningly.

Lynda held up her hands. "Okay, okay, barring a major problem at work, I'll be there."

She wasn't accepting any excuses. If she could get Robert to come, she was going to personally hog-tie Lynda and drag her to the house if her sister gave her any trouble. "Any problem at work on a Friday can wait until the following Monday."

"You know, maybe you haven't changed that much since we were kids," Lynda decided, a half smile playing on her lips. "You were always bossy."

"It's a dirty job but someone has to do it."

Lynda raised her hand, signaling the waiter for their check. "Ready to go home?" she asked Laurel.

Laurel was more than ready, but there was still something she needed to do. "I'd better make a pit stop first." She struggled out of the booth. Baby weight was making a slide out challenging.

It's only going to get worse.

"This baby has made himself at home on top of my bladder and refuses to move."

"Himself," Lynda echoed. "Then you know it's a he?"

"Not yet," she admitted, but then the look of certainty entered her eyes. "But it's a boy, like his brothers. I'd bet on it."

CHAPTER 20

Finished with his breakfast, Jason rose from the table and took his plate and cup to the sink. Since Laurel's unexpected condition had taken them by storm, he found himself doing things around the house just to try to make her life a little easier. It wasn't something he'd done before, but this time around, it seemed like the way to go.

Depositing the dishes, he paused to look at her. She was standing next to the sink, distracted. She seemed uneasy and oblivious to what was going on around her. He knew why. She was due for an amniocentesis this afternoon.

"Want me to be there with you?" he asked.

She turned to him, confused, and he nodded toward the calendar where she'd marked the appointment. That he even took notice of what was written there surprised her. She'd mentioned it to him in passing, but that was when she'd first made the appointment. She hadn't expected him to retain anything about the conversation. Jason wasn't into remembering things like that. Especially when it came to the baby. Most of the time, he avoided talking about their being new parents again. It was as if she was just gaining weight arbitrarily instead of being pregnant.

"Can you?"

Jason shrugged into his jacket, straightening his tie. As hard as it was for him to make peace with this turn of events, he knew how much it meant to Laurel to have him there. "It'll take some shifting around, but I can make it."

She wanted to tell him that it was all right. That she was a big girl—bigger at this point than she was happy about—and that she could do this on her own. But he'd shown such little support that she jumped at the chance to have him with her. To again be that team they'd always been before. Besides, she did feel a little uneasy about this afternoon.

All right, scared—she felt scared. The idea having to face a nurse equipped with a needle that doubled as a javelin, of playing Moby Dick to the woman's Ahab, made her hands and feet turn icy cold and her stomach queasy.

So she gave up the brave facade she always liked to keep up and nodded. "Yes, I'd like that." Laurel took a deep breath, and then let it out, trying to steady her suddenly erratic pulse. "You know, I don't really have to do this," she told him. "There's nothing in the rules that says I have to have this test done."

"Don't you want to be sure that everything's okay with the baby?"

Guilt popped up. When he put it that way, it sounded so selfish on her part.

Because it was.

With a sigh, she nodded. She'd researched the procedure

online to see if anything had changed since she'd had it done twenty-one years ago. There was a short video she could have done without. Now she couldn't get the image of the oversize needle out of her head.

"Yes, of course I do. I just don't relish the idea of being harpooned."

Jason picked up his briefcase from the floor as he chuckled. "You're not that big yet."

"'Yet.' You used the word *yet*," she pointed out dejectedly. God, she'd forgotten how much she hated the outer trappings of this eventual miracle of birth. "It means I'm getting there."

"Of course you're getting there. Laurel, you're just four months pregnant, but you are going to get bigger."

It sounded like some kind of curse being heaped on her head. Laurel closed her eyes.

"Hopefully not in the next two weeks." When she opened her eyes again, she saw Jason watching her quizzically. "The wedding, remember? I have a mother-of-the-groom dress to fit into."

It was obvious that he didn't take this nearly as seriously as she did. "Worse comes to worst, I have a pup tent I can throw over you."

She shook her head in wonder as she straightened his collar. "And to think, I fell in love with you for your sense of humor."

The grin he gave her was positively wicked. "As I recall, that wasn't all you loved."

Laurel sniffed, pretending to ignore the comment. To ignore the memories of the passionate love they used to make before there were rings on their fingers and vows binding their souls. "I was as pure as the driven snow when I married you."

Instead of taking his leave, Jason paused for a minute. He cupped her cheek gently with his hand. The love he felt stirring within surprised him. He'd loved his wife for a very long time, but these rushes of emotion, the same dizzying feelings he'd experienced when he'd first fallen in love with Laurel, were unexpected and surprising. He found himself enjoying them.

"As I recall, the snow was a little slushy as it was being driven." He brushed his lips against hers. "You were a wildcat, Laurie."

"Were?" she echoed, raising an eyebrow.

"My apologies. Still are," he amended. And then he surprised them both as he took her into his arms and kissed her again, this time with more feeling. "My little wildcat."

The smile he received in response was bright enough to melt the aforementioned snow. "Thanks for the 'little.'"

He released her, laughing as he picked up his briefcase again. "Don't mention it."

"Jason?" she called after him as he led the way to the front door. Morgan had left several minutes before for the construction site, so it was just the two of them in the house.

Something in her voice had him turning around. "Yes?"

She joined him at the door, but neither one of them opened it. "Are you having an affair?"

His mouth dropped open. "What?"

Laurel shrugged. "You're different lately." At first distant, then close for a while, then distant again. And now he was offering to come with her for the test, something she hadn't even asked him to do because she didn't want to feel any more abandoned than she already did. What was going on? "You weren't like that during any of my other pregnancies," she pointed out.

He supposed he had been giving off mixed signals, but that was because he'd been feeling them himself. This was change he hadn't bargained for and it had knocked the foundations out from beneath his carefully orchestrated world. "Maybe because, during all the other pregnancies, I was too rushed to appreciate what was happening." He knew it was vague, but it was the best he could do. He didn't want to admit to her that he was anything but confident about what lay ahead. She had enough to deal with. "Too busy to drink in the experience."

She nodded, as if considering his explanation. "So you're not having an affair?"

He searched her face, her eyes, trying to get at the truth. At times he could intuit what she was thinking. At other times, such as now, he hadn't a clue. "Are you serious?"

"Maybe," she allowed, then raised her thumb and forefinger, holding them half an inch apart. "Just a little." She dropped her hand to her side and told him the real reason for her bouts of insecurities. "I feel dumpy."

Instead of answering her, Jason turned her around so that she faced the mirror hanging adjacent to the front door. It allowed a view that went beyond her waist. Standing behind her, he kept his hands on her shoulders forcing her to look at her image.

"If you think that's dumpy," he told her, "then maybe after you have the amniocentesis done, we should take you to Dr. Mayweather," he mentioned the ophthalmologist they'd been seeing annually for several years now, "to have your eyes checked again."

Still looking into the mirror, he watched the smile blossom on his wife's lips. Laurel turned around to face him. The smile had entered her eyes.

"I love you," she told him.

Husbands, one, he thought, pleased and relieved. "Good to know. Now I've got to get out of here." He had his hand on the doorknob. "Two o'clock, right?"

"Two o'clock," Laurel confirmed. "Oh, and by the way." Her words stopped what was about to be a clean getaway. Jason glanced at her over his shoulder, waiting. "I'm having Lynda and Robert to dinner this Friday."

"Robert?" Jason repeated the name. For a moment, it meant nothing to him, brought no images of anyone to mind. And then he remembered. "That's the guy you sold that white elephant to, isn't it?" He opened the door and walked out.

Laurel followed, then locked the door in her wake. "The castle," she corrected, "not 'white elephant.' But yes, that's the guy. Robert Manning. He's the guy whose property your brother and Morgan are working on," she threw in.

Jason had his own theory about this little turn of events. "Feeling guilty?"

She drew herself up to her full height, which mercifully was still more than her width. "No, I don't feel guilty."

"Then you're matchmaking."

She bristled at the old-fashioned word. "I'm merely bringing together two people who might not have the opportunity to meet otherwise."

Jason scrutinized her face. "And this would be a good thing because…?"

Despite the fact that she could almost literally feel Lynda's pain at being alone at this stage of her life, she wasn't undertaking the matchup lightly. "Because I think they're right for each other."

"Then you *are* matchmaking," he said with finality.

She began to protest, but knew that there was no winning with him when Jason took that tone. Besides, arguing would only succeed in making them both late.

"If that's what you want to call it."

As he went to the driveway, he felt oddly tolerant, given his general feelings about things like this. They were damn uncomfortable to say the least.

"What I want to call it is meddling, but you'd probably hit me if I did."

Laurel beamed. "You know me so well."

He paused to look at her for a long moment over the hood of his car. She couldn't read his expression. "Only sometimes, Laurie, only sometimes."

She wanted to ask him what he meant by that but decided to let it go for the time being. He was coming to the amniocentesis and he'd agreed to having Robert and Lynda over for dinner on Friday. That was enough for now.

CHAPTER 21

Blair Memorial Hospital had been part of the community for as long as Laurel could remember. She'd had her tonsils out here as a little girl and all three of her sons had been born here. As she parked the car, she noticed the hospital facilities were twice as big as they'd once been. Several floors had been added to the rest of the extended building. Parking had gone from scattered lots to a four-story parking structure. It hardly looked like the same place she remembered.

It didn't even smell like a hospital anymore, she thought as she entered the outpatient admission area. And even the chapel had been moved. It used to be in the rear of the hospital, but was now immediately visible upon entrance. She saw the light shining through the stained-glass windows on her right and for a moment, she thought about stopping to say a few words in supplication that all would go well.

But she wanted to get this over with, so she went directly to the front desk.

The hospital walls were a soothing pastel-blue and soft gray rugs covered the old black-and-white checkered linoleum. Paintings of pastoral scenes decorated the walls.

Everything to put the prospective patient at ease, she thought.

It wasn't working.

Laurel still felt nervous. Nervous as she gave her information to the blue-smocked, smiling woman who pulled up her preregistration file on the computer. Nervous as she put her wrist out to be tagged.

"Is that really necessary?" she asked, looking at the plastic bracelet that had suddenly been hermetically sealed onto itself—and by proxy, to her. "I'm only going to be here for a couple of hours." She reiterated the words that Dr. Kilpatrick had said to her just the other day. Laurel held onto them like a promise.

"It's just standard procedure," the woman assured her. The receptionist gathered together several in-hospital sheets of paper that further authorized the test and, stapling them, handed them to her. She flashed a brilliant smile. "Don't worry, we're not planning on losing you in the hallway."

Laurel nodded. "Right."

Tearing yet another sheet from a pad, the woman flipped it around for her to see. It was a map of the hospital's first floor. The entire area was honeycombed with more than a score of different rooms for a myriad of labs and screenings.

"Now you follow this line," the woman obligingly drew in said line using a yellow marker. "Until you get here." She made an x with a flourish. "And they'll take it from there. Room one-eighteen," the woman told her, retiring the marker and sitting back in her chair again. "You can't miss it."

Laurel accepted the map, placing it on top of the papers. She glanced again toward the electronic doors. Each time they opened, she'd looked in their direction. Hoping. Being disappointed. She didn't want to make her way to the testing area before Jason got there.

"Um, my husband said he'd meet me here."

The woman nodded. A glint of sympathy entered her eyes. "Everyone has to stop at this desk when they come in. When he gets here, I'll tell him where to go," she promised.

She doesn't believe me. How many husbands and boyfriends promised to come and never showed? Laurel fought off a feeling of being isolated.

"His name is Jason. He's a tall, good-looking man," Laurel described, suddenly wanting to prove to this woman that her husband really *was* going to be here. That maybe other men didn't come when they said they would, but her Jason wasn't like that. He kept his word. *Please keep your word, Jason.*

"Lucky you," the woman said with just a touch of wistfulness. "I'll send Jason over to you the minute I see him come in." Leaning forward, she tapped the map Laurel was holding. "Off you go," the receptionist coaxed.

So, not having any other choice, off she went.

The best time to have the test performed was between fifteen and eighteen weeks of gestation. Laurel had put it off until time had almost run out. It was now or never.

Apparently without Jason, she thought.

No, she told herself, he'd said he'd be here this morning. Jason didn't lie.

But he did get stuck in traffic.

Her phone began to ring in her pocket. She glanced around to see if anyone was around to hear. There were signs posted all through the hospital, thanking people for shutting off their cell phones because the signal could interfere with tests.

Making a quick decision, Laurel darted into the ladies' room. The second the door shut behind her, she pulled her cell phone out of her pocket, at the same time scanning the area. She bent down to see if there were any feet peering out from beneath the stall doors. There weren't. The bathroom was empty.

Laurel flipped open the phone, hoping that it was Jason calling to tell her he'd reached the hospital and that he hadn't hung up yet.

"Hello?"

"Laurie, it looks like I might be late getting to the hospital."

She didn't know whether she detected an apology in his voice, but she did hear frustration. It matched her own.

Laurel leaned against a wall, dropping her purse to the floor. It was starting to feel heavy. She struggled to hide her disappointment. He wasn't going to get here in time. "Oh God, Jason, where are you?" There was background noise, but she couldn't make it out.

"Stuck on the southbound 5, staring at the back of a produce truck." She heard him turning down the radio in the car. "According to the guy on the radio, there was a two-car collision up ahead. I'll be there as soon as I can."

She wanted to ask him why he hadn't left earlier. Or,

better yet, why he hadn't taken the day off to begin with. But that wouldn't change the situation now and being petulant would only wind up creating friction between them.

"Can't ask for anything more than that," she answered, resigning herself to going through this on her own. The outer door opened and a woman entered. She glanced at her with vague, passing interest before going into the stall farthest from the door. "If you do get here," she said halfheartedly, "I'll be in room one-eighteen."

"Not if—when," Jason insisted. "This isn't my fault, Laurel."

She suppressed a sigh. "I know. Look, I've got to go, Jason. I don't want to be late for the appointment."

"Yeah. Well, good luck, baby. And I'm sorry."

"Not your fault," she echoed his words. Laurel flipped the phone shut and this time, closed it.

Baby.

Jason hadn't called her that in so long she couldn't remember the last time she'd heard him say it. Maybe he actually *was* trying to get here. The woman in the stall flushed. Laurel blew out a breath, squared her shoulders and walked from the ladies' room.

Armed with her yellow-marked map, she found the right area in less than five minutes. And that was walking slowly and even pausing to look in the tiny gift-shop window. She gave her name to the receptionist, handed in her paperwork and took a seat on a sofa designed to eat whoever sat down on it.

The wait for her amniocentesis was much too short.

Within seven minutes of handing her paperwork to the

woman at the reception desk, Laurel heard her name being called. Trying to dig herself out of the folds of the all-encompassing sofa without drawing any undue attention, she finally managed to stand.

She raised her hand to get the technician's attention. "Right here."

The next minute, a matronly looking woman in white was at her elbow and she was being escorted to a small, ultimately dark room several feet beyond the reception desk.

The woman handed her a blue-and-white floral one-size-fits-all-gown. "Here, put this on."

"I need to go to the bathroom first," Laurel realized.

"Full bladder?" the woman asked kindly.

"Oh yes." That seemed to be the annoying state of affairs these days, occurring every twenty minutes or so.

"Perfect."

"Excuse me?"

"You need a full bladder for the ultrasound."

Laurel shook her head. "There's been some mistake, I'm here for the amniocentesis."

"I know, dear," the nurse, whose name tag read "Annie," said patiently. "But we need to take the ultrasound so we know exactly where the baby is. Wouldn't want us accidentally impaling the little one, now would you?"

Laurel shivered. She tried not to let her mind go there. "No."

"I'll try to be as quick as possible," Annie promised, beginning to leave.

Laurel looked down at the gown. Funny how a piece of

material could make her feel so vulnerable. "Is it all right if I keep my underwear on?"

The woman smiled. "Sure, just be sure to take off your panty hose. I'll be back in a few minutes. When you're ready, you can get on that." She indicated the narrow, sterile-looking table. There was a fresh layer of paper on in.

"Does it hurt?" Laurel heard herself asking just as the woman opened the door. She remembered that the last time, it had really hurt. Long after the procedure was over.

Annie turned around and gave her a sympathetic smile. "Not so much."

I'll hold you to that, Laurel thought. "Um, my husband is supposed to meet me here," she called after Annie's departing back.

She half expected the woman to give her a patronizing, pitying glance. Instead, she nodded. "I'll let the receptionist know."

And then she was alone.

Laurel's hands felt icy as she slipped out of her dress. Once she took off her panty hose, she stuffed them beneath the dress and left both on top of the nearby chair. She'd just managed to get on the table when the door opened again after one quick knock. Annie had returned. The grandmotherly woman had a broad smile on her face. "Look what I found outside at the reception desk, making a fuss."

The woman stepped aside, allowing her to see just what she had "found."

Jason.

He was at her side the next moment, taking her hand in his. Her husband bent over to kiss her forehead. "Hi, baby. See, I told you I'd make it."

She could have cried.

CHAPTER 22

She stared at him, stunned. "How did you get here so fast?"

"I used the car-pool lane." He made it sound like the simplest thing in the world.

"You brought someone with you?"

Jason hadn't said anything about bringing someone with him when he left this morning, or even when he called earlier. Who could he have brought? Her mother? Lynda? Certainly not one of the boys. Two of them were busy working and Christopher had been rather uncommunicative lately. Ever since she'd told the family that she was pregnant, he seemed to be distancing himself from her, as if he was even more embarrassed about the situation than Luke was. Luke, at least, seemed to be coming to terms with it—as long as she didn't embarrass him at the wedding.

"No," Jason answered innocently. In the background, Annie was moving around, checking instruments, preparing to start the test. And then he grinned. "That's exactly what the cop asked when he pulled me over."

"You got a ticket?" She felt horrible for him. Jason never

got tickets. He was the only one in the family who didn't and he was so proud of his record.

The grin widened. Annie moved a stool over toward him and he accepted the seat with a grateful nod. Making himself comfortable, he continued with his narrative.

"I told him my wife was having an amniocentesis and that she'd bring down the house if I didn't get there in time. He gave me an escort. Nice guy. But we've got to call the baby Darrell when it gets here." Still holding Laurel's hand, he looked over to the woman who had brought him in here. "Did I miss anything?"

"Nope," she answered. "The show's just about ready to start." Slipping on a pair of surgical gloves, Annie parted Laurel's gown, exposing only her rounded abdomen. Taking some gel, she prepared to rub it on the area. "This is going to be a little cold."

Laurel discovered the woman had a gift for understatement. She arched her back at first contact, surprised at just how cold the gel was. It took her several moments to relax again.

"Sorry about that," Annie murmured. She was now passing what looked like a stubby, square wand over her abdomen. "How far along are you?"

Something was forming on the monitor to the left. An overexposed image that resembled an inverted guppy in a pond. Was that her baby? It looked as tiny as a peanut.

"Eighteen weeks."

"You're kind of small for eighteen weeks," Annie commented, watching the monitor as she continued to stroke the wand over her belly.

"I'm trying to eat sensibly this time around."

Annie nodded. "Very smart." Finished, she laid the wand down and picked up a large cotton swab. Very gently she cleaned off the area again. "A lot of ladies overeat, then get depressed when the weight doesn't go once the baby arrives." Turning away, she threw out the swab and reached for the needle. "Now this is going to look a lot scarier than it actually is," she warned just before she faced them again.

The woman had in her hand the largest needle Laurel had ever seen. They'd definitely gotten larger since the last time she'd had this done.

"Not hardly," Laurel breathed.

"Wow." The comment came out before Jason had a chance to stop himself. He cleared his throat, glancing at his wife. "I mean, that's not so bad."

This was definitely *not* a good idea. Laurel froze in place, staring at the instrument. "You want to get on this table instead of me?"

"I'm not the one with the baby, honey," he pointed out gently. And then he took her hand in both of his again. "You'll do fine."

"He's right," Annie told her, getting into position. "And it has to be this big because it's hollow. I need one cc of fluid from the sac for every week of gestation."

Laurel couldn't take her eyes off the needle. "Isn't there some other way?"

"I'm afraid not. This has to reach all the way down to your uterus." Saying that, she began slowly to insert the needle.

"There's going to be a little sting." The woman shifted her eyes to the monitor, watching the image of the baby as she went in further and further. "Just try to relax," she urged.

"Easy for you to say," Laurel ground out through clenched teeth. "That 'little sting' is still there." As the pain continued, she squeezed Jason's hand hard, trying to find a level where she could draw in a complete breath.

"It'll go away in a couple of minutes," Annie promised. Her voice was calm, soothing. "It'll all be over with soon." Annie glanced down at what she was doing, and then back at the monitor again. The tiny guppy seemed to move slightly. But that could have been her imagination, Laurel thought. "And before you know it, you'll be going to her graduation."

"Her?" Laurel cried. She looked at the image, but there was absolutely no hint from that quarter. "It's a girl?" She looked back at Annie. She felt a strange excitement grip her. "I'm having a girl?" Her voice fairly squeaked at the end of the question.

Annie watched the monitor. The image wasn't conclusive. "I really can't tell just yet. Sorry, I was just using a figure of speech. I'm used to girls. I've got five daughters."

"I have three sons," Laurel told her, doing her best to relax a body that felt as stiff as an ironing board. "We," she suddenly corrected herself, squeezing the word out as she tried hard not to scream. The harpoon was going down even deeper than it had originally. Was Annie trying to get fluid out of her toes? "We have three sons."

Annie acknowledged the information with a nod of her head. "So, do you want another boy?"

"Boy, girl, it doesn't really matter. Just as long as the baby's healthy, that's all that counts." She felt like panting, like clawing. This hurt a lot more than the nurse had said it would, even more than she'd remembered.

"Is there something wrong, Nurse?" Jason asked.

The woman glanced in his direction, bemused by his question. "No, why?"

He didn't like seeing Laurel in pain. With his first son, he'd lucked out and been away on business when Luke had decided to come into the world. But he'd been there for Morgan and Christopher. And watching her had damn near killed him.

"Well, it seems like you're an awfully long time with this. I just wondered if that meant that maybe there was something—"

But Annie was shaking her head, stopping him from ending his thought. "We just make sure that we have a good amount of fluid for all the tests and if we rush it, it's going to hurt your wife more."

"Oh God, don't hurry," Laurel pleaded, wishing she could stay Annie's hand.

"You're doing great, honey," the nurse assured her.

"How much longer?" Laurel asked.

"A couple more minutes," Annie answered. And then, very carefully, the woman drew out the needle. With a quick movement of her hand, she dabbed at Laurel's stomach, cleaning up any fluid that might have dripped out. "There," she declared. "Done."

Laurel stared at her, not comprehending. "You said a couple more minutes."

The woman winked, a pleased expression on her face. "I lied," she freely confessed. "This way, you get a nice surprise." She held the needle up, the tip pointing toward the ceiling. "Unless, of course, you'd like me to insert it again."

"No, no, that's okay," Laurel assured her, holding her hands up before her belly. "I feel like a pincushion as it is."

Annie nodded. "All right then, Laurel, you can get dressed now. I'll be back in a few minutes."

As the nurse/technician left the room, Jason took Laurel's hand and helped her up into a sitting position. He looked at her with concern, seemingly half-expecting her to pass out. "How do you feel?"

She stared down at her abdomen. "As if I'd leak if I drank any water."

"You're a lot braver than I am," he told her, shaking his head. "I think if she had stuck that thing into me, I would have passed out."

Now that it was behind her, Laurel could put the experience into perspective. Compared to childbirth, the discomfort of the test had actually been rather minor. It was the needle that had been the most frightening part.

She glanced at the frozen image on the monitor, a replica of the photo that Annie had captured, before she looked up at Jason and smiled. "Then you'd really have a hard time giving birth to this little guy."

"No argument," he told her. Picking up her dress and panty hose, he placed them on the table beside her. "Here, you might want these." His eyes then moved to the gown she had on. "Unless you've gotten attached to wearing that."

"Very funny." Shedding the gown, Laurel quickly slipped her dress on over her head and arms. And then she sighed, gazing down at her legs.

"What's the matter?" Jason asked.

"Just getting up my oomph to put my panty hose on." She began gathering the nylon between the thumb and forefinger of each hand.

He saw no problem. "Why don't you just skip putting them on this time?"

Laurel shook her head. "Because I always feel naked without them."

"Can't have that," he murmured.

Taking the panty hose from her, he put his own thumb and forefinger on either side of the stocking until it was all scrunched in his hands. Then he squatted down beside the table and began to work the material over her toes.

She stared at him. In all their years of marriage, he'd never offered to do this before. "What are you doing?"

"Helping you on with your panty hose," Jason answered simply. It was an effort not to tear anything. The gauzelike material felt as if he could put his thumb right through it if he wasn't careful. Why did women wear these things, anyway?

Annie walked in and then stopped as she took in the sight. She grinned broadly. "Now that man," she pronounced, looking at Laurel, "is a keeper."

Laurel laughed as she leaned forward and ruffled up Jason's hair, the way she used to when they were first married. He looked up at her, bemused. Her heart swelled.

"Yes, I know."

She'd never meant anything so much in her life.

CHAPTER 23

She should have settled into some sort of a comfortable routine by now, Laurel thought as she hurried into the house through the garage. Plastic grocery bags filled to bursting dangled from each wrist as she made her way into the kitchen.

All the other times, she had settled in. Three pregnancies, three patterns. They all ran the same. First she was exhausted, then energized and then she fell into a kind of nesting mode. Each and every time it had been like that. Each phase had lasted approximately three months.

This time around, she seemed to go through the entire cycle every single day. As she deposited all the bags onto the island in the middle of her kitchen, she couldn't help wondering if one morning she was just going to explode.

At this point in the afternoon, she had reached the nesting mode. But she was not moving nearly as fast as she was accustomed to. Or needed to for that matter. An hour ago, she'd been at the Mayfield residence in north Bedford, showing the house, which seemed to have gotten stuck in a time warp circa 1980, to a young couple who, despite the fact that they were just starting out, really, really, wanted to own their own home. She sympathized with that desire, remembering the way she'd felt when she'd first married Jason. She'd wanted her own home more than anything. So, when it came to the young couple, she'd been full of encouragement and content to allow them to wander through the house slowly—until she'd noticed the time.

Robert and Lynda were due at the house in less than three hours.

Which meant that she needed to shop, cook and get ready in approximately two. Laurel felt exhausted just thinking about it.

With apologies, she had hustled the young couple back outside, told them to think about it and see if they could come close to Mrs. Mayfield's asking price. Since the house belonged to a seventy-four-year-old widow who was looking to relocate, she'd told them there was definitely some room for play between what Mrs. Mayfield was asking and what she might be willing to accept. Laurel had delivered her suggestion as rapidly as possible, spurred on by visions of undercooked veal, an overly tart apple pie and a dining room table surrounded by some very unhappy, disgruntled dinner guests.

She had shopped the same way, flying down one aisle and up another in the supermarket located two miles from her home. She'd made it in and out in less than half an hour.

But now that she was finally home, with everything she needed housed somewhere in the five bags she'd barely managed to drag in, Laurel felt as if all the air had suddenly been sucked out of her. God, but she wished she could tap into something that would make her feel more like her old self instead of merely a two-dimensional version of herself.

She heard a noise behind her and turned around. The house was supposed to be empty. The tall, lanky frame of her youngest was in the doorway. He looked as surprised to see her as she was to see him.

"Christopher, I didn't know you'd be home."

He made a little vague movement with his shoulders and then addressed his answer to the wall. "Class got canceled."

Laurel began to unpack the various bags. "Good, I could really use some help. I'm running behind." Which, in Laurel-speak meant that she wasn't going to be early, the way she usually was.

But Christopher was already backtracking, making his way to the garage door. "I got plans, Mom."

She stopped unpacking and turned around to face him. He wasn't about to get away so easily. It was time they had this out. The help she was asking for was only an excuse. "Which you didn't have before your class got canceled."

Christopher frowned, temporarily lost in the face of her answer. "Yeah, but—"

Ordinarily, she let things slide. But not this time. She needed to be a little tougher with "her baby," she realized. After all, he was twenty, almost twenty-one. Not exactly a child anymore.

"Look, I need a little help here. Half an hour of your time, that's all I'm asking." She pinned him with a look that he could feel even when his eyes were averted from hers. "Is that such a big deal? There was a time when you used to hang around me all the time."

The reminder made Christopher petulant. He was trying to pretend that part of his life never happened. "I was ten."

"And a lot less complicated," she recalled. Laurel banked down the ache that suddenly rose up in her throat. Instead, she tried to focus on unpacking the groceries.

"Yeah, well—" he shoved his hands deep into the pockets of his jeans "—things were a lot less complicated then."

And you were a lot less embarrassed to let the world know you even *had* a mother, she added silently.

"You know," Laurel continued out loud as she set the contents of each bag out on the island before deciding where to put it, "there were times back then when I thought you were almost hermetically sealed to me."

He snorted. Absently, he picked up the jars of sauce and placed them inside the pantry. "How did you stand it?"

She smiled at him, a fond expression on her face. "The part that didn't worry about you becoming too attached to me loved it."

Christopher shrugged, disinterested. Disgusted. "I grew up."

"Good," Laurel declared cheerfully. The last bag empty, she folded it and stuck the lot into one of the drawers next to the sink. "Then you can reach the top shelf for me when I need it." She started to take out the dinnerware and then decided she could do that *after* the meal was in the oven. "I've got your aunt Lynda and a man I went to school with coming for dinner tonight and I'd really rather not hand them frozen entrées on a stick."

"Ma—" The single word he drew out fairly dripped with protest.

How long was he going to continue being embarrassed by her condition? "I promise not to give birth while you're here."

The look on his face was pure disgust, but he held his tongue. He was brooding again, she thought. Her sunny boy had turned into the Grinch—and she couldn't stand it anymore. She paused for a moment, searching his face for some sign of the boy she had once known. The one who kept climbing on her lap and vying for all her attention. He was still in there, somewhere. At least she hoped so.

"You want to talk about it?"

Like everything else that had gone on between them lately, the question made Christopher look darkly uncomfortable. "Talk about what?"

"About why you're so mad at me," Laurel answered simply.

He made an annoyed, unintelligible sound. "I'm not mad at you."

She begged to differ on that point. "You leave the room every time I come in, keep to yourself and have hardly said five sentences to me in almost four months." Christopher turned away from her. "You're either mad at me or you think I have the plague." She got in front of him, refusing to be ignored any longer. "Christopher, I'm your mother and I love being your mother, but you have to understand, I am more than just that."

His eyes seemed flat when he looked at her. But she thought she saw a glimmer of something beneath. Hurt? Sadness? "Yeah, I know, you're a hotshot real estate agent."

That wasn't the point she was trying to make. She resented the tone he used. It bordered on insolent. "I'm also a woman, married to a wonderful man I'm very much in love with—"

He pretended to put his hands on his ears in order to block her out. "I don't need the birds-and-the-bees speech right now, Mom." His eyes swept over her belly unintentionally. "You took care of that little thing for all of us."

She resisted the temptation to put her hand on his shoulder. "So it is about the baby."

"No, it's about me," he finally shouted. "It's about how embarrassing it is to have your senior-citizen mother running around, pregnant."

She felt her temper spiking. Another outward sign of the hormone mutiny that was going on inside of her. She struggled to keep it all in check.

"You never were good in math, Chris. I'm many years shy of being in that category and besides, 'senior citizens' don't like being referred to by that term anymore. I hear they prefer 'seasoned citizen.'" She pushed a bag of potatoes toward him. "Here, peel these for me." Her mouth curved whimsically. "I'm too feeble to be trusted with a knife."

Christopher opened his mouth, frustrated. "I didn't mean—"

She cut him off. "Yes, you did. But you're wrong. Except for a few extraneous aches and pains I have now that I didn't have twenty-one years ago, when I was carrying you," she deliberately emphasized, "I'm still in pretty good shape. Forty-five today is not the same thing as forty-five ten, twenty years ago. Forty-five is still young and vibrant these days."

A knife in one hand, a potato in the other, he was about to begin his KP duty when he stopped, horrified. "Are you telling me that you're going to have another baby after this one?"

Hearing him, she didn't know whether to laugh or cry. The very idea of having a fifth child made her feel like doing both. She shook her head. "Oh God, no. Four children is more than enough, thank you."

Laurel pulled a very worn recipe book out of one of the drawers. She knew the recipe she was preparing tonight by heart, but it was comforting to have the actual directions somewhere close by. Just in case she forgot something.

Opening the book and setting it on the counter, she looked over toward Christopher. "I'm going to need a frying pan and also a large pan." She pointed toward where she kept the items. "And a smile."

That only succeeded in producing a frown. "What?"

"You heard me, mister. I've hardly seen you in four months. Since I've somehow managed to commandeer you for the next half hour, I'd like you to smile so I can remember my son the way he used to be."

Christopher made no reply. Instead, he gave her a sideway glance and what looked like a grimace.

"Close enough," she murmured. "You used to look like that when you were a little guy and had gas."

She didn't catch what he said next, but she thought maybe it was better that way.

CHAPTER 24

The minutes chased each other around the clock. Christopher made no attempt to talk and only answered in single syllables when she put a question to him. Laurel was left wondering if she should say something about his attitude, or just let it go and hope that it would work itself out.

She had another four and a half months of being pregnant to go and she wasn't sure she could stand that. Jason seemed to have finally come around, but that could only be temporary again. God, but she felt lonely out here, adrift on this "older" mother-to-be float she was on.

She was about to make another stab at a conversation when the house phone rang. Christopher looked up, a prisoner hoping to either be paroled or escape.

"Cut the potatoes into pieces after you finish peeling them," Laurel instructed before picking up the receiver. "Hello?"

"Mrs. Mitchell?" a warm voice on the other end of the line asked.

She tried to place the voice as she answered, "This is Laurel Mitchell."

"Mrs. Mitchell, this is Annie Wise from Blair Memorial.

I was the one who performed the amniocentesis on you at the hospital earlier this week."

"Yes, I remember." Laurel wiped her free hand against the towel on the counter, then took the receiver and held it with both hands, bracing herself. A thousand butterflies had suddenly been let loose inside of her stomach, doing barrel rolls. "Is there something wrong?" she asked.

Out of the corner of her eye, she saw Christopher's head jerk up in her direction. The knife he'd been using slid out of his hand, onto the counter. He had her full attention.

And Annie Wise had hers.

"No, nothing's wrong," Annie told her cheerfully, warmth radiating from every word. "I'm just calling to tell you the test results."

"Which are?" The question was all but strangled. Laurel had stopped breathing.

"That the baby is fine," Annie assured her.

"Fine?" Laurel echoed, so relieved that she was having trouble processing the word.

"As in everything seems to be in order and perfect," Annie laughed. There was a slight pause and then she asked, "Would you like to know the baby's sex?"

The question caught Laurel off guard. She thought she already knew the baby's sex. After all, three tries, three boys. Any sense of mystery had evaporated when Christopher had made his way into the world. She'd felt certain that if she had twelve babies, they would all be males.

A smile played across her lips. The woman obviously

enjoyed telling parents if they were going to have a boy or girl. Why rob her of that after she'd set her mind at such ease?

"Sure, why not?" Laurel replied whimsically. She saw Christopher shifting, looking at her curiously. "What is it, a boy or girl?"

"Girl."

Laurel felt as if a bomb had just detonated at her feet, rendering her deaf. Or at least, incapable of hearing properly. "Excuse me?"

"A girl," Annie repeated. She could hear the woman chuckling to herself. "You're having a girl, Mrs. Mitchell. In case you've forgotten, that's a softer version of a boy."

Laurel felt as if her throat had turned into the perimeter of the Mohave Desert. "You're sure?"

Christopher had rounded the island and made his way over to her, concern etched onto his face.

"Mom, what is it?" he asked.

But she was busy listening to the woman on the other end of the line. Listening and trying to understand.

"Ninety-nine percent," Annie was saying. "I'm forwarding the results of the test to your doctor," she continued.

"Okay." Laurel felt numb. Utterly and completely numb. A girl. She was having a girl. "That's fine," she heard herself say although she had no recollection of forming the words. No recollection of thinking or rendering coherent answers. The word *goodbye* appeared of its own volition, as if it was preprogrammed to appear at a certain interval.

"Mom, what's wrong?" Christopher asked again.

Laurel blinked, looking down at the receiver. It was just lying there on the island. She needed to hang it up, she realized. Picking it up again, she walked over to the wall unit and hung it up. The receiver fell off, clattering to the tile floor.

She stared down at it.

"Mom?"

Now more than a tinge of concern was locked inside the word. Christopher put his hands on her shoulders, much the way his father would, and tried to get her to look at him. To come out of the trance she was obviously in.

"Mom, what's wrong?" he repeated. "Who just called? What did they say?"

She looked at him, trying to pull her surroundings into focus. Trying to think coherently. It was a struggle. "It's a girl."

His fear prevented him from taking her answer on the simplest level. Laurel Mitchell was a pillar of strength, a woman who could push on and do what needed to be done while battling a 102-degree fever because her kids were sick and needed her. She had never, ever even once, to his recollection, fallen apart.

To see her like this made the foundations of his newly constructed independent world wobble dangerously. "What?"

Laurel blinked again, coming around. Letting the sunshine in. A warmth had begun to radiate all through her. "I'm having a girl, Christopher. *We're* having a girl," she amended because everything she ever did had ultimately been for and about the family. As the words finally started to sink in, a smile began to blossom on her lips. "You're going to have a sister."

Relief was ushered in with confusion. He'd never thought about the new addition being female. A little sister to watch over. Something cute and pink that was vulnerable and needed protecting.

His mouth dropped opened. "You're kidding."

"I wouldn't know how anymore," she said honestly, far too shell-shocked to make anything up. A euphoria was gradually taking hold. A thousand fragments of thought began crowding into her head. Her eyes widened as she suddenly realized that she and Christopher were the only ones who knew this wonderful thing. She clutched at his arm. "Your father, I have to call your father."

"You want to sit down first?" Christopher separated himself from her for a moment, bolting toward the row of counter stools on the other side of the island. He dragged one over. "Here, sit."

He wasn't asking, he was telling. The next moment, when she made no move to comply, he gently pushed her down onto the stool. A thousand and one thoughts came rushing at her, all demanding equal time. Laurel felt as if she was being pulled in all directions.

"I can't sit. I have a dinner to get ready." She slid off the stool. She'd tell Jason later. It felt good to savor the news for a little while. Like her own personal secret.

Hers and Christopher's, she thought, slanting a look toward him.

"What do you need?" Christopher asked.

"You're actually offering to help me?" A minute ago, he was set to escape the second her back was turned. What a difference the promise of a female on the scene can make, Laurel thought fondly. Of course, this one was little more than the size of a peanut, but still, it was a girl. A female.

She was going to have a daughter.

Laurel hugged the thought to her as she felt herself beaming from the inside out.

"Don't make a big deal out of it," Christopher warned, going to retrieve the frying pan she'd asked for before the phone had rung.

She did her best to suppress her pleased smile. "Of course not."

But it was a big deal. A very big deal because by his very offer, Christopher had just forgiven her for being human. It was a very nice victory.

Laurel took a breath, remembering the recipe. "I need bread crumbs, milk, a plate and a bowl. And oh, oil for the pan," she added as Christopher placed the large frying pan on the dormant burner.

With a nod of his head, Christopher went to the pantry and then the refrigerator, taking things out one at a time and piling them onto the counter. Curious, he looked at her over his shoulder.

"Aren't you going to call Dad?"

"Yes, of course." She glanced at the clock. It really *was* getting late—by anyone's standards and not just hers. "But I think I'll get the veal started first."

And then Christopher said something that really surprised her. "I can do that."

She tried to remember if she'd ever seen him do anything more complicated than pour cereal out of a box into a bowl. "Do you know how to bread veal?"

"No," he admitted ruefully.

She smiled. At least he'd offered. "Watch and learn." She poured milk into a bowl and shook the bread crumbs out onto a plate. Once she had the breaded veal in the frying pan, she could try calling Jason.

"Um, Mom?" Christopher asked as he watched her dip the separate pieces of meat into the bowl of milk, then deposit them one by one into the bread crumbs she'd spread out on a plate.

"Yes?" She turned each piece over twice, then removed it from the bread crumbs.

"Am I the first person to know about the baby being a girl?"

Her eyes met his. For a second, there was a moment of bonding. She could literally feel it. *Just like the old days*.

"After me, yes, you are."

He nodded, watching the fillets as they began to sizzle. "Cool."

Very cool, she thought happily, looking up at her son.

CHAPTER 25

He brought Laurel flowers. Pink carnations because they were her favorites, although he had actually wanted to bring roses. Roses to him had always seemed to be at the top of the flower pyramid and he thought the occasion demanded roses. But the flowers were for her, not him, so he brought her what he remembered she liked, congratulating himself on being able to summon that small tidbit.

"Jason," Laurel called, hearing the door open and close, "is that you?"

The next moment, she found herself wrapped in a fierce embrace and literally lifted off the floor. She knew flowers were involved, because she could feel them against her back and smell them as Jason spun her around the room.

Laurel braced herself against his shoulders. "Careful," she warned with a laugh. "You really don't want a pregnant woman getting sick all over you."

"You say the sexiest things," he told her, setting her back down. "These are for you." He held the bouquet out to her.

She felt herself tearing up and blinked hard to keep the tears back. Jason never understood tears of joy—they confused him.

"They're absolutely beautiful, Jason. Here, let me put them in water."

She stopped everything and went to retrieve the vase she kept on the bottom shelf of the pantry. The vase she hadn't used since she couldn't remember when.

Jason leaned against the sink, watching her fill the vase with water. He felt like bursting inside. "A girl, huh?"

Laurel shut off the faucet and smiled as she looked at him. "A girl." Taking the vase over to the far side of the counter, she placed the flowers into it.

"And she's healthy?" Jason shifted out of the way as Laurel brought a spoonful of sugar to the vase and dropped it into the water. It was to keep the flowers fresh longer.

Shifting some of the flowers, she gave the arrangement one last finishing touch and then returned to what she'd been doing before Jason came in. "Healthy as a horse."

He glanced at the tray of hors d'oeuvres and stole one. "A healthy girl horse." Jason popped the tiny ham-and-cheese pastry into his mouth. "Just what I always wanted."

Laurel looked at him, a tenderness budding in her breast. For a moment, everything else was put to the side as she cupped his cheek. "You always wanted a girl."

Despite his teasing her about having his own baseball team, Jason had never been one of those macho men who had a driving need to stamp his image on a perfect miniature of himself. Never really cared about ensuring that his family line would continue on to the next generation. In his heart of hearts, he'd confessed when she'd found herself pregnant a second time, that if he had a choice in the matter, he wanted girls. When Christopher arrived after the third pregnancy, he'd adjusted to the idea that the only female in the house was going to be Laurel. And he was all right with that.

But now all that was changing.

He'd thought she was putting him on when she'd called him this afternoon. He was just about to go into a presentation with a campaign he'd spent the past six weeks working on for a new sports drink. His mind had gone completely blank once he had realized that Laurel was serious. By the time he walked into the meeting, he'd been running on such an adrenaline rush, he hardly remembered anything he said. Except that his presentation had been a huge hit. The client had just assumed he was high on the product rather than on his life. Contracts were signed, hands were shaken, and all Jason could think of was that, after all this time, he was going to have a daughter.

He wanted to celebrate that fact.

He glanced at the table in the other room. It was set for four. Not his number of choice right now. "Any way we can scrap this dinner party and go out, just the two of us?"

Any other time, Laurel would have jumped at the idea of the two of them going out. It didn't happen very often these days. But everything was all set. Her sister and Robert would be arriving soon.

"Oh, honey," she protested, "I don't know when I can corner Lynda and Robert again without making it seem like a big deal." She wiped her hands on a towel. "And that would make it awkward."

He picked up another tiny pastry and bit into the shell. "I take it that Lynda knows that this is a setup?"

Laurel gave him a look. "She's my sister, Jason. She's not stupid."

Jason polished off the remainder of his hors d'oeuvre and brushed his hands together. "And she's okay with that?"

Laurel swept away the crumbs on the counter, fallout from his sampling, with the flat of her hand. "She's not thrilled, but she wants what we have."

Amused, Jason raised an eyebrow. "College loans to pay off?"

Laurel laughed, slapping his hand away as he went to pick up still another hors d'oeuvre.

"The kids to go with those loans." She moved the tiny puff pastries, spacing them further apart so that they still managed to fill the tray. "I think my pregnancy really hit her hard."

Jason turned toward the sink and rinsed off his fingertips. "I'd say welcome to the club, except now I don't feel like I've just been torpedoed."

"And you did before?" He'd hidden that well from her, she thought.

He lifted a shoulder and let it drop. "A little," he admitted. "I'm sorry I behaved like an ass."

All he had to do was apologize and she would have forgiven him anything. "It's behind us, now." *God willing.*

"You've got to admit that at our age—my age," he amended tactfully, "an unexpected pregnancy is not at the top of the list of things you find yourself generally worrying about."

"And there's still nothing to worry about," she assured

him with a smile. For a second, she covered the swell in her abdomen with her hand. "We girls are doing fine."

Where was all this emotion coming from? he wondered. He could feel it welling up inside of him. "Can't ask for more than that." He kissed her forehead.

Laurel smiled as she shook her head. "Oh, you can do better than that."

"Yes." Jason locked his arms behind the small of her back and drew her to him. "I can." To prove it, Jason lowered his mouth to hers, this time kissing her with feeling.

"Get a room, you two, the product of your loins is coming through," Christopher announced, walking back into the kitchen. He held one of his hands up against his temple, as if to shield his eyes.

Laurel and Jason drew apart just far enough to break lip contact. Feeling incredibly content, she leaned her head against Jason's chest and he closed his arms around her protectively.

"So, what do you think about all this? About the baby being a girl?" he elaborated when Christopher said nothing.

Christopher shrugged, doing his best to look nonchalant. "It's okay."

Laurel knew better. Beneath that careless facade, Christopher was excited. She'd seen it in his eyes when he'd first found out that he was getting a sister. She looked up at Jason. "He has your gift of understatement," she told her husband.

"You got anything for me to eat before I head back to the dorm?" Christopher asked. He looked at the tray he'd watched his mother prepare earlier. "Or is all this for your guests?"

"There's always food for you," Laurel told him. Stepping away from Jason, she moved the tray of hors d'oeuvres toward her son.

"Hey," Jason feigned indignation, "when I took one, you slapped my hand away."

"You took three," she corrected. "And it's because you're one of 'the guests,'" she reminded him. "You get to eat this in a few minutes. Besides, if we don't feed him," she looked affectionately at Christopher, "he might not come back."

Meanwhile, Christopher had worked his way to the refrigerator and was now stocking up on goods he planned to take back to the dorm with him. Arms full, he pulled out a bag from the bottom drawer and deposited his loot.

"You think?" Jason teased, only to have Laurel smack his shoulder with the flat of her hand. He'd seen it coming and had braced his arm for contact, causing his biceps to bulge.

He had the physique of a man half his age, she thought with pride.

"That the best you got?" Jason teased her.

She raised her chin. "I'll show you the best I've got later."

Christopher slipped the plastic grocery bag handle over his wrist and put both hands to his ears. "Please, not in front of the children. And on that note," he announced, dropping his hands to his sides again, "I'm out of here."

Christopher took two steps toward the front door, then stopped and looked at his mother. "Don't do too much," he told her.

"Excuse me?" she asked.

"You always do too much, push yourself too hard," he said, frowning. "Why don't you take it easy for a change?"

Her eyes were bright with humor. "Are you offering to clean up for me?"

"I'll send Morgan," Christopher deadpanned, walking away. He shifted the grocery bag to his other hand. "After all, he's the one who lives here."

"And so do you," Laurel called after him. "Anytime you need to."

"We could invite Luke and Denise to come live with us, too. Run a modern-day Ponderosa. I can be Ben Cartwright and you can be Hop-Sing."

Laurel frowned as she looked up at him. He'd just awarded her the position of the cook on the classic program. "Hop-Sing?"

"It's the best I can do, unless you want to be Hoss. They didn't have any women on the show," he reminded her.

She was aware of that. She loved the old program anyway. "They would have if I had anything to say about it."

He laughed, pulling her back into his arms. "You know, Laurel Mitchell, you are something else."

She grinned broadly. "About time you found that out."

CHAPTER 26

The doorbell rang just as Jason was lowering his mouth to kiss her.

He raised it again, a disgruntled expression on his face. "Your sister always did have the worst timing," he muttered, releasing his wife and backing away.

Laurel smoothed back her hair and checked the front of her dress to see if there were any smudges or traces of food on it. "It could be Robert," she pointed out.

"Hate him already."

"Stop that," she chided, moving swiftly to the cupboard and retrieving a large serving platter. "Now be a good host and go open the front door."

"What'll you be doing?" he asked.

She indicated the dish she was holding. "I'll be putting the veal parmesan on a platter."

"Aye-aye, Captain." Jason offered her a smart salute before he went to see which of the two guests was at the door.

She heard him open the front door, heard the soft murmur of voices exchanging greetings. But seconds ticked by and no one came into the kitchen.

"Who is it?" Laurel called out.

The exclamation of joy that sounded one step removed from a scream gave Laurel her answer. She placed the platter on a warming tray that was almost as old as her marriage. She managed to flip the dial to the on position just as Lynda and Jason walked into the kitchen.

She looked at her husband accusingly. "Jason, you told her." The single sentence vibrated with disappointment.

"I couldn't help it. She dragged it out of me." He gave Laurel a look that was so innocent, it was comical in nature.

"How?" Laurel wanted to know as she entered the living room, carrying the tray of hors d'oeuvres before her.

Jason took the tray out of her hands and placed it on the table. "She said hello."

As she began to say something, Laurel found her available air whooshing out of her. She was enfolded in a fierce, warm embrace that threatened to decrease the size of her rib cage. Lynda's arms were locked around her like a vise.

"A girl," she cried, beaming. "Does Mom know?"

Laurel shook her head. "Not yet. I just found out this afternoon and I've only told Jason and Christopher—he was here when I got the phone call from the hospital," she explained, in case Lynda wondered why she'd let one of her sons know and not the others.

"Mom is going to be over the moon about this," Lynda said.

"Please, she's too old for long trips," Laurel quipped. "I'll figure out a calm way to tell her."

"With Mom," Lynda pointed out, her voice following

Laurel into the kitchen, "there is no calm way." Looking down at the platter, she helped herself to an hors d'oeuvre. She raised her head just in time to see Laurel's reproving look as she walked back into the living room. "What?"

"I was hoping to keep most of the tray intact until Robert got here." At this rate, between Jason and Lynda, everything on the tray would be gone before Robert arrived.

Lynda seemed to debate putting the small pastry back, then applied their childhood touching rule—touch it, it's yours—and popped it into her mouth. She grinned as the flavor spread out on her tongue.

"Speaking of whom, when is he—" Before she could finish the question, the doorbell rang. Lynda froze, turning a lighter shade of pale. "Never mind," she whispered.

"It'll be fine." Laurel squeezed her hand reassuringly. Hers was warm, Lynda's was icy, she noted. "Just be yourself."

"That product isn't marketing well these days," Lynda muttered, more to herself than to either her sister or her brother-in-law.

Laurel hurried out of the kitchen to answer the door. "Say something to her," she urged her husband as she went passed him.

Jason suppressed a sigh and gave Lynda an encouraging smile. For the most part, he liked her, always had. She was like the little sister he'd never had. "Maybe you just need a new marketing area," he told her, slipping his arm around her shoulders and very gently escorting her back to the living room.

Just in time to see Robert Manning walk in.

Like Jason, Robert was wearing a suit. Unlike Jason, he didn't look as if he'd spent the past forty-eight hours in it, pitching ideas to his backup team and getting frustrated. On the contrary, he appeared fresh and crisp. And very dynamic.

"Wow," Jason heard his sister-in-law murmur under her breath.

"If you like that sort of thing," he allowed. Dropping his arm from Lynda's shoulders, he stepped forward, his hand out. "Hello, I'm Jason Mitchell. Laurel's husband."

"Yeah, I know." Robert smiled warmly, taking the hand that was extended to him and shaking it. "You're one lucky guy," he told his host with an honesty that Jason found disarming.

Laurel quickly took over the introductions. "Robert, this is my sister, Lynda Taylor. Lynda, this is Robert Manning. Robert and I went to school together," she prompted when faced with Lynda's dazed expression. Her sister looked as if she'd just had a spell put on her by a renegade fairy godmother.

Leaning forward, Robert took Lynda's hand in his. "I see good looks run in the family."

His smile was warm, as were his eyes when he met hers.

Lynda felt herself melting. And her mind rendered a complete blank. Coherent thoughts refused to form in her head. The man was just too good-looking for words. A glib lawyer with a sharp, legal mind, she suddenly felt as if she was ten years old, wearing mismatched shoes. Her confidence plummeted.

She glanced over at Laurel. "I thought you said that he was a geek," she protested. Too late, she realized how that had to sound. She forced herself to face her sister's guest, knowing that she'd inadvertently insulted him. Even though she had meant the complete opposite.

"Reformed geek," Robert said before Laurel could find her tongue. Humor highlighted his features. Far from insulted, he seemed really amused. Almost pleased, Lynda thought. "I've joined GA."

"GA?" Jason repeated.

"Geeks Anonymous," Robert supplied. "I've had a few setbacks, though," he confessed, looking at Lynda. "They found me solving quadratic equations in the closet a couple of times and once, when no one was looking, I designed a new software package."

The self-deprecating humor put her at ease. Lynda heard someone laughing and realized a moment later that the sound was coming from her.

"Can I get you something to drink?" Jason asked, slipping into the role of host.

"Maybe later," Robert demurred. He turned toward Lynda again. "I've got a feeling I'm going to need a clear head tonight."

It was at that point that Laurel began to feel rather pleased with herself for bringing this evening about. She caught Jason's eye and smiled smugly just before she turned on her heel to walk back into the kitchen. "Dinner will be ready in five minutes," she promised, then disappeared.

Belatedly, Lynda came to life. "Um, let me help," she called after her sister.

"Go back into the dining room," Laurel whispered

urgently. "If I need help, I'll call Jason." Lynda made no move to leave. "I want you out there, Lyn."

But Lynda shook her head. "He's too pretty."

Granted, Robert Manning could be the poster boy for late bloomers, especially in light of his awkward high school years. But she didn't see what Lynda's shaky protest had to do with her hiding out in the kitchen.

"So?" Picking up the platter, she handed it to Lynda. Since her sister insisted on being here, she might as well be of some use.

"So, I can't expect someone like that to pay attention to someone like me."

"And just why not?"

Lynda sighed. "Because I'm me, that's why not." When she realized Laurel was still waiting for an answer that made sense, she added, "I'm terminally boring."

Something, no doubt, Dean had drummed into her head, Laurel thought angrily. "Now you listen to me, Lynda Rae Taylor. You are *not* boring. You're bright, funny and witty. And beautiful. I will not stand and listen to you run yourself down that way. If this 'terminally boring' thing is something that Dean said to you, or made you feel, then it just proves he was a loser with no taste. If it makes you feel any better, Bobby Manning was the guy most of the girls wouldn't have been caught dead around in high school—and now look. He's successful, well-off and teeth-jarringly good-looking. And all those people who were nasty to him are nowhere on the map."

Laurel realized that she sounded as if she was pontificating and stopped herself. Instead, she gave Laurel a long, hard look the way she used to when they were growing up together. "Now I'm your big sister and I order you to go back out there and have a good time. Or else."

Lynda sighed, turning back toward the living room, the platter of food before her. "If only it was that easy."

To her surprise, although not Laurel's, once Lynda relaxed, really relaxed, she discovered that it actually was that easy.

CHAPTER 27

Jason walked out of the bathroom and over to the window. The temperature in the house had dropped in the evening, but it was still warm. He took off the window's safety lock and pushed open the sash. He'd had to walk by Laurel to do it. There was no missing her expression. She was smiling from ear to ear.

"Pretty pleased with yourself, aren't you?" he asked as he crossed back to the bed.

She stood on the opposite side, taking off the decorative pillows and placing them against the bureau. Jason slept on the left, she on the right. It had been that way ever since they'd gotten married. She paused for a second, considering his question. "Are we talking about the baby, or the dinner?"

Jason lifted the comforter on his side and pushed it down to the foot of the bed. It was way too warm for down comforters, no matter how much he liked the feel of one. "Well, seeing as how it wasn't possible for you to deliberately determine the baby's sex on your own, I'd say I was talking about the dinner."

She got into bed on her side, spreading the pale blue sheet out until it was smooth. "The food was rather good, wasn't it?"

"We're not talking about the food and if you were any more smug, I think you'd burst," he said.

Unable to hold back anymore, Laurel turned toward him as he got in and grinned. Jason was right. She was very, very pleased with herself. Everything had gone off without a hitch. Lynda held back at first, but Robert didn't seem to mind. He drew her out until, by the end, they were both talking, their voices blending and dovetailing, as was the sound of their laughter.

To say that she felt triumphant was a vast understatement.

Laurel wiggled a little, as if burrowing a space for herself on the mattress. She would have loved to hug her knees to her chest, the way she usually did while sitting up and talking in bed, but for the time being, those days had passed.

"He did seem to like her, didn't he?" She shifted slightly, trying to find a comfortable position. That was becoming less and less of a possibility, she thought. "Give me the male point of view."

He told her what he knew she wanted to hear. That it was also true did help the situation. "Yes, he seemed to like her."

Laurel looked up toward the ceiling, seeing beyond it in her mind's eye as she visualized the sky. She pumped one arm down in a sudden, victorious motion. "Thank you, God."

Jason understood that his wife was happy the dinner hadn't been a disaster, but he saw no reason for the degree of enthusiasm in Laurel's reaction. Has she always been this emotional during her pregnancies? He couldn't remember.

"Lynda's only thirty-five, Laurie. It's not like she's desperate." She could only shake her head. "Spoken like a man."

"That's the whole point, isn't it?" he asked. "I thought you were asking for a male point of view."

"Just about another man, not my sister—"

A hint of a smile tugged at the corners of his mouth when he asked as seriously as possible, "So you don't want me to tell you that Lynda's hot?"

Laurel's mouth dropped open. She knew her sister was pretty. More than pretty. They both took after their mother who had been first runner-up in the Miss California contest years ago. But Jason had never commented on Lynda's looks before. Ever.

"You think Lynda's hot?"

"Sure," he said innocently, doing his damnedest not to laugh out loud. "Not as hot as you, of course."

"Now you're just backpedaling."

Jason gave up trying to look stone-faced. "As fast as I can. How am I doing?"

She shrugged carelessly. "Verdict's still out." And then, because she couldn't help it, because within every woman, no matter how open, how understanding, beat the heart of a competitor, she asked, "You really think my sister's hot?"

Jason sailed right past what obviously had become an incriminating sentiment. "Which is why I said she's not desperate."

"Women who want families start feeling desperate as the number of their single friends decreases and the number of candles on their cake increases," she told him. She could see that he didn't really believe her. "Men age better," she elaborated. "There's no stigma attached to a man in his forties.

He's still young, virile, on the prowl. People regard a woman of the same age as having been passed over. She's passé." Laurel sighed, shaking her head. Feeling bad for countless faceless women who were up against that kind of prejudice. And thankful that there, but for the grace of God, went she. "It's not a fair world, Jase."

Smiling, Jason drew Laurel close to him. Lynda might be "hot," but it was Laurel who got his blood going, Laurel who filled his heart. Funny how he could go for months, taking all that for granted until it suddenly leaped up and hit him between the eyes with the force of a two-by-four.

"Aren't you glad you found me?"

She laughed. He made it sound as if he'd been hanging on some clearance rack. "Oh, I remember it well." She laid her wrist to her forehead melodramatically. "There you were, in the bargain bin, cast aside by Heather Daniels, alone, forlorn."

Jason kissed her forehead, stopping her before she was off at full gallop. "Your details are a little off, but the bottom line is still the same."

There were times when she thought they were on the same page but they weren't. So she asked, "Which is?"

"That you saved me from a horrible fate—a life of clubbing and partying. A different woman on my arm every night."

Laurel nodded her head. "Empty, shallow existence," she agreed.

He laughed softly as he slid down on the mattress. "My sentiment exactly."

Laurel remained sitting. Looking down at him, she pressed

her lips together, debating asking. Finally, unable to help herself, she gave in.

She asked. "You really think Lynda's hot?"

Jason raised himself up on his elbow. Now he sincerely regretted his earlier assessment of Lynda, even though it was true. This was going to haunt him for a while, he decided. He only hoped that eventually, it would die down. But for now, he had a method to handle it.

"I guess there's only one way to shut you up."

He was already snaking his arms around her. "What's that?"

Jason didn't answer her. Taking his wife into his arms, he showed her instead.

Two weeks later, in the middle of preparing breakfast, Laurel dropped several sheets of paper in front of Jason, just on top of the newspaper he was reading. Picking up the sheets, he glanced at them. There was a smiling baby in the upper left-hand corner.

"What's that?" he wanted to know.

Why don't you read it and find out? She put the question to him silently. Laurel had already crossed back to the kitchen counter.

"It's a schedule of different Lamaze classes being offered at the hospital," she finally said, even though it was right there on the top, written in black and white with a smiling baby as an emblem.

He continued looking at the sheets of paper in his hand, not seeing them, not turning them. "Lamaze?" he echoed in disbelief.

Maybe he thought she was getting ahead of herself. "I know it's a little soon," she agreed. She poured the oatmeal she'd prepared into a bowl. The sight of oatmeal made her sick, but Jason seemed to love it. Turning, she placed the bowl in front of him, then moved over the maple syrup. "Most people attend somewhere in their third trimester, but it's never too early to register. Spaces fill up fast."

He pushed the pile of stapled papers away. "For God's sake, Laurie, you've had three kids. You could teach the damn class if you wanted to." He sprinkled two tablespoons of sugar and then about a quarter of a cup of maple syrup into the otherwise-bland concoction and began mixing it. "We don't need to attend any Lamaze classes."

She could sympathize with his reluctance. She wasn't exactly thrilled, either, but there was no getting around it. "Hospital rule, Jase. If you want to be in the delivery room, you have to get certified that you took the class. Besides, it's been over twenty years since we went to one of those."

"And what, they've discovered a new way to give birth in that time?" He added a little milk to the cereal, which had already begun hardening. "I don't think so."

She hadn't thought about his not attending. She wanted him with her. In class and especially in the delivery room. But he was getting that stubborn look on his face.

"Honey—"

Jason gave up trying to scan the morning paper, but as to the other matter, he remained firm. "Listen, I don't want to go and have a bunch of barely out of puberty couples staring at the 'old couple.' They'll think we're in the beginning stages of Alzheimer's and wandered into the class by mistake." He saw the exasperated expression on her face and raised one hand, not in surrender, but in the spirit of compromise. Sort of. "If you want to go, go ahead, I'm not stopping you. But me, I'm just not up for that."

"I can't go without a partner."

He shrugged, turning his attention back to his breakfast. "Fine, ask Lynda to go with you."

"Lynda's life has suddenly gotten very full," Laurel informed him. A matter he would have known if he bothered to listen to what she told him. Lynda and Robert were seeing a great deal of each other now and she for one couldn't have been happier. "And besides," Laurel added, annoyed, "she's not my husband."

"What do you mean, full?"

"She's seeing Robert on a pretty regular basis. With any luck, this will continue—and don't change the subject."

He thought that was part of the subject. There were times when a woman's mind—his woman's mind—completely mystified him. And now he was getting a pint-size version as well. Life was really going to get confusing.

"One thing at a time, Laurel," he cautioned. "We have the wedding this weekend," he added when she eyed him quizzically.

"I don't need reminding of that," she retorted.

The closer the wedding came, the more beset she was by mixed emotions. She was extremely happy for her son and yet she found herself unaccountably battling a sadness that seemed to loom larger with each passing day. She was at a loss as to how to shake it off. This pregnancy had certainly come at a bad time.

Jason was surprised by the edge in her voice. He left the last bit of oatmeal in his bowl and pushed the bowl away. "Something wrong?"

She didn't bother trying to mask her feelings. "Other than you making me feel as if I had two feet in the grave, no."

Tact and quick thinking had always been his saving graces. "Sorry, I wasn't thinking of you, I was thinking of me."

How could he possibly think of himself as old? "Well you're still gorgeous. And if there're any single mothers-to-be in the group, you'll probably wind up being hit on." She sighed, sitting down at the table opposite him. Reaching out, she put her hand on his. "Tell me you'll at least think about it."

"Will that get you to stop talking about it?" he asked.

"Yes," she said quickly. Then, because they had never lied to each other, she added, "For now."

He sighed. "At least that's something. Okay, I'll think about it," he promised.

She smiled at him as if she'd already won her victory.

She probably had, he thought darkly.

CHAPTER 28

Adjusting his jacket sleeves, Jason walked back into his bedroom. The wedding ceremony was starting in less than two hours and Laurel had disappeared on him, which wasn't like her. They needed to get moving.

He found his wife sitting on the edge of the bed, the two sides of the dress she'd chosen to wear pooled about her distended waist like a silver skin that had been shed.

Laurel was in tears.

He knew it.

Jason sighed and shook his head as he knelt down beside her. Up until now, she'd been a trouper and he thought they'd get through this without a hitch. He should have known better. He placed his hand over hers. "Honey," he said gently, "you've known this day was coming for a long time now."

She shook her head. "That doesn't make it any easier to put up with," she squeaked. "I tried so hard."

Yes, yes, she had, he thought. Even at the wedding rehearsal, she'd remained dry-eyed, laughing and talking instead of being sad. It had given him hope that they could get through the ceremony without having her cry. "And you did a great job."

Laurel looked at him as if he'd lost his mind. "What?"

She was worse off than he'd thought. Just when he thought he knew her inside and out, another door opened and out stepped a new Laurel.

"Think of the bright side, Laurie. Like the old saying goes, you're gaining a daughter."

She wasn't gaining a daughter, she already had one, albeit the baby was still forming. "What old saying?"

Jason continued to speak softly, all the while acutely conscious of the minutes that were ticking off in his head. He absolutely *hated* being late. "The one about not losing a son but gaining a daughter."

It took her a second to absorb his words. "What's that got to do with anything?"

He was getting a little desperate. "I thought it might help you not feel sad."

Couldn't he see what she was dealing with? Was he blind as well as dense? "What would keep me from being sad is if I was five—no, ten pounds lighter."

It suddenly dawned on him that they weren't talking about the same thing. "Wait a minute, back up here." He rose to his feet again. "Just why are you crying?"

Frustration filled her. She'd had a figure once, a waist and small hips, and now they were gone. Who even knew if they were coming back? "Because I can't zip up this dress."

"You're not crying because Luke's getting married?"

"No," she cried emphatically. "Denise is a sweet girl—away from that barracuda of a mother of hers—and Luke loves her. I'm happy for both of them." She took a deep breath, willing herself to deal with this. She wasn't going to get anywhere feeling sorry for herself. "But I'm really unhappy for me because it looks like I'm going to have to go naked to the ceremony."

He was relieved to hear her make a joke. As long as she had her sense of humor, there was hope. "In that case, you won't be the only unhappy one."

She pretended to glare at him, wondering if, under the banter, he was being serious. "What?"

He raised his hands in surrender. "Just trying to lighten the mood, honey. Okay." He gestured for Laurel to get to her feet. "Stand up. Let me take a look at this."

Laurel exhaled a huge sigh. After a beat, she rose to her feet and then turned her back to him. The zipper's tongue was still where she'd left it, lodged at the small of her back. It defied all of her efforts to get it to slide up her spine.

"The dress fit just fine when I brought it home from the bridal shop three weeks ago." Laurel placed her hand over her abdomen. She hadn't thought she'd gained that much weight, but obviously, she must have. "This is going to be the first thirty-pound baby born at Blair Memorial Hospital."

And at least she hadn't lost her knack of exaggerating. "You're not that big," he chided his wife. Taking hold of the zipper, he placed his other hand on the swell of her hip and began to pull. "Okay, hold your breath."

"No, you take in a breath, then let it all out," Laurel told him and then followed her own instructions. "Okay," she urged him through clenched teeth, her hands on her hips as she tried to move the material there closer to her spine to give him more play.

Jason pulled. Hard. The zipper resisted, then finally, as he continued to work it slowly up, it rose up past what had once been her waist. Ordinarily, the few times he had helped Laurel with a tricky zipper, it was smooth sailing once he got to the area just beneath her shoulders.

Not this time.

It was touch and go, pull and tug.

"Careful, don't tear it," she warned. "It's very delicate."

"Luckily, you're not," he muttered. He continued maneuvering until finally, the zipper made it to the top of the summit. The dressed was zipped. "Done," he announced, more than a little proud of his accomplishment. He stepped back to admire a job well done. "You'll be fine if you don't breathe for the next eight hours."

The dress felt like a tourniquet. She looked at herself in the mirror. Happily, it didn't look like a tourniquet. "Not what I want to hear," she told him.

Jason always liked to have a contingency plan at his disposal. Now was no different. He looked around the room, then went to the bureau and began opening one drawer after another as he searched.

"What are you looking for?" she asked.

Just as she asked, he found it. "This." Jason pulled out the silver shawl he'd accidentally come across the other day while looking for a fresh pair of socks. "Take this with you in case the zipper decides to make a break for it."

She stared at him, impressed. The shawl actually did match her dress. "Since when have you become so resourceful?"

He spied a purse on the nightstand. Since it was small, he assumed she was taking it to the wedding. Her everyday purse was the kind that she could have smuggled a small pony in and no one would have been the wiser. Once he fetched the purse, he handed it to her.

"Didn't I ever tell you? I was a Boy Scout." He threaded her arm through his and began to head out of the bedroom with her. "All of three weeks."

That didn't sound like him. Jason usually stuck things out. At least for a while. "What happened?"

He smiled as he remembered. Now that thirty-five years had gone by, his short stint was funny, although it hadn't been at the time. "I accidentally set the park bench on fire in the campgrounds. The counselor wasn't very understanding. I quit the next day."

She loved when he told her about things that had happened to him when he was a little boy. It made her feel closer to him. "Glad you stick to things a little longer these days."

He looked at her for a moment, his eyes communicating what he would have had trouble putting into words. "When I find something worth sticking to, it's easy." And then he put it behind him. "Let's get a move on, honey. We don't want to be late."

No, we don't, she thought. Who knew how long the zipper would last?

* * *

"Dress giving you trouble?" Jason whispered the question in her ear a little less than an hour and a half later. They were standing in the front pew of the right side of Our Lady Queen of Angels Church. The groom's side.

The strains of the wedding march had just begun to fade away. Denise was standing beside Luke and Laurel was staring at their backs. Blinking back tears.

A thousand thoughts crowded her head. Luke, age three, leaping out of the bathtub and running madly around, with her chasing right behind him, his gleeful laugh echoing through the small house. Luke, age five, standing in front of Los Naranjos Elementary School on his first day, holding on to her hand so tightly her fingers were numb. Luke, all of nine, begging for one more story so he could fall asleep before the monsters came for him. Luke, twelve, sharing his first heartache with her as Megan DeAngelo dumped him for someone else. Luke, sixteen, waving at her as he drove away for his first solo drive, his driver's license still warm in his pocket.

Where had the time gone?

"No," she answered Jason with lips that hardly moved. The tears were stinging her eyes. She took a slow, shallow breath. "It seems like only yesterday I was pushing him out, and now look—"

"He got out," Jason concluded.

The priest had begun to speak. *Here it comes.* Laurel took out a handkerchief, preparing for the waterworks she knew were inevitable. "He's not my baby anymore," she whispered.

"No," Jason agreed, leaning in so that only she could hear. "He's Denise's. But he'll always be your little boy."

The words made her heart swell. She glanced at Jason as a tear escaped. She doubted that she had ever loved him as much as she did right at this very minute. "You think?"

"I think," he responded.

She pressed her lips together as she drew in a long breath. Her firstborn was a man now. And he was getting married.

How had it all happened so fast? In just the blink of an eye.

Laurel moved her hand to her abdomen, spreading her fingers out over it protectively.

You're not getting married until you're thirty, you got that? she silently told the daughter who had yet to be.

In response, she thought she felt the baby move. No, that wasn't a move, that was a kick. A definite kick. The first of many tonight, she knew. Laurel smiled to herself. It was comforting to know that even while she was letting one go, another one was coming on to the scene.

And this one, Laurel had a feeling, was going to be a scrapper. But that was all right. She found herself looking forward to the matches.

CHAPTER 29

Jason wrapped his fingers around hers. The musicians at the reception had finally decided to try their hand at a slow number—either that or their fingers were worn out by all the fast songs they'd been playing for the past forty-five minutes—and he thought it was safe to ask Laurel to come out on the dance floor. She loved to dance and he knew if she were on the floor for a fast song, she'd do her best to keep up. And the baby might suddenly arrive several months prematurely.

But slow dances were different. Slow dances didn't require excess energy. What did require energy, he discovered, was attempting to hold his wife close. Her stomach was a definite roadblock here. The fact that the baby was kicking her—and now him—didn't help matters any.

Jason smiled down at her.

"What?"

"Dancing with you is definitely a challenge tonight." As Laurel eyed him quizzically, he glanced at the general vicinity of her stomach, then back to her face.

Laurel leaned into him as best she could. It was like attempting to get close with a small beach ball lodged between them.

"That's what keeps a marriage interesting," she told him, a smile playing on her lips. "The curveballs that are thrown."

"Is that what this is, a curveball?"

"Well, it's certainly not anything either one of us reckoned on," she reminded him.

They were in agreement there. Jason smiled to himself. It was nice to feel as if they were on the same side of things for a change. Laurel had been edgy lately and still so prone to crying that it made him nervous. He was accustomed to her being a rock, the harbor that his ship sailed toward over choppy seas. Lately, the harbor had been periodically shut down for repairs.

It made him appreciate her and realize what it was he had that other men didn't.

Jason looked over toward where Luke was standing with Denise. They had their heads together and were laughing. It made him remember his own wedding. He realized that he was a little envious of all they had before them.

When he turned back to Laurel, he saw that she was watching him, a curious expression in her eyes. He wasn't about to admit to the sentimental feeling that had just wafted through him. Instead, he sought refuge in being glib. "Well, one down, two to go."

"Three," she corrected him.

Jason laughed. "I don't think that one is going to be ready to 'go' for quite some time yet."

Laurel gazed at Luke and Denise. Luke was leading Denise out onto the floor. He stopped to kiss her softly. Laurel could feel herself tearing up again. That made four times already. She would have thought she'd be dehydrated by now.

"God, I hope not."

Ever the prepared husband, Jason reached into his pocket and pulled out his handkerchief. He handed it to her. "Just how much water do you have in you, woman?" he asked. But his voice was soft, tolerant. Even if he didn't understand it, he was used to her crying at moments that didn't, in his book, merit tears.

"Allergies," she sniffled, turning her head away. She offered him back his handkerchief.

Jason stowed it in his pocket until next time. "How come these allergies only seem to act up whenever you look in Luke's direction or say something about the wedding?"

She shrugged. "Must be his cologne."

Rather than scoff, Jason nodded, his expression neutral. "Must be." And then he laughed. "You know, you're an awful liar."

"That should make you feel very secure."

His eyebrows drew together in marked confusion. "How so?"

"Well, if I'm a terrible liar, and you can see right through me if I do lie, then you know I've never lied to you."

It took him a moment to unscramble that. "Unless it's all an act to lull me into a complacent state."

Laurel laughed. He was giving her way too much credit.

The music stopped and the band leader said something about being back after a ten-minute break. Jason took her hand and led her back to their table.

"Yes, I am diabolical like that, on occasion," she admitted sarcastically, addressing the "confession" to his back. "I guess then you'll never know if I'm being on the level."

Jason stopped just shy of their table. Two of the other couples were there and he didn't particularly want to be overheard, even though what he had to say was harmless.

"I guess there's only one solution."

"And that is?" she asked gamely, not sure she liked the gleam in his eye.

"Simple." He pulled out her chair for her. "Stick to you like glue so that you can't do anything to lie about."

Laurel nodded as she took her seat. "Sounds like a plan to me. Especially since I have to go to those Lamaze classes."

They'd joined the others at the table too soon. Leaning over and keeping his hand before him so that no one could see his lips, he told her, "Slight change of plan."

"Too late." She sounded both cheerful and final.

He knew that tone meant she had made up her mind and if he wanted any peace in his life, he was going to have to go along with it. She didn't use it often, but when she did, she couldn't be blasted away from her decision.

Still, he wasn't about to throw in the towel, either. "We'll talk."

Laurel frowned. She knew what he was telling her. That he'd talk, she'd listen. But not this time. When she'd had the other three, she'd been fairly into securing peace at any price. Not that Jason was a tyrant, but there were times when she let him get his way and she was not happy about it. But for the sake of harmony and in order not to rock the boat around her sons, she'd gone along with things when that happened.

This time around, for all intents and purposes she was carrying an only child. Almost. One and a half sons were out of the house. Christopher returned only when he had a bag of laundry in his hand or when his cupboard was bare. With this particular pregnancy, for reasons she had yet to sort out, she felt completely empowered. Jason's equal in every way but one. And with that, since it was childbirth, she felt superior.

That put her slightly ahead of Jason.

She was going to win this argument when it came down to the wire, she promised herself.

"Yes," she responded with feeling, her eyes meeting his. "We will talk about this further."

As the days went by and the time for the Lamaze classes drew closer, Jason felt that he was not being humored so much as whittled away. No matter what the conversation, Laurel found a way to turn it back to what she regarded as their unfinished debate.

It was only unfinished to her since she hadn't heard the answer she wanted. As far as he was concerned, the discussion was terminated. He wasn't going. Wasn't going to relive classes that had been etched into his brain almost a quarter of a century ago. There was no way he was about to sit there and feel like some octogenarian who was the covert object of pity, not to mention unabashed curiosity. Especially not to get a mere certificate qualifying him to stand there and watch something he really didn't want to watch in the first place: Laurel in pain.

Yes, it was all well and good to welcome a baby into the world, but it would make things a hell of a lot easier if that baby just stepped off a bus or deplaned at one of the local airports. Watching his wife writhe in pain, alternately biting back screams and turning red, pushing, was not his idea of a good way to spend half a day—or night.

But saying as much was not getting him anywhere. Laurel was nothing if not relentless. She might lack energy in other areas, but when it came to arguing, she was utterly tireless.

"C'mon, Jase," she pleaded when he turned her down for what seemed like the millionth time at the breakfast table. There was less than a week left before classes were to begin. "This is going to be your last time to see this."

He raised his eyes from the newspaper he really wasn't reading. "Promise?"

Sitting opposite him over a plate of waffles that had grown cold, Laurel gave a little shrug in response. "Unless you get me pregnant again."

He snorted at that possibility. "Once that baby comes, I'm not going near you until you're seventy. I'm assuming you won't be fertile by that time."

She smiled brightly at him. "You could always get a vasectomy."

The very thought sent a shiver down his back. "That's a discussion for another time." He raised the paper up again.

"Okay, fine." Determined, she put her hand on top of the

newspaper, pushing it down until she could see him again. "But about the discussion we *are* having—"

He sighed, abandoning all attempts at grabbing a few minutes for himself before he had to leave. "You're having it," he pointed out. "I'm just being nagged."

He knew she hated when he said she nagged, Laurel thought. He'd said that on purpose. But she refused to be baited or get sidetracked. There was something bigger at stake here. "You'll never forgive yourself if you miss this."

He'd seen Morgan and Christopher come into the world. Two out of four were pretty good odds in his book. "I'll chance it."

"Do you actually mean to tell me that if I asked you, really asked you, you'd say no?"

He did his best to ignore the hurt he saw in her eyes. "I thought you were asking me," he said. "Was this just a trial run?"

But she wasn't smiling. "This isn't funny, Jason, I want you to come with me." Laurel pressed her lips together, a part of her fearing rejection. "I need you to come with me."

He gave it one last try. "What about Lynda, or your mother? Or Jeannie?"

Her eyes never left his face. She said the same thing to him now as she had when he'd originally suggested the substitution. "They're not my husband."

Jason could feel himself losing ground. It was literally slipping away beneath his feet. "Granted, but they're a lot more up to this than I am."

"Jason, please," Laurel entreated softly.

And that was his undoing. That small, pleading voice meant only for him. "Oh, all right," he sighed. "Sign me up."

She smiled then, one of her incredibly radiant smiles. The kind that made him think of sunshine. The smile that had made him fall in love with her in the first place. "I already did."

CHAPTER 30

The hospital corridor leading to the room where the Lamaze class was being held was brightly lit. There was absolutely no chance of missing their destination, Jason thought glumly. Especially since there was a large sign posted right by the open door.

He was even more glum once they walked in. The room was already more than half filled with couples. Couples who looked as if they hadn't even been born when he and Laurel had gotten married. He couldn't have felt more uncomfortable than if he were actually living one of those nightmares where he walked into his office wearing just his underwear.

"When did they lower the legal age to get married in this state?" he whispered to Laurel as she led the way in.

Besides her regular two-ton purse, she was carrying a small knapsack with a bottle of water strapped to its side and the mandatory pillow that she'd brought from home. It looked as if she was on an African safari. And he'd been relegated to the post of one of her lowly bearers, trailing humbly after her.

For two cents, if it wouldn't mean stranding Laurel, he would have turned around and left.

Less than two cents, he thought darkly, glancing at one couple who didn't seem old enough to attend their senior prom.

"They didn't," Laurel told him cheerfully. Staking out a spot off to one side of the room, she let her pillow drop to the floor and set down her knapsack beside it.

"Sure looks that way to me," Jason insisted gloomily. "Laurie, I'm warning you, the first person who gets up to offer me his seat, I'm out of here."

He was referring to the chairs arranged over on the opposite side. She imagined they were for when the exercises were over. She turned to her husband, hoping to get a few words of support from him. The very things he was complaining about were the things plaguing her. She felt like a fish out of water here. An old fish. He was supposed to make her not feel that way. But instead of being bolstered by him, she was busy trying to raise his self-esteem.

She supposed, in an odd sort of way, trying to raise his spirits did keep her from dwelling on the fact that she was the oldest mother-to-be in the room, probably by a good ten years if not more.

"Nobody's going to offer you their seat, Jason," she insisted through clenched teeth.

"You owe me," he told her.

"Fine," she retorted gamely, "you can have my fourth-born."

Because only a few of the couples were sitting on the floor, she left her pillow and backpack to mark her space and crossed to the table against the wall farthest from the door. There was literature about childbirth stacked on both ends of the table. The rest of the table was devoted to neatly arranged snacks and an army of small paper cups filled with what appeared to be orange juice.

"Just like in Little League," Jason commented, two steps behind her. "Seems kind of fitting." He picked up a cup. "Wonder if I ever coached any of these people?"

He'd been a T-ball coach for all three of their sons when they played. T-ball was typically played by six-year-olds. Laurel suppressed a sigh. "Age is only a number."

He used the paper cup to block his mouth and mask his words. "Some of these people look as if they just learned their numbers."

"You can't tell that just by looking at them. You look ten years younger than you are. Maybe some of these people are ten years older than you think they are," she pointed out.

"That still makes them a hell of a lot younger than us," he commented. Laurel rolled her eyes.

"Class, would you all take your places, please? We're about to start," a cheerful young woman announced to the gathering. She had medium blond hair, a shade darker than Laurel's, and she wore it pulled back in a ponytail. Her eyes were lively and she had the kind of mouth that was quick to smile.

"They just sent in the cheerleader," Jason whispered to her as they made their way back to the area where she'd left her pillow. "The first piece of entertainment for the evening is to watch the women lowering themselves to the floor," he quipped affectionately as he held her hand and helped her sit down.

Laurel shot him an exasperated look.

The young woman conducting the class scanned the room to make sure that everyone was on the floor. Satisfied, she continued.

"My name is April O'Brien. I'm a registered nurse and I've worked the maternity ward at Blair Memorial for five years now. I've taught these classes for two. When you and your spouse or significant other finally come crashing through our doors, ready to party—" she smiled at each couple individually "—chances are that I'll be the nurse on call offering smelling salts to your not-so-better half."

She was tolerable, Jason decided. Her next words changed his mind.

"I'd like to go around the room and have you each introduce yourselves."

"Okay, done. We're out of here," he muttered into Laurel's ear. He made a move to get up. But she caught his hand, throwing her full weight behind it to hold him in place before he could get to his feet.

"You walk out that door," she told him as firmly as she could, given that she was whispering, "I get the house."

Jason was stunned. "Are you threatening me with a divorce?"

"You betcha."

One look into her eyes told him that, for once, she wasn't kidding, just desperate. With a sigh, he relented and sank ck down the quarter of an inch he'd risen. "You really owe me now," he told her as a couple close to them announced that they had met the night of their high school graduation party. Two years ago.

"I'll think of something," Laurel promised.

"It wasn't so bad," Laurel said two hours later.

Class had let out and they walked to the parking structure where their car was housed. There was a cool evening breeze, a welcome event after the unseasonable heat of the day. September brought with it hot devil winds from the desert, commonly known as Santa Anas, but tonight, the winds had died down.

"No," Jason allowed grudgingly. In the name of husbandly chivalry, he was juggling both her pillow and her knapsack, and wondering how women managed to carry everything and still hold on to an assorted number of children, the way Laurel had when their band was young. "I suppose not."

All in all, it hadn't been as bad as he'd anticipated. He'd found some common ground with a few of the fathers, talking about the upcoming series that was about to be played between the Angels and the Yankees. Baseball was a great equalizer. He'd actually found someone who knew as much about the game, and its history, as he did. It made the second hour pass a lot more easily.

Reaching their car, he unlocked her side first. His door opened automatically.

"And I do appreciate it," Laurel told him. She covered her stomach with her hand, as if to protect it as she slowly lowered herself onto the passenger seat. "It really wouldn't have been the same without you, Jason."

He inclined his head in mute acknowledgment, then glanced at her abdomen. "I guess I owed it to you, seeing as how you wouldn't have to be here in the first place if it wasn't for me."

Finally, she thought.

Laurel allowed herself a smile before she struggled with the seat belt. To her surprise, Jason leaned over and adjusted the belt for her, then slipped the metal tongue into the slot. "I really felt awful for that one woman."

She referred to one woman attending class without a male partner. Instead, she'd brought another woman she'd introduced as her best friend.

Jason started the car. "Maybe she was better off with this friend than with her husband."

Laurel shook her head. "Wanda's not married."

"Just because she wasn't wearing a ring doesn't mean she's not married." He drove out of the structure. "Remember how swollen your fingers got when you were carrying Morgan?"

"No ring," she confirmed. When he looked at her quizzically just before heading onto the road, she said, "I talked to her during the break—while you were talking baseball strategy."

Leave it to Laurel to gravitate to the underdog, he thought. It was one of the reasons he loved her. "So, what's Wanda's story? They break up?"

"No, they're still together. His name is Paul. Paul's just squeamish." She slanted a glance at him before continuing. "She told me she envied me, having my cute husband right there."

Jason raised an eyebrow. "Cute? She called me cute?"

Laurel grinned. She knew he'd warm to that. "Yes, she did."

He nodded, thinking. "Hmm, maybe I can talk to her boyfriend for her, tell him how he'll regret not being there years later."

"That's what I said."

"You volunteered me?" he asked incredulously.

"No." And then she added, "But that's because I knew you'd volunteer yourself."

He wondered if he'd just been set up, then decided it didn't really matter. That was some of the small stuff his father had once advised him not to sweat. Life was a lot bigger than that.

Jason again noted Laurel's profile and felt himself smiling. The older he got, the smarter his father seemed to get. He sincerely hoped that was a universal truth.

CHAPTER 31

Dr. Rachel Kilpatrick pushed her stool back, away from the end of the exam table and its metal stirrups. Rising, she pulled off her rubber gloves, stepped on the little lever that made the wastepaper-basket lid rise and tossed the gloves away. She smiled, as if pleased with the examination.

"You can get up now."

Draped in a sheet of white paper embossed with blue flowers, her wide skirt hiked up past her hips, Laurel propped herself up on her elbows, not without effort.

"Not easily," Laurel muttered audibly, angling her way up into a better sitting position. She deliberately ignored the hand Dr. Kilpatrick offered her, afraid that she might prove to be too much for the diminutive doctor if she really allowed herself to rely on the woman's strength to pull her the rest of the way up.

The obstetrician made a few notes to herself in Laurel's file, then closed it. Holding the folder to her chest, she leaned back against the counter and turned her attention to her patient. There was genuine compassion in her eyes.

"So, how are you doing?"

Upright now, dangling her feet over the side of the table, the paper sheet still tucked about her waist and parts lower, Laurel looked at her doctor, amused. "Isn't that supposed to be your job, to tell me how I'm doing?"

Dr. Kilpatrick played along, although they both knew what she was really asking. "Well, all your vitals are great. The baby is thriving and seems to be doing quite well. And you've gained less weight than I thought you would. I'm very proud of you, Laurel," she said with feeling.

Laurel looked down at the mound that seemed to her to actually be growing by the moment. "Then why do I feel like such a lead weight?"

The doctor's expression told her that she sympathized. Dr. Kilpatrick had had two pregnancies and knew firsthand all the highs and lows that were involved with that state. The woman smiled at her. "It's in your head."

"No," Laurel contradicted, "it's not. It's in my stomach."

Rather than argue the point, the doctor laughed and then changed the subject. She flipped open the file to a page near the front. "I hear you've signed up for the Lamaze classes."

She hadn't mentioned anything to the doctor about taking the classes. She wanted to keep that under wraps until she received her certificate—just in case Jason suddenly decided to bail on her. She'd known the doctor forever, but that still wouldn't change the embarrassment she'd feel if Jason decided to quit attending classes for some reason.

"I see news travels fast," she commented, trying to sound nonchalant.

Putting the file down on the counter, the doctor shoved her hands into her deep pockets. "It's a closed community and I like keeping track of my mothers-to-be." She eyed Laurel carefully. "So, how are the classes going for you?"

There was essentially nothing new to be gleaned. It was all coming back to her in vivid color, especially after the video they'd been forced to watch last week. "All right, I guess."

Dr. Kilpatrick remained leaning against the counter with her back. "And how's your husband taking it?"

Surprisingly well, she thought, especially in light of the way he'd been so adamantly against attending classes to begin with. "He's adjusted," Laurel told her. She fixed her skirt, allowing it to pool down over the paper sheet. "More than I thought he would. He's found some buddies amid the expectant fathers." She smiled fondly. "Baseball nuts, like him. Frankly, I think they're all huddling together for mutual support. They've kind of made Jason the head father, because this is his fourth time around." And that pleased her. Although he was the type that didn't really want any limelight, she firmly believed everyone needed to be acknowledged once in a while. This was Jason's once in a while.

The doctor nodded, her blue eyes intent. "And you?"

She took a deep breath before answering, as if to fortify herself. These days, she caught herself taking a great many deep breaths. The baby seemed to be sitting on everything that made life a little easier. "I just want this to be over with. I feel like I've been pregnant forever." It wasn't a new sentiment. A rueful smile slid over her lips. "I miss my feet. And

I'm not too crazy about the way my belly button is turning out," she concluded with feeling.

The doctor laughed. "Well, according to the chart, it's not all that far away now. Another two and a half months and you'll be back on your way to regaining that figure I've always envied."

Much as she wanted to believe the woman, Laurel shook her head. "You're just saying that to bolster my morale."

"No, I'm saying it because it's true. A lot of women let themselves go after the second baby. You've had three and have gone back to your original, trim weight each and every time."

"That's because I had the boys so close together. Chasing after them, I never had a chance to eat more than a bite at a time."

The doctor laughed. "Whatever works." She straightened. "So, any questions?"

Laurel wiggled a little farther to the edge of the table. Her toes almost touched the single step she'd used to get up on the table in the first place. "Yes, how do I keep my sanity?"

"Ah, the secret of the ages," Dr. Kilpatrick teased. "One day at a time, Laurel, one day at a time." About to head out the door, the file under her arm, the doctor paused. "Are you still working?"

Laurel nodded. The room was cold and she could feel her abdomen getting goose bumps. "Why, are you thinking of moving?" She thought for a second, reviewing the newer properties in her head. "I have a really nice ranch that's fresh on the market."

"No," the doctor said. "Simon and I like the house we're in just fine. It took us years to break it in." She looked at

Laurel seriously. "I was just wondering if perhaps you're not taking on too much right now."

"You just said I was fine."

"Your blood work is fine, but that doesn't mean everything's perfect." She seemed to search Laurel's face. "Are you letting yourself get enough rest? If you weren't working—"

"I'd be busy sitting around, watching my stomach grow and getting very neurotic about it," Laurel said. And then she smiled. "Trust me, Doctor, I need to work."

Dr. Kilpatrick nodded. "Just a suggestion, Laurel, nothing written in stone. If you change your mind, or want to take a leave of absence early, all you have to do is ask. I'll be happy to write you a note to give to your boss."

Just like in school, Laurel thought. It felt like only yesterday—and a hundred years ago at the same time.

"I appreciate it, Doctor, but no, I really do need to work. I like working," she added with a wide smile. "And, I've discovered that people tend to trust a pregnant Realtor." She hadn't been working during her other pregnancies, so this was something new for her. "They think I really do know what I'm talking about when it comes to schools in the area and how safe the neighborhood is."

"Well, don't you?" Dr. Kilpatrick asked.

"Sure," Laurel replied. "But now I really *look* as if I do."

Dr. Kilpatrick laughed. One hand on the door, she began to turn the knob. "Okay, I'll leave you to get dressed."

Laurel looked over to the panty hose peeking out from beneath her purse on the chair. Getting those on took her ten minutes all by themselves. However, going without hose was not an option. She was wearing a skirt today and she absolutely refused to go barelegged when she wore a dress or a skirt. It was something her mother had drummed into her head when she was growing up until she'd embraced it as her own mantra. But it certainly made getting dressed difficult these days.

"No restrictions?" Laurel asked just before the doctor left the room. With Christopher, because she'd flirted with toxemia near the end of her pregnancy, there had been a whole host of dos and don'ts she had to contend with.

Dr. Kilpatrick paused in the doorway, thinking. "Just one. Remember not to go hang gilding in the desert."

"I don't think you really have to worry about that," Laurel assured her.

"Good." Dr. Kilpatrick pointed the top of her pen at her as if to reinforce her words. "Okay, next appointment, two weeks from now," she said, and walked out.

They'd stepped up her visits, Laurel thought, easing herself off the table. She pushed the paper that had followed her down back onto the plastic top. From one every other month, to one a month and now one every two weeks. In her last month, she knew there would be visits scheduled for each week.

Until D day.

Laurel took her panty hose and planted herself in the chair. She began the taxing task of coaxing the nylon onto her toes and then up her legs.

The baby was due just before New Year's. She smiled to

herself as she managed to get one leg on before turning to the other. Jason had liked that part. It gave him a new deduction to use on his tax form. Except this time, she promised herself, rising to her feet and pulling the panty hose up the rest of the way, he was going to do something novel, something he hadn't done before. He was going to learn to enjoy diapering his new tax deduction.

CHAPTER 32

She missed her energy.

These days, any energy that materialized seemed to be in her head. Energized thoughts would scatter in several directions as she made plans, laid down schedules, promised herself deadlines. Her body, however, failed to keep up with any of it.

This was what someone had in mind when they'd said that the spirit was willing but the flesh was weak. Her flesh was not only weak, it was exhausted.

Laurel found herself longing for sleep the minute she opened her eyes in the morning. Not exactly the frame of mind she needed to get things accomplished. And there were always things to accomplish.

Pregnant or not, she still had a household to run, a job to go to each morning. Listings did not care if you had the energy level of a snail that had just been run over by a truck. They needed to be moved. Clients needed to be shown properties. Houses, even perfect ones, did not sell themselves. She had a reputation to maintain, one that she had worked long and hard to create. She was proud of it. Proud that she had come in the Bedford agency's top seller four times in the past six years. Her pregnancy shouldn't change anything.

But oh, God, how she longed to put her head on her desk and close her eyes for just a minute.

Or thirty.

There were tiny bursts of energy, followed by incredibly long spates of exhaustion. This was even worse than the early stages, which had been pockmarked with exhaustion.

Pouring herself a cup of herbal tea, Laurel paused to lean against the counter. She took in a deep breath. It didn't help.

"Something wrong?" Jeannie asked. She was right behind her, intent on filling her oversize coffee cup with dark brew. But her face was lined with concern as she looked at Laurel.

Laurel shook her head. Nothing was wrong, at least, no more than usual, she thought. "I feel like Rip van Winkle just before he first leaned against the tree and fell asleep for twenty years."

Concern turned to sympathy. Jeannie took the coffeepot and emptied the contents into her large mug. "That bad, huh?"

Tossing the used tea bag into the wastepaper basket, Laurel nodded. "The baby kept me up half the night, kicking."

Jeannie tasted the brew she'd just poured and made a slight face. For Jeannie, the coffee was always too weak, even when it was mud. "She's getting ready to blow that Popsicle stand and kick her way out of solitary confinement," she declared.

"I'm not due for another month," Laurel reminded her, taking a sip of her tea.

She stifled a shiver. God, but she was not looking forward to the end of the process. As much as she wanted to have the pregnancy over with, that was how much she didn't want to have to face labor. Time had muted the memory but hadn't completely erased it.

"Maybe she doesn't know that," Jeannie pointed out. She patted Laurel's belly. "I doubt if there's room inside there for a calendar."

"Very funny." She began to walk slowly back to her desk, aware that each time she passed, she garnered looks from the other agents. Sympathy and curiosity all mingled together in the eyes of her colleagues. "The nursery's not ready yet," she told Jeannie.

Jeannie looked at her, curious. According to Laurel, the project had been undertaken several weeks ago. "How's that going, anyway?"

Laurel pressed her lips together. In about five years, this was going to be a funny story. Right now, it was just an exasperating one. "Jason has all the cans of pain opened."

Jeannie snorted as she sat down at her desk. "Going that well, is it?"

There was no point getting herself worked up, so she laughed. "He keeps meaning to get to it. And every time I pick up a brush, he has a fit. Says the fumes aren't good for the baby."

Jeannie glared at her over the rim of her mug. "He's right."

"Thank you, expert," Laurel replied loftily. She lowered herself onto her chair, then took another sip before continuing. "But neither is it good to come into the world and stare at walls that have the remnants of tape on them. Luke had all four walls completely covered in posters."

When her oldest had moved out on his own, she'd left the posters up, silently thinking that if Luke decided to come back home for a while, the way so many of his generation did, he might welcome familiar sights. But he didn't move back. The months fed into one another and the posters continued to linger. Now that Luke had gotten married, she needed room for the baby.

Jeannie waved a hand at Laurel's words. "She'll survive," she promised. "My father was the last of ten. He said that when he was born, they had no room for him so he slept in a drawer for the first three months."

Now there was a story she wasn't about to pass on to Jason, Laurel thought. "As long as no one closed the drawer."

Jeannie grinned.

Laurel put down her cup, her eyes widening. She hadn't been serious. "You're kidding."

"Nope. His older brother Kyle did, once. He was jealous of all the attention the new baby was getting. Luckily, my grandmother saw him shut the drawer. She came running to my dad's rescue. To hear my dad tell the story, Uncle Kyle couldn't sit for a week."

There was no one at the house to be jealous of the baby. She thought of Christopher. He still wasn't exactly thrilled about all this, but he was too old to act out that way, thank God. "Lily's not going into a drawer."

Jeannie raised an eyebrow. "Lily?"

She'd forgotten that she hadn't told Jeannie about their decision. It had taken Jason and her all this time, since they had first known about the baby, to come up with a name they both agreed on.

"That's what we've decided to call her. Just the other night," she confided, then added, "Lily was Jason's grandmother's name."

"Nice."

Because she knew her, Laurel could hear the trace of sarcasm someone else might miss.

"That'll keep your grandmother-in-law always close to you."

She felt duty-bound to defend the late woman. "She was a very nice woman. She died shortly after we were married." To placate her mother, whose feelings were liable to be hurt at being passed over, they were going to use "Debra" as a middle name.

Jeannie nodded thoughtfully before taking another long sip of her coffee. "Thus proving the old adage, only the good die young." And then she grinned wickedly. "I can lend you my mother-in-law in case you miss having one."

"I still have one, we're talking about his grandmother," Laurel reminded her. Jeannie went into great lengths describing all of the older woman's shortcomings. "And as for your mother-in-law, why would I want the lady from hell?"

"I had to try," Jeannie quipped. She turned toward her computer, then paused and glanced back at Laurel. "You have any plans for lunch?"

Laurel thought the question was a little premature. "It's only nine o'clock, Jeannie."

The woman's wide shoulders rose in a half shrug. "I don't

like putting things off to the last minute. Besides, if I have lunch to look forward to, it makes the morning go by faster." She turned her chair around to face Laurel and peered at her over the top of the reading glasses she'd just lowered to her face. "How about it?"

She was supposed to have lunch with Jason today, but he'd abruptly backed out this morning, telling her he needed to put in extra time on his new presentation. So, she was free. "No, I don't have plans."

Jeannie grinned, pleased. She turned back to her computer. "Now you do."

Laurel smiled to herself. It had been a long time since she'd gone out to lunch with Jeannie. Things had gotten so hectic and her supply of energy so limited that she often found herself working through lunch, an ignored sandwich on her desk, sitting on an island of wrinkled aluminum foil. There was no other way to catch up on her paperwork.

"Okay," Laurel agreed, "it's a date. Provided the Kellers make up their mind between now and noon," she added, murmuring the words out of the side of her mouth just as the couple in question entered the office.

Jeannie looked over toward the front door and shook her head. Wade and Leticia Keller had been coming into the office every other day or so now for the past two months. They had already gone through several other agencies before walking into Bedford Reality Company. Laurel hadn't even been their first agent. They had used up two Realtors before they had been passed on to her.

"If anyone can sell them a place, it's you," Callaghan had told her when he informed her of the change.

Laurel wasn't so flattered by the words that she couldn't see through them. No one else at the agency had enough patience to put up with the overly picky pair. Gamely, she had agreed to work with the couple. It had earned her the undying gratitude of no fewer than three of the other agents who had feared they were going to be behind the eight ball.

As far as Laurel was concerned, she had nothing but patience. It came from raising three children and bracing herself to raise one more. She had learned a long time ago children either taught you patience, or the fastest route to the pharmacy to fill a new prescription for Valium.

With effort, Laurel pushed herself up to her feet, then picked up her leather-bound notebook. She met the couple halfway.

"Ah, Mr. and Mrs. Keller. You're not going to believe this, but I just got in a new listing and I think this just might be that dream house you've been looking for."

"Liar," Jeannie muttered under her breath, audible enough only for her to hear.

Laurel managed to keep her smile in place as she approached the couple. "We'll take my car," she told them.

"Well, of course we will," Mr. Keller replied coolly. "You stand to make a sizable commission off us. The very least you can do is pay for gas."

As she led the way out, Laurel wondered if California convicted pregnant women for committing justifiable homicide.

CHAPTER 33

The moment Laurel walked into the real estate office, Jeannie was up on her feet, slinging her purse straps over her right shoulder and pushing in her chair.

"Wow, I was getting worried that they ate you alive. Any luck?" The question came out as an afterthought.

God, but did she feel bushed. Laurel glanced around the room and noticed that it was almost empty, except for Hank Wilson, who was sitting all the way in the back, munching on his customary peanut-butter-and-jelly sandwich. It looked like everyone else had already gone to lunch.

"They're 'thinking about it,'" Laurel answered with a huge sigh, sinking gratefully into her chair. "I showed them five more houses besides the new one." She did her best to distance herself from the morning's events but it wasn't easy. "It got to the point that I seriously regretted not having an ejection seat installed in the car." She opened her bottom drawer and dropped in her purse. "God would have trouble keeping his temper with those two."

Jeannie bent over and retrieved the purse from the drawer, holding it out to her like a freshly saved treasure. "Well, we'll have a nice lunch and you can forget all about those people. They're probably not going to buy anything anyway."

She was beginning to think that herself. The Kellers were what was commonly referred to in the industry as Lookie-Lous, except a little more upper-crust.

"Probably," Laurel agreed. She took back her purse but made no effort to get up. At this point, she doubted if she'd ever get up again. "Look, Jeannie, would you mind very much if I took a rain check on that lunch? I'm just too exhausted to go out again—or even to get up again."

Jeannie stared at her for a moment as if she'd transformed into Wiley Coyote and had just discovered that she'd walked two extra feet than there was ground. Said knowledge was going to instantly send her plummeting down the ravine.

"Yes, I mind," Jeannie finally said.

The answer stunned Laurel. Jeannie was the last word in easygoing. She went along with everything. Usually. "What?"

"I've been looking forward to having lunch with you all week." Jeannie seemed hurt.

"We can send out," Laurel told her. "My treat."

Again, Jeannie surprised her by shaking her head. "It'll take too long." She got behind Laurel's chair and turned it around to the door. "It'll be faster just to go."

Laurel sincerely hoped that Jeannie had no intention of tilting the chair and dumping her out onto the floor. She grasped the armrests, just in case, her purse strap wrapped around one arm. "Not the way I've been dragging."

"I'll drive," Jeannie volunteered with a touch of eagerness

that Laurel found incredibly strange. Her friend didn't care for driving and begged off whenever humanly possible.

Now it was Laurel's turn to stare. "And if I still say no, are you planning on carrying me out of here?"

"If I have to," Jeannie answered matter-of-factly. And then her voice softened. "C'mon, Laurel, you're getting into a rut and you need to snap out of it."

"And you think going out to lunch is going to snap me out of it?"

"It might." Jeannie's purse strap slipped off her shoulder and she pushed it back up again, her eyes never leaving Laurel's face, never relinquishing its pleading look.

Oh well, what would it hurt? Laurel decided. And maybe she'd wind up regaining some of her energy back.

Surrendering, she shook her head as she slipped the strap of her oversize purse back up on her arm. "You know, if you demonstrated this much drive when you're showing houses, you might sell a lot more and get on Callaghan's good side."

Jeannie snorted, leading the way to her car. Having come in early, she'd secured a spot against the building. It was a short walk. "Callaghan doesn't have a good side."

"That's true." It was incredibly sunny, one of those days that had people labeling Southern California paradise. The middle of October and it was crisp, clear and warm. She felt better just being outside. "So, now that you've managed to pry me away from my chair, where is it we're going?"

Jeannie unlocked the pristine white Toyota Echo. Three years old, it was in the same mint condition as the day it was purchased. Planting herself in the driver's seat, she waited for Laurel to get in and buckle up. "I thought we'd try someplace new for a change."

"New?" Laurel echoed. These days, she was rather cautious about what she consumed. Ever since she'd gotten pregnant, food didn't seem to like her the way it once had. "As in guaranteed to give me a case of heartburn?"

Jeannie smiled as she turned the key in the ignition. "Don't worry, honey, I kept your delicate condition in mind. Besides, this is your favorite kind."

"Chinese food?"

"The Red Dragon," Jeannie told her. It was a new restaurant that had opened a month ago in a freshly renovated strip mall not too far from the office. She spared Laurel a look. "They even have bland food on the menu to soothe the expectant mama's tummy."

Laurel hated baby talk. "Now you're just getting nauseating."

Jeannie laughed, backing out of her spot. "Sorry, being thoughtful has that effect on me. You'll like it, trust me."

Trust me. Whenever people said that, it inevitably made her feel uneasy. "Well, since you're driving," Laurel said philosophically, "I guess I'm going to have to."

The moment they got to the street, they were engulfed in traffic. It was almost noon, the time of day when everyone who worked hit the road in either an attempt to get some necessary shopping done or go to a restaurant, hoping to mentally get away for a half hour or so. Today seemed a little worse than usual.

Laurel shifted in her seat. She put her hand between the shoulder strap and her throat in an attempt to keep from being strangled by the seat belt. "You know, it's not too late to turn around and order takeout from the office."

Rather than answer, Jeannie gunned her motor and began weaving in and out of the lanes of traffic. For a robustly built woman, she had chosen a rather compact vehicle as her mode of transportation. Getting in and out of the Echo was a complete challenge—for her and definitely for any pregnant woman who dared to enter. But the upside of driving a car the size of an extralarge crayon box was that it barely needed the space of a whisper to get in and out of crowded lanes. In addition, it could turn on a dime.

"You afraid of a little traffic?" Jeannie teased, working her way through a third lane change.

"No, I'm afraid of dying in a little traffic," Laurel answered. She had her hands out flat on the dashboard in an attempt to remain upright, besting gravity so as not to tilt right or left with each maneuver that Jeannie executed.

Her friend slanted a quick glance in her direction, chuckled and promised, "I'll get you there in one piece, Laurel."

She had her doubts about that. Her wrists felt as if they were going to snap off. "You drive like this on the way back from lunch and you're going to have to have the inside of this car steam cleaned," Laurel warned.

"Duly noted." The next second, Jeannie was shifting into yet another lane.

Laurel sucked in her breath as they barely made it into the

lane, avoiding the rear bumper of a semi. It was going to take a while for her heart to crawl down from her throat.

"Jeannie, why are you playing hopscotch on the road? They won't mind if we're a little late getting back from lunch. Callaghan wasn't even in the office when we left. He won't be able to say anything about our taking too long."

Jeannie didn't seem to be listening. She was intent on watching the road. Or what was up ahead. Suddenly, like Columbus's lookout in the crow's nest, spying land for the first time in months, she pointed triumphantly. "There it is."

"There what is?" With the ongoing thrill-a-minute ride, she'd forgotten about their destination.

Laurel forced herself to look ahead. They were nearing the newly renovated strip mall. To her knowledge, restaurants there were little more than storefronts. Most came and went in the blink of an eye, leaving behind a little debris and no memories.

And then again, maybe not this time. Business, apparently, was good and Laurel noted how crowded the parking area was.

She heard Jeannie murmur "damn" under her breath and assumed she was frustrated by the crowded lot. "Okay, how about going to a restaurant across the street?" Laurel suggested. The older strip mall on the other side of the thoroughfare looked fairly empty from here.

Jeannie didn't answer. She had zeroed in on the lone parking space in the area.

"Ah, here," she announced. The next second, she'd executed a ninety-degree turn and tucked the car into a space that was the size of an enlarged shoe box. Jeannie beamed broadly as she turned off the engine.

Thank God, that was over. "So, you charge extra for the ride?" Laurel mumbled, only too glad to get out. Her knees felt wobbly and disconnected. She imagined sailors had the same reaction walking out onto the dock after months at sea.

Jeannie surprised her by threading her arm through hers to ensure that she remained upright. "You'll feel better once you're inside."

"I'll feel better once I'm home, in bed," Laurel countered. Jeannie yanked open the wooden door and drew her inside.

Whatever else Laurel might have wanted to say was drowned out the next moment as approximately twenty women simultaneously cried out, "Surprise!"

CHAPTER 34

Stunned, Laurel pulled back as the wall of noise and cheer washed over her. She couldn't go far because her arm was still tucked through Jeannie's and the latter had a firm grip on her.

"Omigod, Jeannie, what did you do?" she cried, turning in amazement toward her best friend.

"Got into your PDA and invited every woman you know," Jeannie freely confessed with a wide grin. "Surprised?"

"That's one word," Laurel allowed. "Stunned, amazed, overwhelmed would be others."

She tried to make out faces in the dimly lit entrance but failed. The next minute, she was being swallowed up by the crowd and led off to the rear of the restaurant.

She saw Denise with her cousin and several of her friends—but mercifully, not her mother, Sarah. And then, just as she entered the banquet room, she spied the other women from her office. So that was where everyone had gotten to.

Her sister and mother moved to the foreground, each taking a side. Jeannie brought up the rear. She couldn't turn and flee if she wanted to, so she allowed herself to enjoy what was happening: this was her baby shower.

"How long have you been planning this?" she asked Jeannie, raising her voice to be heard over the crowd.

"A couple of weeks," Jeannie answered.

Laurel strained to hear her. The noise in the small room was almost deafening, especially since the voices of the maître d' and a waiter were added to it and both were conversing in Chinese.

"And you never let anything slip," Laurel marveled, raising her voice even higher. Jeannie's previous record for keeping a secret had been an hour. "You're getting better."

Jeannie laughed. "Why do you think I was avoiding you so much?"

"Eyes front, Laurel honey, you don't want to trip now, do you?" her mother coached.

For the time being, Laurel decided to let her mother baby her. What would it hurt?

The Red Dragon restaurant was a great deal larger than it appeared from the outside. It was still narrow, but the actual footage went deep. The shower was being held in the rear banquet room. A huge rectangular table dominated the area. Silvery balloons with babies splashed across them shared space with fierce red dragons painted on the wall.

The chaos seemed rather appropriate, since this baby had come crashing into her life, completely unexpected and unannounced.

"Sit here, dear," her mother instructed, directing her to the head of the table. "The place of honor."

Everyone else quickly found their seats.

It was like a game of musical chairs without the music, Laurel thought, watching them. Her mother, Lynda and Jeannie were seated closest to her while everyone else, including Denise and her cousin Beth, filled in the rest of the places around the table. Over in a corner was a table piled high with colorfully wrapped gifts.

The noise began to die down and little by little, all eyes turned toward her.

Laurel felt herself growing emotional. She hadn't expected this. Her last shower had taken place twenty-one years ago and it had been, she thought, her *last* shower. She'd planned to have this baby quietly.

Yeah, right. Think again.

She looked at the sea of faces all focused on her. All giving up a bit of their precious time for her.

Laurel was at a loss. "I really don't know what to say."

"I do. Let's eat," Jeannie declared, waving over the servers who began by bringing in trays filled with appetizers.

Those were followed by the main course, a choice of one of three entrees, all of them numbering among Laurel's favorites: shrimp in lobster sauce, sesame chicken and Moo Goo Gai Pan. Fortune cookies followed twenty minutes later, before the actual three-tier cake was wheeled in. Unlike the food, the cake had been brought in from somewhere else.

Laurel was coaxed out of her chair with applause before she went to cut the cake. After taking the first cut, she surrendered the knife to the waiter, who smiled as he took over. Servings were quickly cut and handed out.

"I ran out of space ten minutes ago," Laurel lamented, looking down at the plate that the waiter had placed before her.

"Oh, but you have to try it," her mother enthused, almost finished with her piece. "It is by far the best cake I've ever eaten." She beamed. "It came from this lovely little Bavarian bakery in Costa Mesa. Lynda discovered it."

Laurel looked at her sister. This was something new. "You're scouting out bakeries, Lyn?"

She tried very hard to keep an upbeat note in her voice. When Lynda and Dean divorced, her sister had barricaded herself with a supply of ice cream that could have fed a small village for a year. Had Lynda and Robert broken up and Lynda was turning her attention to cake instead?

"I am."

There was such a positive note in her sister's voice, Laurel felt compelled to ask, "Why?"

"How else am I going to find the best bakery to handle making the wedding cake?" Lynda asked the rhetorical question in between bites of her piece.

Laurel exchanged glances with her mother, but Debra Taylor seemed as surprised as she felt.

"Wedding?" Laurel breathed, mentally crossing her fingers so hard she felt cross-eyed. "What wedding?"

Lynda raised her head and looked at her, the smile on her lips bordering on sly. "My wedding."

Debra's fork slipped from her fingers, clattering to the

plate before it finally fell to the floor. Her eyes were huge as she regarded her second daughter.

"Your what?" she whispered.

Sly vanished, immediately replaced with excitement. Lynda's eyes were actually sparkling. "My wedding."

Debra splayed her hand over her small chest. "Lynda, you wouldn't tease an old woman, would you?"

"I'm too happy to tease anyone," Lynda laughed. And then she faced her sister. "I'm going to owe you for the rest of my life, aren't I?"

Lynda was marrying Robert, Laurel thought. She didn't know she could feel so happy for someone else. If she didn't feel as if she weighed a thousand pounds, she would have gotten up and danced around the room. Instead, she abandoned the to-die-for cake she'd just begun to sample and grabbed both of her sister's hands, squeezing them.

"Even beyond that," Laurel said, laughing. She pulled her sister into a hug with her mother throwing her arms around both of them. "Why didn't you tell me things were going that well?"

"Because I didn't want to jinx it," Lynda answered when she finally got a little breathing room. She was positively glowing, Laurel thought. Wait until she told Jason. "I was afraid if I said it out loud, it would all go away."

"And he asked you to marry him?" Debra asked.

That was her mother, the fact checker.

Lynda nodded her head vigorously. Opening her purse, she took out the ring box she'd been carrying around with her, waiting to spring the news on her sister and mother. She slipped the ring on and held up her hand for viewing.

Laurel pretended to shade her eyes. "Oh God, some light-house is looking for its beacon."

Tears sparkled in Debra's eyes as she hovered over her younger daughter. "I'm speechless," Debra cried.

"This is the best present you could have given me, Lyn. Mom, speechless. Who would have ever thought it?" Laurel said.

Obviously, too happy to take offense, Debra merely waved her hand at Laurel and dabbed at her eyes with the handker-chief. "My baby's getting married again."

"For keeps this time," Lynda added softly, looking at the way the ring caught the overhead lighting and cast out spar-kling beams all around the room.

Bracing her knuckles against the tabletop, Laurel pushed herself into a standing position and looked down at the long table. "Everyone, I have an announcement to make." It took a few seconds for the din to die down and for all the women to turn in her direction. She savored her next words. "My sister Lynda is getting married!"

The news was greeted with exclamations of surprise and shouts of congratulations. Several women rose and came over to their end of the table.

Amid the sound of interweaving conversation, Laurel saw Denise timidly raising her hand, obviously hoping to get her attention. She made eye contact with her daughter-in-law and raised a quizzical brow. Denise mouthed something that was lost in the noise.

Laurel cupped her hands around her mouth and called out, "Louder," to her. She saw the girl slowly rising to her feet.

Oh God, please don't let this be bad, Laurel thought, trying to fathom the strange expression on the young woman's face. Since the wedding, Denise had gotten progressively closer to her, confiding that, after all these years, she finally felt as if she had a real mother. Was this something about Luke?

Again, Denise mouthed something, but she still couldn't hear her.

Puzzled, Lynda leaned into her. "What's Denise saying?"

"Probably something to congratulate you," Laurel guessed. Taking a breath, she rose to her feet again, longing for the day when she could do it without so much effort. "Everyone," she declared, "my daughter-in-law has something to say."

Denise seemed embarrassed at the attention focused on her. She gave the impression of someone who wanted to fold up into herself and disappear.

"C'mon, honey, just spit it out," someone to her right coaxed.

Denise fixed her gaze on Laurel. It was apparently the only way she could get through this. And then she said, "I'm pregnant."

The next moment, she was engulfed by the other women at the table even as Laurel slid bonelessly back into her chair. Stunned for the third time in less than an hour.

CHAPTER 35

It seemed to Laurel that the fit behind the steering wheel of her car was getting tighter and tighter every time she got in on the driver's side. She'd pushed the seat back as far as she could to still work the pedals. What she needed was longer arms and legs.

Either that, or a smaller stomach.

Too late for that, she thought. God, but she felt she'd been playing the part of Dumbo's mother for the past ten years. She couldn't imagine Denise getting this way. The girl was a stick. And now she was a pregnant stick.

Wow, Denise pregnant.

Luke, a father, double wow.

Her baby was having a baby.

She'd tried to call Jason to tell him the news, both about Denise being pregnant and about Lynda getting married. But each time she pressed his number, his cell was either busy or out of range. All three times.

Where *was* he? Why wasn't he answering his cell?

Maybe he'd come to his senses and had decided to run away. And then she smiled to herself. No, Jason was one of the good guys. He'd proven that by going with her to those Lamaze classes when he didn't want to. He'd stick by her no matter what. And having a baby at forty-five was one of those things that came directly under the heading of "no matter what."

Laurel jammed on her brakes as an SUV drifted into her lane, cutting her off. For a second, as she swallowed a few colorful adjectives about the driver's mental capacity and listened to her own heart pounding, she struggled to calm down. This afternoon, for the most part, was a blur.

She did recall hugging Denise in the restaurant. Her daughter-in-law had clung to her and whispered "I'm scared" into her ear while everyone else had swarmed around to congratulate her.

At the same time, Jeannie had looked at her and quipped, "It must be catching. Remind me not to drink the water."

She'd told Denise not to worry, that she would be there for her every step of the way. Denise had turned out to be a good match for Luke after all. Sweet, caring, not a thing like the woman who had given her life. Probably by proxy, Laurel mused, knowing what she did about Denise's mother.

Mother.

A bemused smile played on her lips as she squeaked through a yellow light. She was going to be a grandmother and a brand-new mother almost at the same time. If she wasn't careful, she could find herself being overwhelmed, trying to live up to all her responsibilities. Being there for everyone.

She'd raised three sons, she could do this.

And how about Lynda? she thought with pride. Getting married again. If she knew her little sister, Lynda was going to need help with the wedding.

So much happiness, Laurel mused, so little time.

Keeping her eyes and her mind focused on the road was getting to be a challenge. She found that she kept drifting off mentally, making snippets of plans. God knows she was pleased beyond words.

And her mother, well, her mother had turned into the personification of joy right before her eyes. And why not? Laurel grinned to herself. Lynda getting married to not only a decent, good-looking guy but a rich one as well. Just proved that all good things came to he who waits, or in this case, she.

Laurel picked her cell phone up from where she'd left it on the passenger seat and pressed number three for Jason. It rang several times before stopping at four.

Jason's disembodied voice asked her to please leave a message.

"You never listen to your messages anyway," she accused the cell—and Jason by proxy—as she ended the attempt.

Closing the cell, she dropped it back on the passenger seat. What if she'd gone into early labor? Granted, that would be *really* early, but you could never tell. If she *did* go into labor, she'd have to rely on one of her sons or someone else to get her to the hospital—provided she could reach someone, she thought. All those phones out there and none of them being answered.

In this day and age of technological marvels, she sometimes felt that all they did was provide more ways to get frustrated. Most likely, if she did go into early labor and need a ride to the hospital, she'd wind up out on some corner, trying desperately to hitch a ride. And just who in their right minds would pick up a desperate, pregnant woman?

She was getting carried away again, Laurel chided herself. It was happening a lot lately. She'd never been a withdrawn person by any definition, but ever since this last pregnancy had overtaken her, she'd become a walking bundle of emotions. They seemed to go bouncing all over the place at the slightest provocation.

This too shall pass, she told herself.

Turning right at the corner, Laurel drove down the cul de sac and then turned left at the second house from the end, pulling up into the driveway. She was home an hour earlier than usual. That was Callaghan's gift to her. He'd told her that she could make her own hours from now until after the baby arrived.

Twenty minutes after he'd told her, she was on the road home, her vehicle overflowing with packages. The women at the shower had all helped load up her car with gifts. At the time, there'd been almost too many hands helping.

Now, of course, there were none available, she realized as she got out of the vehicle and surveyed the back seat. It was completely stuffed, as was the trunk. For a moment, her can-do attitude almost got the best of her and she unlocked her trunk. She'd never been one to wait around until someone came by to help. Whatever needed doing, she'd always it done herself. But as she picked up the first box, she changed her mind.

For once in her life, she was going to play the role of the helpless little woman. For once, she was going to have the men in her life fetch and carry for her instead of doing it all herself.

Christopher's car was parked at the curb. Unless one of his friends had come by to pick him up, that meant he was home. Which in turn meant that he could be pressed into service and unload the car for her.

She liked that idea.

"Christopher, are you around?" Laurel called out as she unlocked the front door. Nothing but silence met her in response. Removing the key from the lock, she raised her voice and called again. "Christopher, could you come here a second?"

Still nothing.

Laurel sighed. Her initial thought had been right. Someone had come by to pick Christopher up for whatever it was that kids his age did.

People, she corrected herself. For whatever it was that *people* his age did. Christopher wasn't a kid anymore, even though she thought of him that way. Thought of them all that way. Her kids. Her babies.

Laurel shook her head. She was getting as syrupy as a greeting card.

The remedy for that was work, she decided. There was dinner to see to. Even though food was the last thing on her mind, Jason would be hungry. And so would Morgan once he got home.

She was just going to go into the kitchen to get herself a drink of water, and then she could get started unloading the car. All except for the bassinet, she qualified. The bassinet was a lovely item her mother had picked out for her, all frills and laces and perfect for a little girl.

Until Lily decided to be a tomboy. Like her.

Lynda had been the one for laces and frills. Growing up, they couldn't have been more opposite. Lynda wanted laces, she had wanted a catcher's mitt for her tenth birthday. Her mother had been depressed, her father elated.

Laurel was almost in the kitchen when she heard the noise. Something had dropped with a clatter, followed by a string of words she wasn't going to allow the baby to hear until she was at least in college. Maybe not even then.

When had Christopher learned how to swear like that?

"So, you *are* home," she called out.

Obviously he'd wanted to pretend he wasn't, but too bad. It was about time she got him to help her out a little. He'd been withdrawing from her more and more ever since she'd gotten pregnant. She knew that on some level, he felt betrayed, but he needed to get over that. She thought he had when he'd found out she was having a girl, but obviously, she'd been mistaken.

She missed her last-born, missed the talks they used to have. Missed his sunny laugh. She hated that they didn't seem to connect very often anymore.

With effort, Laurel made her way up the stairs. She was about to head toward Christopher's room when a second noise stopped her. The sound wasn't coming from his room. It was coming from the room next to the master bedroom. From Luke's former room.

Had he decided to come back for some unknown reason? Oh God, what if he and Denise'd had an argument over the new arrival? He would have called, she insisted.

Laurel crept forward toward the room that had been designated to be the baby's. The logical thing to assume was that, despite all his complaints, Christopher had decided to do a little work on the room. She doubted a burglar would be knocking around in there.

Puzzled and curious, she made her way to the room.

The smell of paint greeted her several feet before she got to the threshold.

There was plastic sheeting everywhere she looked. The rugs and furniture that huddled in the middle of the room were covered with it. And there were her men, rollers in their hands, their coveralls sprinkled with pastel pink.

Jason saw her first. "You're early," he accused. "You weren't supposed to be here for another hour."

She pressed her lips together, her throat temporarily clogged with emotion. They were painting the baby's room. All of them—Jason, Morgan and Christopher. It went straight to the head of the line as the best present she'd ever received.

"Then I would have been forced to think that elves did this, because the men in my family have a habit of putting things off." She sniffed, blinking back the moisture that was forming along her lashes. "So this was why I couldn't get through on your cell this afternoon." She lifted up the phone he'd placed on a shelf. It was turned off.

"This is why."

Putting the phone back down, she picked her way carefully over the plastic on the floor. One wall was being turned into a mural, with nursery rhyme characters playing in a field of clover. Giving vent to his artistic side, Morgan was doing the honors. Right now, he was working on Jack and Jill.

"It's beautiful." She looked over her shoulder at Jason. "Thank you."

"Hey, don't thank me," he told her. "This was all Christopher's idea. He was the one who called us and shamed everyone into helping."

"Yeah, we thought he was going to pull a Tom Sawyer on us," Morgan added, dipping his roller into the pan on the floor, "until he joined in to do his share."

"Christopher?" Miracles really *did* happen, she thought. She crossed to him. "Put your roller down so I can hug you."

He seemed completely embarrassed. "Don't get all mushy on me, Ma."

"I'm pregnant," she reminded him. "I have a free pass to get mushy any time I want."

"Well, okay," he muttered, setting down the roller as she'd asked. "But make it fast. The paint's going to dry funny if I don't finish."

She saw right through him. Emotion embarrassed him, just as it once had his father. To let him save face, she said, "Yes, dear," just before she hugged him. Hard.

Because of the hour—six—the restaurant hadn't gotten crowded yet. Without the din of voices to drown it out, she could hear the soft music being piped in. The song playing was vaguely familiar, although the name eluded her.

It didn't matter.

What mattered was that they were here, that Jason had suggested this last "date," bringing her to the restaurant that they'd been frequenting for years. He'd proposed to her here. And this was where she'd first told him that she was expecting Luke. More than any other spot, the Rainbow's End was their "special place."

"I'm so glad Christopher finally came around," Laurel said. She closed the bright red menu and set it aside. She already knew what she wanted. The owner subscribed to the theory that if it isn't broken, don't fix it. Nothing had changed on the menu in the past four years, except for the prices.

Jason grinned. Work on the nursery had been completed more than two weeks ago. Laurel was still talking about it. He liked seeing her so happy. "It was bound to happen sooner or later, especially since this time, you're having a girl."

She hadn't thought that the baby's gender really made that much of a difference to Christopher, only that he was embarrassed that his parents were sexually active and the world knew about it because she was pregnant. "Do you think that has anything to do with it?"

Jason paused to give their orders to the waiter, then picked up a roll and began to butter it.

"That has everything to do with it. A little boy," he continued, "even though he's initially someone to teach and guide, eventually represents competition. A little girl, however, is a little Kewpie doll to our sons."

That would be setting progress back by fifty years. Laurel set down her diet soda and rolled her eyes. "God, I hope not."

"At least for the first five years. You've got to give them some space to enjoy having a little girl in the family."

Laurel sighed slightly. "In five years, Lily will be spoiled rotten."

He finished his roll just as the waiter returned with their meals. Jason moved his bread dish aside to make room for the plate. "That's the plan."

She didn't know if he was kidding or not, but visions of tantrums and pouting flashed through her head. "That is *not* the plan. You don't want to have to deal with the fallout when our 'spoiled rotten' daughter reaches her teens."

Jason was teasing her. She could see it in his eyes. They were smiling. "All right, so just how long can we spoil her?"

She had an answer ready. "Until she's on solid food."

Jason knew better. She was always the first one to melt

around a baby, but he played along. "You are a hard woman, Laurel Mitchell."

She stopped eating long enough to look down at her distended stomach. Had it ever been really flat, or was that just a faraway dream? She sighed. "Not now, but I intend to be." Laurel thought of it in terms of a day-by-day routine. It felt daunting already. "It's going to be hard to get back into shape, isn't it?"

"I don't know," he deadpanned, sinking his fork into his mashed potatoes. "I've never been a pregnant forty-five-year-old woman before."

"Neither have I," she countered, shifting slightly in her seat, "and that was an opening for you to say something supportive."

Jason raised an eyebrow. The longer he was married, the more convinced he was that every woman should come with her own manual. Just when he thought he was on the right track, someone switched the route. "It was? Sorry. You know, I do better with a teleprompter."

Amusement curved her mouth. "I'll keep that in mind." Damn, she really wished the baby would settle down. Each time she opened her mouth to take a bite, Lily would execute a high kick. Was she trying out for the Bolshoi Ballet? "So what do you think of being a grandfather?"

"Love the concept," he told her, "hate the name."

She thought of her own grandfather. He'd died when she was twelve, but he'd seemed ancient to her even though he'd only lived to be sixty. There was a built-in image with the label, one that brought to mind white hair and soft food. She understood Jason's reluctance to embrace it.

"We'll come up with a better name," she promised. The next second, she felt her eyes water as Lily kicked again. If there'd been two of them inside her, she would have sworn they were having a rumble.

Jason shrugged as he continued eating. "We've got time."

"That's what you said about Lily and, look, I'm about ready to pop." In fact, she added silently, it felt as if she was doing that right now.

He seemed unfazed. "We've still got a month."

"We," she repeated. As if they were actually going to go through this together. Men were so loose with their words sometimes. "Which part of the labor do you want to take? The beginning or the end?"

Jason nodded, taking her point. "We'll shoot for it," he answered glibly. "Rock, paper, scissors."

Her mind made an involuntary side trip down memory lane. "You might have to shoot me if this one is anything like Christopher." She shivered. "Ten long hours of absolute hell."

He remembered better than she probably thought he did, Jason thought. He hated seeing her go through that. "There's always a C-section," he reminded her.

There'd been a story on the local news the other evening. A lot more women were going that route these days than ever before. To her it was a last resort, to be done only if the baby was in danger. Despite the pain involved, she wanted to have Lily naturally, the way she'd had her others. Laurel was convinced that it had helped to create a lasting bond between her and each of her sons. If possible, she wanted to be awake and lucid when Lily drew her first breath, not half-unconscious.

"We'll put that on the back burner," she told him, then caught her breath as another really sharp pain telegraphed itself through her, starting at her navel. For Jason, she forced a smile to her lips as she shifted in her chair for the umpteenth time. This time, she gripped the armrests as she did so. She could feel herself sweating. Southern California in November was not as cold as most places in the country, but it still didn't usually have the kind of weather that induced perspiration.

Now that she thought about it, she hadn't been able to really get even marginally comfortable for the past two days.

Just as she placed her hand on her stomach, she felt another strong jolt. "Of course, there might not be any need to consider a C-section. Lily just might kick her way out."

He put down his knife and fork and looked not at her eyes but at her stomach. "Baby's being active again?"

"She'd have to be shot with a tranquilizer gun to go down to 'active.' This isn't active, this is a class-five hurricane that I have inside of me." There it went again, another shock wave. "A hurricane training to be the next welterweight champion of the world."

He was almost finished with his meal. What was left could be taken home, as could hers. He noticed Laurel had hardly eaten any of her dinner.

"Do you want to go home?"

She shook her head stubbornly. "No, this might be the last time we get to go out to eat as a twosome for a very long time. You're going away on business next week and by the time you get back, I might be so large, I won't fit into anything except for a U-Haul."

Reaching across the table, he placed his hand on hers. "You're exaggerating again. You're not even as big as you were when you had Christopher." He saw Laurel grin. "What?"

"I think you're finally getting the hang of this supportive stuff."

He withdrew his hand and picked up his fork again. "Slow and steady, that's my motto. Okay, we'll stay. But if you start feeling sick, tell me and I'll take you home, understood?"

"Understood."

Lily seemed to settle down then. For almost fifteen minutes. But just as the waiter was bringing out the dessert, the baby went into high gear, kicking even harder than before.

Laurel put down her fork. She was starting to feel like one of the astronauts in *Alien*, just before the creature popped out of their chests. Granted that in her case the center was a little lower, but the feeling, she was sure, was the same.

It began to feel very warm in the restaurant again. There were more people now and the noise level had gone up, contributing to the odd feeling that was beginning to wrap itself around her.

"You all right, Laurie? You look a little pale."

Jason's voice sounded distant. She forced herself to focus

on it. Forced herself to sound as if nothing was wrong when she was beginning to feel that it might be.

"Pale is my natural color," she quipped. "That's why there are seven little men following me everywhere."

"No, paler," he insisted, leaning over the table and peering at her face. "You look paler than usual. Are you sure you're all right?"

"I'm eight months' pregnant, Jason. I haven't been all right for about two months now."

Jason shrugged, letting the matter drop. He raised his hand, signaling for the waiter to come with their check.

"You know best." He wasn't about to get into an argument over it, not with her hormones out of kilter. She could go from zero to banshee in less than sixty seconds and he for one was not about to get caught in the crossfire.

"Um, Jason?"

Hand still raised for the waiter, Jason glanced at her. Her voice sounded odd. "Yes?"

"Could we go now?"

"That's what I'm trying to do, honey. Soon as I get the waiter's attention."

"Sooner."

"What?" Jason looked at her, puzzled. "Why?"

She pressed her lips together, taking a breath. It didn't help. The pain just became sharper. So sharp she couldn't speak for a moment. And then she did.

"Because my water just broke." There was no shifting away from the pain. "Jason, I'm in labor."

CHAPTER 37

"No, you're not," Jason retorted with feeling once he regained the use of his tongue. "You're just eight months' pregnant, Laurie. You *can't* be in labor." All three of their other children had arrived at least a couple of days past their due dates. There was no reason to believe that Laurel's pattern had changed.

Another wave of near-immobilizing pain began speeding toward her. Laurel shrugged her shoulders helplessly in response to Jason's protest. He could protest all he wanted to, she knew what she knew. The baby was coming. Very soon.

"I know exactly…how pregnant…I am," she told him, gritting her teeth. "But…Lily…wants…to be…different. She…wants…to…be…early." Every word was an effort. With each one she uttered, Laurel fought back a cry of pain.

The owner of the Rainbow's End, Aldo Grimaldi, a restaurateur for the past twenty-nine years, was drifting from table to table, as was his habit each evening, asking patrons if everything was to their liking. As he approached Laurel and Jason, his warm smile froze, then disappeared, replaced by a look of concern. He knew his regulars by name and Laurel and Jason were two of his oldest customers.

The dapper-looking man quickly made his way over, stopping at Laurel's chair. "Is anything wrong, Mrs. Mitchell?"

"I'm about to...give you...another patron," Laurel managed to gasp out just as the waiter arrived in response to Jason's summons. Staring at her, the young man turned white as an old-fashioned sheet. "In a...matter of minutes...I think." She pressed her hand to her abdomen, as if that could somehow magically keep her baby where it was.

Jason never took his eyes off her. "I need the check," he told the waiter. "Now."

Aldo waved his hand, making the matter go away. "Never mind that, my friend. Consider it on the house. The only thing you need to do is get your lovely bride to the hospital."

"My...thoughts...exactly," Laurel ground out.

Perspiration had formed a ring along her hairline. Her bangs had begun to stick to her forehead. All around them, diners were watching them. She just wanted to be able to get out, to make her way to somewhere private, before Lily's birth became a public affair.

Aldo nodded, digging into his pocket. "I'll have my driver take you," he offered, already on his cell, making the call.

But Jason shook his head. There was no time to wait for someone to come. From the look on Laurel's face and the way she was breathing, every second counted. "I've got my car in the lot."

Aldo was not the kind of man who took no for an answer or was easily dissuaded.

"You need to be focused on your wife, Mr. Mitchell. Ryan

will get you to the hospital." Before Jason could ask who Ryan was, the man had materialized before his employer. The driver was a tall hulk of a man whose every movement seemed to make his uniform strain at the seams. His face appeared to be chiseled out of stone. "Ryan, this lovely lady is about to bring another life into the world. Get them to—" Aldo paused, looking at Jason to fill in the destination.

But it was Laurel who answered, all but crying out the name. "Blair…Memorial."

Ryan nodded. The chiseled face softened as he witnessed Laurel's pain. "That's just five miles away. You'll be there in no time flat."

"Maybe…not so…fast," Laurel amended. Trying to get to her feet, she felt her knees buckle. Her hand splayed out onto the table to keep from falling over. Jason was quick to catch her from behind, keeping her upright.

"Lean on me, honey," he urged.

To both their surprise, Aldo's personal chauffeur intervened.

At the last minute, just before picking Laurel up in his arms, Ryan looked to Jason for approval. "If it's all right with you?"

It would have been the more manly thing to decline the offer, to say something to the effect that he could take care of his own wife, and then pick her up himself. But Jason knew that he would struggle beneath Laurel's weight and that would only make her more uncomfortable. Ryan looked as if he could bench-press tractors in his spare time as a recreational outlet.

Laurel's welfare came above all else, including his own ego. Jason nodded. "Sure."

She didn't want some strange man carrying her. But before she could lodge a protest, Laurel felt herself becoming airborne. The restaurant owner's chauffeur had just picked her up as if she weighed next to nothing.

Any comment about his strength faded as another wave of pain washed over her, growing progressively more powerful. Laurel tried very hard not to dig her nails into Ryan's shoulders.

This is bad, Laurel thought. Someone had scrambled up and was opening the outer door ahead of them. The last time she'd felt pain this intense and this often, she was just minutes away from pushing Christopher out.

The hospital seemed like an entire state away.

"Am I hurting you?" Ryan asked. He was moving as gently as he could while still trying to hurry. Jason was bringing up the rear.

She didn't answer the driver's question. There had always been something extremely competitive about her, something that forbade her from admitting how weak she felt and how much pain she was in. All she could do was blurt out, "Hurry."

Laurel was barely aware of being deposited onto the spacious back seat of the stretch limo. She was acutely aware of the fact that she was desperately trying to fight the urge to push with all her might.

As she clenched her hands into fists at her sides, Jason was climbing into the limousine. He took the seat beside her as the driver's-side door slammed shut. The next second, the limousine took off. Laurel released a ragged breath.

"We'll be there soon, Laurel," Jason promised, taking her hand in his. "Just hang on, honey."

Laurel pressed her lips together. If there was anything she'd learned with her other pregnancies, it was that babies came when they wanted to. "I don't know…if I…can…Jason. She wants…to…come out."

"Breathe, honey, breathe." He was shaking his head, negating her words, even as he issued instructions. "You remember. You can't pant and push at the same time. C'mon, honey, do it. It's just a few more minutes to the hospital." Then, feeling that she might want to have him keep her company, he began to pant, illustrating what he'd just told her to do. "Like this."

As he continued to pant, Jason saw the lights out of the corner of his eye. Red lights. A whole slew of them. Taillights glowing like fireflies on a holiday in the dead of night. The next moment, he felt the limousine slowing down.

"What's the matter?" he called out to the driver.

There was barely suppressed annoyance in the man's deep voice. "Traffic jam."

"There can't be," Jason cried. But it was Friday night on Pacific Coast Highway. *Not* to expect a traffic jam fell into the realm of fairy tales.

"Hold on," Ryan advised.

The next moment, they felt the car tilting slightly. Just before they took off.

The red lights remained where they were. They did not.

The passage was bumpy. Jason realized that Aldo's chauffeur had angled the limousine slightly so that they were now driving on the shoulder of the road. Since it was so narrow, two of the car's wheels were running along Pacific coast Highway's hilly terrain.

Each time they hit a bump, Laurel sucked in her breath.

Jason's heart stood still as he monitored her every movement. "Out," he coached, "not in. Out!" Again, he demonstrated.

Laurel was holding onto his hand for all she was worth. She knew she was squeezing too hard, but she couldn't make herself stop. It was as if holding her husband's hand, not the panting, was helping her cope with the pain and keep the baby back.

"The...doctor," Laurel cried.

"She'll be there."

But she shook her head. He didn't understand. How could Dr. Kilpatrick be there if the doctor didn't know she'd gone into labor? "Call...her!"

He'd forgotten about that. Jason felt around for his cell phone. Locating it in his inside pocket, he pulled it out and hit the number that Laurel had preprogrammed into his cell only the week before.

He got the doctor's answering service.

"No, I want Dr. Kilpatrick. A message?" he echoed the question the woman on the other end of the line asked. "Yes, I want to leave a message. This is Jason Mitchell. My wife Laurel's in labor and we're on our way to the hospital. We'll be there in five minutes. The baby might be there in six. Yes, six. Tell her to hurry."

Jason flipped the phone closed. Taking a look at Laurel's face, he wasn't sure they actually had six minutes left.

CHAPTER 38

When Laurel looked back on it later, all the events of the evening leading up to her daughter's debut seemed to blur, rushing together at the speed of light.

However, at the time the big moment seemed to transpire at a painfully plodding pace. Even the wild ride to the hospital. Ryan made it there in under ten minutes. The moment he brought the limousine to a screeching halt in the parking area reserved for emergency room vehicles only, the driver came barreling out of the vehicle and ran through Blair Memorial's electronic doors. The doors barely had enough time to part far enough apart to allow him entrance.

Watching him, Jason had the impression that the man could have smashed right through them without so much as pausing for a second to recover.

Ryan was back almost in the next heartbeat, followed by a nurse and a short, thin orderly. They were maneuvering a gurney between them.

If it weren't for the driver, Jason thought, they'd still be stuck in traffic. And Laurel would be giving birth on Pacific Coast Highway. With only him in attendance.

God, they had dodged a bullet with that one.

"If we were having a boy, we'd name him after you," he told Ryan, gratitude pulsing in every syllable. Beside him, the medical team gently lifted Laurel onto the gurney.

In response, the chauffeur grinned broadly. "Ryan could work for a girl." He put his two fingers to his cap and took several steps back, getting out of their way as the orderly and nurse turned the gurney back toward the E.R. entrance.

"Tell Aldo we said thanks," Jason called back to him as he hurried to keep up with the gurney and, more importantly, with his wife.

"You Mr. Mitchell?" the slender blond nurse asked.

"We're the Mitchells," Jason answered, instinctively knowing how much providing a united front meant to Laurel, especially at a time like this.

The nurse nodded. They crossed the threshold and kept on going. "Dr. Kilpatrick called," she informed him. "She's on her way." The nurse looked down at Laurel. "Hang in there, honey. The doctor left instructions to take you directly to the delivery room."

Aware of the precise way that the wheels of any enterprise turned, regardless of how dire the situation, Jason glanced back over his shoulder toward the reception desk. They'd hurriedly bypassed it on their way to the elevators.

"Don't I need to fill out forms?"

It was Laurel rather than the nurse who answered his question. "I...already...pre...registered a...week...ago."

He shook his head. The woman never ceased to amaze

him. Despite everything that was going on, she was always efficient. He'd been taking that for granted the past few years. He shouldn't have, he thought. And there was no better time than now to tell her. Because now was all they ever had.

"You are a wonder, Laurie." Jason felt his smile freeze as Laurel started to squeeze his hand so hard he was positive she was breaking blood vessels in the process. "Bad?"

"On a scale...of...one to ten...it's...a...twelve," she panted.

She was soaked, he thought. With his free hand, he took out a handkerchief and wiped her brow. Checking the numbers, he watched the floors pass slowly and longed for a way to speed up the car.

Laurel gurgled, swallowing a scream. "Why doesn't this go faster?" Jason demanded.

"Be happy it's not getting stuck between floors," the orderly told him.

The very thought made Jason's heart freeze.

But then the next moment the elevator doors were dragging themselves open. Jason breathed a sigh of relief. As soon as the doors were apart, the orderly and nurse pushed Laurel's gurney out onto the maternity floor.

Hurrying alongside of the gurney, Jason took Laurel's hand and squeezed it. "It won't be long now," he promised.

"Not...long." He didn't realize that she was contradicting him and not just echoing his words until she screamed out, "*Now!*"

It felt like forces greater than she were acting on her body. Laurel found herself helpless to do anything but push.

The nurse was horrified to see Laurel tense her body. "Wait!"
But it was beyond her power to comply. "Can't!"

The delivery rooms were located all the way down the hall.
At this point, it might as well have been in the next county, Laurel
thought. Thinking quickly, the nurse steered the gurney into
the first open room she saw. For a change, the maternity floor
was relatively inactive and there were more empty rooms
than occupied ones.

"Get the doctor!" the nurse shouted to the orderly. But
by the time the young man had raced out and down the
hallway, Laurel could feel the baby pushing her way out,
ready or not.

"Jason! Jason…she's…heeerrre!" Laurel cried, grasping for
her husband's hand again.

"Right here, Laurie, I'm right here." Remembering what
he'd learned in class, rather than take her hand, he got behind
Laurel and propped her up so that she could be in a better
position to push.

"Wait for me," the nurse told them, quickly moving to the
opposite end of the gurney. There wasn't even time to transfer
Laurel to a regular bed. "You two can't have all the fun."

The nurse barely took her place and stripped away Laurel's
underwear. The baby appeared immediately behind the
cotton material, eager to take her place in the world.

"I'm here!" Dr. Kilpatrick declared, still slipping on her
blue operating-room livery. "And so, apparently, is your junior
miss," she noted, looking down at the baby the nurse was
holding in her hands. She grinned, looking back at the ex-

hausted mother. "You do-it-yourselfers are going to put me out of business." Picking up the surgical scissors, Dr. Kilpatrick held them out to Jason. "Would you like to cut the cord?"

But Jason shook his head. "I'd rather be on this end, with Laurel." Very gently, he removed his hands from beneath her shoulders and laid her back down on the gurney. "You did good, honey."

Her heart was racing so fast it was difficult for her to catch her breath. She was only marginally aware that Jason had taken out his handkerchief and was wiping her brow. She felt as if she'd been turned into a giant puddle.

"I can't believe it's over." The baby made a noise. Eager to see her child, Laurel attempted to prop herself up on her elbows.

"It's over," Jason assured her. Holding Laurel up, he looked over at his new daughter. "And she's beautiful."

Yes, she was, Laurel thought as she watched the nurse clean her up. "You know, Ryan's not such a bad name for a girl. What do you think of Lily Ryan?"

"It's different," Jason agreed. Overcome with emotion, with the harrowing thought that if there had been any complications, he might have lost her if not for the efforts of a man he didn't know, it took Jason a moment to get control over himself. "You can call her anything you want, Laurie."

"Lily Ryan Debra," Laurel whispered, nodding her head. "Lily Ryan Mitchell." It had a nice ring to it. "We need to call the family," she suddenly realized.

He nodded as the nurse, having wrapped a receiving blanket around the baby, tucked the infant into his arms.

Emotions he couldn't begin to identify erupted all through him as he looked down upon the brand-new life he was holding.

"In a minute," he whispered. Jason raised his eyes to look at his wife. "Right now, I'd like to just enjoy this moment, this child, with you. Alone."

It occurred to Laurel, as she watched her husband with their daughter, that that was one of the nicest things Jason had ever said to her.

Lying back, she opened her arms. "Don't hog her," she told him.

"Sorry, it's just that she's so tiny. So perfect." His eyes met Laurel's. "So much like you."

Very carefully, he transferred the baby into her arms. And it was at precisely that moment Laurel realized that what the doctor had told her was true. Some things were even better when experienced the second time around.

* * * * *

Don't miss Marie Ferrarella's next story,
HER LAWMAN ON CALL,
available February 2007
from Silhouette Romantic Suspense.

Every life has more than one chapter
and NEXT offers another great lineup of titles
in the coming months.

For a sneak preview of
BLINK OF AN EYE by Rexanne Becnel,
coming to NEXT in February,
please turn the page.

What should I do? I gripped the driver's side headrest.

Go drown yourself. That's the plan, isn't it? So go do it.

In three feet of water?

Except that those three feet looked like they would soon be four. Or more. "Just wait," I muttered. "Just wait a little longer."

Within fifteen minutes the water was over the seat cushion and rising, almost as deep inside the car as outside. I shivered as my capris soaked up the chilly water. Was I going to drown in a Toyota with the doors locked and the windows up? Or would I get out of the car and head toward the lake and deeper water? Assuming I didn't drown before I got there.

That's when a dog slammed into my front windshield. Somehow it righted itself, scrambling around for footing on the wet hood. Then it stood there, spraddle-legged and terrified, staring me straight in the face.

I heard one yelp—or maybe I saw it. Either way, when the next wave sent the animal sprawling, sliding off my car, I didn't stop to think. I shoved the door open, lunged through the opening and into the water, and somehow caught the animal by the tail.

I managed to get a hold of the dog's collar just in time. The next thing I knew, we were both underwater.

It wasn't rainwater, but salty, brackish water. Don't ask me why I noticed that. But as I came up sputtering, with Fido still in my grasp, I knew that the worst had happened to New Orleans. Hurricane Katrina had caused one of the levees to break.

Between the tearing winds, the punishing waves and the debris missiles from the hurricane that followed, I could easily have just let go. Given in. Given up.

But I couldn't.

It was because of the dog.

He was a medium-sized mutt, black and white, totally nondescript like a million others. Mainly, though, he was petrified with fear. He'd decided I was his salvation and kept trying to climb into my arms because the water was too deep for him to stand in.

Unfortunately, between the wind and the waves, it was too tough for *me* to stand in. Tree branches, lawn furniture, street signs, garbage—it was like being inside a giant washing machine set on spin.

One thing I knew: avoid the cars. Because if one of them pinned me to a tree, I was a goner.

I know, I know. Five minutes ago I'd wanted to be a goner. And I still did. But I needed to save this dog first.

I could barely keep my eyes open; that's how harshly the winds whipped around me. Like a drowning blind woman, I flailed around looking for something solid to cling to. Then

I slammed into a fence. And the gate led to a house. Somehow I dragged myself up the steps. The minute Fido's feet hit something solid, he was out of my arms. Right behind him, I crawled up the long flight of steps, out of the water and onto a porch. There I curled into a ball in a corner against the house. Fido, wet and stinky, wormed his way into my arms and that's how the two of us spent the next few hours. He shivered and whimpered uncontrollably. I shivered and alternatively cried and cursed.

You'd think someone who wanted to be dead wouldn't be afraid of anything. That she would stand up to the storm, beating her chest and screaming, "Come and get me, Katrina! Come and get me!"

But it was terrifying. It seemed like hours went by with no change.

Fido finally stopped shivering, but he kept his anxious brown eyes on me, as if I might disappear if he looked away. Who did he belong to? And why on earth had they left him behind?

He wore a collar with a tag that identified him as Lucky.

Lucky. Yeah, right! Lucky to be huddled on somebody's porch with a crazy woman while the whole damned city returned to the sea.

She had nothing to lose…

With a hurricane bearing down on New Orleans, the failed nurse-turned-waitress viewed it as an opportunity—to escape her tattered life. It was time to rebuild—her life, her city— on a foundation of hope.

Blink of an Eye

USA TODAY bestselling author
Rexanne Becnel

Available February 2007
TheNextNovel.com

It's never too late to take that flying leap

Two friends set off for the Tuscan countryside to heal wounds of the past. Through the strength of their friendship, both women discover they can face the future and embrace its limitless possibilities....

Late Bloomers

by
Peggy Webb

HN78

Available February 2007
TheNextNovel.com

This February...

Catch NASCAR Superstar **Carl Edwards** *in*

SPEED DATING!

Kendall assesses risk for a living—so she's the last person you'd expect to see on the arm of a race-car driver who thrives on the unpredictable. But when a bizarre turn of events—and NASCAR hotshot Dylan Hargreave—inspire her to trade in her ever-so-structured existence for "life in the fast lane" she starts to feel she might be on to something!

HARLEQUIN® *Romance*.

What a month!

In February watch for

Rancher and Protector
Part of the Western Weddings miniseries
BY JUDY CHRISTENBERRY

The Boss's Pregnancy Proposal
BY RAYE MORGAN

Also in February, expect
MORE of what you love
as the Harlequin Romance line
increases to six titles per month.

SRJAN07